Kiamichi Storm

Book Two

of the

Kiamichi Survival Series

C.A. Henry

ISBN-13: 978-1533465689

ISBN-10: 1533465681

Cover by Hristo Argirov Kovatliev

Maps by Cassandra N. Bailey

Editing by Hope Springs Editing

Dedication

In honor of my mother, Ruth Evelyn Harless
Henry

and

In memory of my dad, Emil Maurice (Chuck)
Henry, Sr.

The world needs more parents like them.

Acknowledgements

Many thanks to Hristo Kovatliev for doing my covers for this series, and to Cassandra Bailey for the great maps and floorplans.

Thanks also to Russ Henley for answering all my questions about big trucks.

Rocky Keys, your expertise on radios, antennae, solar panels, and rigging up gadgets from what seems like junk was priceless. Thank you.

Dr. Nancé Hicks, thank you for allowing me to pick your brain on the medical aspects of this book, and for taking the time from your busy life to be a beta reader, as well.

Speaking of beta readers, all mine know very well how much I need them. My sincere thanks to Laura "Eagle Eye" Gibson, and Jennifer "Hawkeye" Murray for catching so many mistakes. Scott Kenney, you are one in a million, and I appreciate your help more than I can say. Jinnie Lettkemann, your critical evaluation has made me a better writer, and I hope we will become friends.

And thanks to my dear husband Jack for listening to lots of crazy ideas and helping me brainstorm, and for supporting me in this endeavor, even though it means we eat out a lot and have a dirty house.

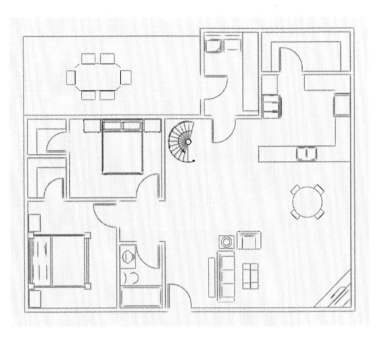

First Floor of the Lodge

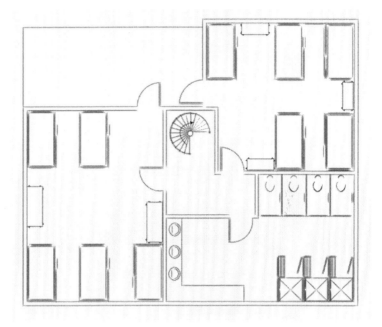

Second Floor of the Lodge

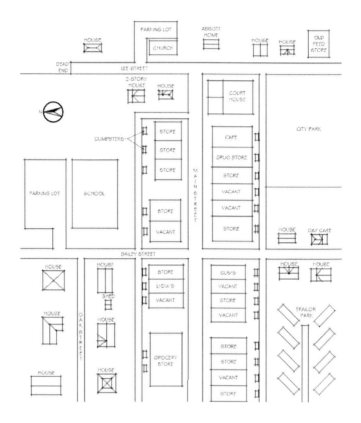

The Town of Kanichi Springs

Population before the Collapse: 472

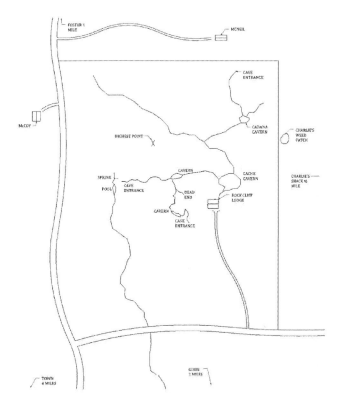

The Lodge Overview

The Story So Far . . .

A freelance editor of survival manuals and prepper fiction, Erin Miller moved to Kanichi Springs from Tulsa, following the death of her beloved Uncle Ernie. He left her a house in town and a hunting lodge in the wilderness. It took Erin a while to find the secret door in the pantry that led her from the lodge to a system of caves and caverns, the largest of which Ernie had filled with supplies.

While running errands in town, Erin was accosted by a parolee in front of the courthouse, and a handsome giant of a man named Tanner McNeil rescued her. He and Erin became friends, and Tanner devoted himself to making the relationship something more. When she discovered signs that someone was skulking around the lodge,, he let her have his favorite dog, Blitz, the very best of the police and personal guard dogs he trained.

Just as Erin was settling in and making new friends in the tiny town, a series of terror attacks on US and British bases in Afghanistan triggered a retaliatory strike by rogue US pilots, resulting in a total embargo against the US by members of OPEC. Terrorists then hit refineries and pipelines, as well as oil storage facilities, bridges, and the electrical grid in the US, causing a breakdown of the American economy and chaos in the cities.

Erin's friends from Tulsa, forced by riots and fires to evacuate, came to stay with her at the lodge, then several others joined them. Richie Baxter, the local pharmacist, was forced to abandon his store due to addicts demanding drugs. He brought his entire inventory of medications to the lodge. Shane Ramsey saved Erin and Tanner from an armed prison escapee, and was invited to join the group. Micah Phillips, a young street kid, and Gus Jenkins, who owned the mechanic shop in town, came as well.

Gangs of convicts, escapees from the nearby state prison, wreaked havoc on the area, and the group from the lodge fought one such gang, killing all but the leader, a convicted rapist and thief, and the same man who had threatened Erin the day she met Tanner.

The Characters   (alphabetically by last name)

Ken and Terri Abbott – preacher where Erin attends church and his wife; parents of four

Richie Baxter – owner and pharmacist at Richie's Drug

Dana and John Benoit – Tanner's sister and brother-in-law; parents of Zeke and Tucker

Lydia Clark – Erin's friend; divorced; owner of a gift shop in Kanichi Springs

Clint Ellis – an NSU student who got caught up in a convict gang by accident

Charles Farley – former sniper in Vietnam; grower of premium quality marijuana

Angie Foster – ER nurse; wife of Nolan; mother of Paul, Quinn, and Amaya

Nolan Foster – retired Marine; husband of Angie

Heather Gibbs, Hunter Gibbs - Jimmy's twins; sophomores at OSU

Jimmy Gibbs – widower; son of Lee and Naomi; father of Hunter and Heather

Lee and Naomi Gibbs – Erin's neighbors and friends from church; Jimmy's parents

Gus Jenkins - the town mechanic

Barry Kline – deputy sheriff in Kanichi Springs

Rose and Will Lapointe – Tanner's sister and brother-in law; parents of Gina, Isabelle, and Wyatt

Manuel "Sarge" Lopez – sergeant in the National Emergency Recovery Corps in

Pueblo, Colorado; former Army Ranger

Sarah Logan – Erin's friend; a high school science teacher

BJ and Frances Martin – Jen's parents

David and Price Martin – the "Martin Menaces"; Jen's brothers; NSU students; NERC troopers

Jennifer Martin – Erin's best friend; car salesperson; daughter of BJ and Frances

Julia McNeil – Talako's wife; Tanner's grandmother; a Choctaw wise woman

Talako McNeil – Tanner's grandfather; Choctaw Council member

Tanner McNeil – breeder and trainer of police and personal protection dogs

Ian McClure – Tanner's best friend; owner of a furniture store in McAlester

Mac and Claire McCoy – a trucker/ ham radio operator and his wife; parents of Kyra

Micah Phillips – a kid whose foster parents died, leaving him alone in the world

Shane Ramsey – Tanner's friend; martial arts expert

Ollie Simmons – convicted rapist and burglar; leader of a gang of escaped convicts

Vince Sullivan – lieutenant at the prison; Ian's friend

Noah Thomason – a young fellow from Texas trying to get home from Okmulgee

Chapter 1 – Early September

Charles Farley crept through a forest lit only by the quarter moon. It was a few minutes past 5:00 a.m., according to the fluorescent dial on his watch. That trusty Timex required winding every day, but he had been doing it for forty years and the old timepiece still worked. He had left the lodge a little after 4:00, dressed in camouflage clothing from head to foot.

About a hundred yards from his destination, he slowed, easing forward with as much stealth as a man in his late sixties could muster, careful to avoid brushing against bushes and stepping on sticks that might make a noise. Charlie had a touch of arthritis, but otherwise, remained in remarkably good health. His eyesight, in particular, was excellent, and he could shoot almost as well as he had as a sniper in Vietnam. Today, he hoped that good luck would join with his good vision, because he had a hankering for pork. Wild hogs were fairly abundant in the area, and Charlie knew some good places to hunt.

Inching forward the last several yards, he threw out some potato and apple peels with the butt ends and greens from several carrots, then slipped into a nearby ground blind he and his buddy Gus had constructed a few weeks earlier, nestled in the arms of a grove of young pine trees that bordered a clearing. He placed a small green cushion, one that Frances Martin had made for him, on an upturned bucket that served as a seat, and settled in to wait. Two game trails crossed about twenty yards in front of his blind, which was near a stream. For the past several days, Charlie had come to that crossing to toss out any food scraps that he could collect. He had seen deer and hog tracks, and he knew that the hogs had been eating the little offerings he left for them.

Them pigs are alert and got noses like a bloodhound, but they don't see worth a durn, he thought. *I hope they don't get wind of me and spook today, but if I don't see one, I'll try for a deer. Sure got my mouth ready for pig, though. Be a nice change.*

Charlie had showered with a scent-killer body wash that Tanner let him use, and laundered his camo in the creek near the lodge, hanging it out on some cedar trees so it would absorb their natural scent instead of the aromas of humans and their cooking. He even chewed some of Tanner's chlorophyll gum to neutralize his breath.

He sat motionless, listening intently to the nearly silent forest. The air was unusually still; the quiet was deep and profound, but Charlie's patience paid off. Just minutes before sunrise, he heard the grunts and snuffling of feral hogs looking for food.

Four big sows came into the clearing, along with several younger pigs of various ages, including a litter of piglets that were maybe a couple of months old. As the light from the rising sun began to illuminate the forest, Charlie picked out the biggest sow, took a couple of deep breaths, and slowly raised his Excalibur crossbow. The sow moved a bit, sniffing out scraps on the ground, and turned slightly, giving Charlie a good angle to bring her down. He let out his breath and fired the bolt into the sow's side, right behind the shoulder.

At the sharp *thunk* of the shot, the pigs scattered in all directions, the sow running about thirty yards before she stopped. She stood still for several seconds, as though she wasn't sure what had happened, then she shook, staggered a few steps, and dropped. Listening intently, Charlie waited until he was certain that the sow was down for good before moving around or making any noise. After about fifteen minutes, he felt sure she was dead.

Charlie used his handheld radio to contact Gus. "How 'bout some pork roast for supper?"

"Sounds good to me. I'll bring the game cart and be there in a bit."

Charlie stood and stretched, then exited the blind to get a closer look at his kill. She was dark red, with the long snout that is typical of feral hogs. He estimated that she weighed about 180 pounds. He got out his hunting knife and went to work, field dressing her.

Times sure has changed, he thought. *Not too many years ago, they was shootin' these pigs from helicopters and leavin' 'em lie on the ground, just to get rid of 'em. Hogs can tear up a pasture or destroy a crop overnight, but now, folks is glad to see 'em, not bein' able to run to the store and buy meat whenever they feel like it. They taste just as good the pork from the store, but the meat is leaner. Sure gonna be good to have some pork to eat.*

When he finished, Gus had still not arrived, so Charlie walked down to the stream to rinse his knife blade and hands. He knelt, swishing his fingers in the cool water. He rubbed at the blood, then shook his hands and held them out to air dry in the gentle breeze. He caught a whiff of dead meat, and glancing around, saw something large and dark lying on the ground under a hickory tree some distance across the stream. Stepping on rocks, he crossed the shallow stream and approached the tree, a feeling of dread coming over him. When he understood what he was seeing, his jaw clenched in anger at the same time that his stomach seemed to rebel. He swallowed hard several times, trying not to vomit.

Three bodies, or what was left of them, lay sprawled on the rocky ground, crawling with maggots and flies. Their clothing was torn and covered with dried blood. Edging closer, Charlie could see from the round holes in their clothing and skulls that each of them had been shot repeatedly. Each one wore a badge that said "Kanichi Springs Police Department".

"Charlie? Where are you?" Gus called.

"Over here, Gus. Found somethin' real bad."

Gus crossed the stream, and when he realized what Charlie had found, a look of horror claimed his face. He stared for a long moment, then looked at Charlie as if he was begging him to say it wasn't real.

"Dear Lord, that's our cops. All of them," he whispered.

"This was no accident, and for sure not natural causes. Them officers was murdered. See them bullet holes and the blood on their uniforms? Somebody wanted 'em dead. Got 'em out here somehow and shot 'em."

"It's a terrible thing. Chief Johnson was a good man, and those two were just young fellows. I don't think either one of them was thirty yet. What a shame."

Charlie started looking all around, examining the ground near the bodies, and Gus asked him why. "Any evidence is probably gone, with all the rain we've had. These bodies have been here a while."

"I'm just lookin'." Charlie used his booted foot to move some leaves aside, and scanned the area carefully. "Hey, check this out." He pointed at something shiny near Gus's foot. "There's a cigarette lighter."

Gus leaned over and picked the old lighter up. He turned it over, then his eyes met Charlie's.

"This belonged to Deputy Kline. I never saw him that he wasn't turning it over and over in his hand. You think he killed these men?"

Charlie stared at the scorpion design on the lighter. "I always thought he was dirty. If he didn't kill 'em, he was likely here when it happened. His body ain't here, so he was in on it. Had to be."

"What should we do now?"

"Haul that porker back to the lodge and tell the others. We gotta bury the bodies, what the critters didn't eat. These boys deserve a decent burial."

"It's a wonder that there's anything left to bury. I don't think it was the pigs been eating on them. Maybe it was coyotes. Wild pigs wouldn't leave anything but the teeth behind, and human meat isn't their food of choice. There's plenty of other stuff for them to eat this time of year, and they wouldn't just nibble on 'em and leave the rest, if they was hungry enough to start 'em in the first place. Guess whatever it was hadn't had time to get around to finishing them off. They just ate some of the soft parts."

The two old friends crossed the stream and, with some difficulty, loaded the sow onto the game cart, then headed home, taking turns pulling the cart. The lodge was a beehive of activity when they arrived. Mac McCoy had brought his wife and young daughter over. They were just getting out of their truck when Angie and Nolan Foster arrived at the same time that Gus and Charlie pulled the game cart into the yard. Several of the group's members were waiting on the porch.

"What's goin' on?" Charlie wondered.

"Claire's in labor. Her water broke about an hour ago," Angie explained. "Sarah, would you take Kyra and keep her occupied for a while? Val, we'll need water boiled, and clean towels. Erin, are there baby things in the cavern?"

Mac interrupted. "We've got a bag in the truck with diapers and baby clothes."

"How far apart are the contractions?" Angie asked.

"About three minutes, a little less."

Erin ran out to the truck to retrieve the bag while Mac and Angie got Claire settled on Erin's bed.

The other men gathered around Charlie and Gus, talking about the big sow and offering to help with it. The two older men waited until the hog was hung and all the women were out of earshot before mentioning the dead police officers.

"Charlie found something else out there that you need to know about. Charlie, tell them."

"I went to the stream to wash the blood off my hands, and found the cops from town. They're dead, all three of 'em. Murdered. Hard to tell when, but not real recent. Critters had been at 'em, but we could still tell they was shot several times each."

A shocked silence fell as Charlie spoke. Tanner finally asked the question that was on everyone's mind. "Any idea who did it?"

"We found this." Charlie thrust his hand out and opened his fist. "Right beside the remains." The old silver lighter gleamed in the sun.

"I always knew he was bad," Tanner muttered, and the others agreed.

Vince looked confused. "Who? Who are you talking about?"

"See that lighter? Just about anyone in this part of the county would recognize it. Barry

Kline, the deputy assigned to our area, carried it. Not in his pocket. In his hand, and he fiddled with it constantly, turning it over and over, rubbing it with his fingers. I don't know where he got it or why he carried it all the time, but he had it for years." Tanner shook his head. "It's hard not to jump to conclusions. He may not have pulled the trigger, but it's a good bet that he was there, so from now on, everyone needs to be on the lookout for him."

"He always seemed arrogant to me. Liked to throw his weight around, be the boss. I've talked to a lot of people who had problems with him. Never did do his job, if you ask me." Gus frowned. "The only laws he ever enforced were traffic laws, and then, only if you were on his bad side. Anyone who crossed him got stopped soon after, and got a ticket. I don't remember him ever solving a crime of any kind, not a theft or vandalism or anything else. The only crime solving was done by the city cops or the state police."

"I heard rumors about him at the prison," Vince commented. "Some of the inmates talked like he was their friend; others made fun of him. I don't remember hearing any of them say the kinds of things about him that they usually said about officers. If they didn't hate him or fear him, that tells me that he wasn't a good cop."

"So what are we going to do about the bodies? Every vehicle we have is short on gas." Ian scratched his head. "We can't just leave them out there."

"We'll think of something," Gus assured them. "We have to."

Mac burst out of the lodge's front door. "It's a boy! I have a son!" he called to the men, his huge grin splitting a face that was wet with tears of joy.

Some of the men called out congratulations and started toward the lodge, but Tanner stopped them long enough to murmur, "Let's keep this quiet around the women and Mac, at least for now. Let them celebrate this birth without ruining their memories of the day."

The others nodded, then crossed the clearing to shake Mac's hand and slap him on the back. Angie came out and placed the new baby in his father's arms. Tanner picked Kyra up so she could see her new brother. Everyone gathered around to admire the little guy, who had a headful of red hair just like his daddy's. Mac leaned down with him so that Blitz, Major, and Flash could sniff him and get acquainted.

Mac straightened, so proud he felt like he would burst. "Claire's doing great, and my boy is healthy and strong, His name is Ford Allen, after Angie's grandpa and my dad. This is surely a day full of blessings," Mac beamed.

Little Ford blinked a few times, then yawned.

"Daddy! He doesn't have any teeth!" Kyra gasped.

After the laughter died down, Mac explained to Kyra that her brother was fine, that his teeth would grow in soon. She looked skeptical, but finally agreed to wait and see.

Chapter 2 – The Next Morning

"Mac, please. For the sake of Claire and the children, move in with us," Erin pleaded. "It's just not safe for you at your place."

Mac rested his arms on the glass top of the patio table and stared off into the forest for several seconds. The trees that seemed so thick from a distance, or from the top of the mountain, were actually not close at all; instead, most were several feet apart. Rocky terrain and the lack of sunlight beneath the thick foliage kept the undergrowth to a minimum.

Erin cleared her throat to regain Mac's attention. He turned to her, his expression stubborn. "Not yet. We're doing fine. Now that the convict gang is dead, there's not as much danger as you think. I can take care of my family."

"Oh, Mac, I know you can, under normal circumstances, but things are far from normal. Ollie Simmons may still be in the area, and there are other convicts who escaped from the prison. You can't stay awake all the time, and neither can Claire. And the two of you can't fight off a hungry mob. What about all those refugees you told us about, the people leaving the cities? They've got to be getting desperate by now."

"Last I heard, there were groups of folks walking out of Tulsa and Oklahoma City in every direction. Most are staying on the major roads, which I personally think is dangerous. There's been looting and scavenging, but I have only heard of a few murders. Most folks are not turning into monsters, at least not yet. That could change, I know, but it hasn't so far. Of course, it may just be that nobody has discovered the bodies.

"I also heard about some so-called 'religious' cult out in California. They dress all in black, and roam around inviting people to join them, but when anybody refuses, they make them into slaves. Word has gotten around, so most folks are frightened into joining up. Supposedly, they believe the collapse is a punishment from the gods, and they believe in several gods. I didn't get many details on that, but it sounded like they borrowed some from Celtic and Norse myths and mixed them all up together, then added in some sexual perversion for good measure.

"I only listen on my radio lately. I very seldom say anything, and when I do, I never drop even a hint about where I am or what we've got. We're far enough into the boonies that I'm sure we'll be okay. I appreciate your offer, Erin, but we're going home as soon as Claire feels up to it. We need to get out of here before you girls spoil our kids any more than you already have." His wry smile told her he was kidding.

"Okay, Mac, but the offer stays open. You don't have to ask. If you need to come here, or need any kind of help at all, you've got it. Now what else have you heard lately from other places?"

"It's bad in the big cities. Really bad. Huge gangs have divided up the cities and are engaged in constant turf wars. There's hardly anything to eat anywhere, and the stores have all been looted. The gangs raid each other's territory and steal whatever they can, including women and young girls. In areas where there are lots of Muslims, they have either barricaded themselves in, or gone into hiding. Some folks blame all Muslims for the actions of the governments in the Middle East. They act like all Muslims are terrorists. I have mixed feelings about that. If Islam is a peaceful religion, why didn't the ones who weren't 'radicalized' speak out against the violence? I knew a few Muslims, and they seemed like nice folks, but their beliefs seem to me to be incompatible with America's way of life. I don't blame them all for what happened, but I do wonder about why they didn't take a stand against terrorism.

"Even in less populated areas, things are rough. I heard two guys talking about upstate New York. One said that he is living in an abandoned cabin in the woods. He has some food stored, but he's eating it cold. He even ate raw meat from a rabbit he trapped."

"Yuk! Why'd he do that?"

"He would have had to cook outside on an open fire. He said that the aroma of meat cooking might attract people who would kill to get food, so he just doesn't cook. I don't know how folks will stay warm this winter. The smoke from a fire would be visible during the day, and at night, people could see the glow from even a little fire from a long way off. He said that hiding out is the best way to stay alive."

"I'm glad that there aren't any huge cities around here. Dallas is too close, if you ask me. Millions of people lived in the Metroplex before the collapse. I wonder how many are still there."

"From what I gathered just listening, they had a really big exodus the first couple of weeks, then there was a spell of pretty serious violence. Looting, killing, gangs – it was dangerous to go outside at all, and that drove even more people to flee. Right after that, the sickness started. It wasn't just one disease, either. From the description I heard, it sounds like something respiratory, and something else that causes severe vomiting and diarrhea. Probably thousands of people have died already, and there aren't enough people left to dispose of all the bodies. Rats are everywhere. The sewers are backed up. People can't flush because there's no water, so diseases are bound to spread. Any standing water quickly becomes contaminated with human and animal waste. People are just pooping and peeing wherever they happen to be. They're having to drink water from the river and the creeks, but rain has washed their poop into the water. Without clean water, people are bound to get sick. I guess the smart ones were the ones who got out, although who knows if the places they went are any better?"

"And those refugees may be in our neighborhood soon. Promise me, Mac, that if you feel like it's becoming unsafe at your house, you'll come here."

"I promise that if we see any bad guys, or we feel threatened, you'll be stuck with us for the duration. We'll live in one of those caverns you told us about."

"No, you won't! I'll be happy to move upstairs and bunk with the girls. Your family will have that bedroom."

Erin held up her hand to stop Mac's protest. "Don't argue with me, Mac. It's a done deal. Claire and the kids don't need to be sleeping in a cave that stays so cool all the time. Now, if you'll excuse me, I think my knowledge of diseases is in need of improvement. I'm going to the cache cavern and see if there's a book about contagious illnesses. Maybe there are steps we can take to avoid getting sick. Knowing Uncle Ernie, there'll be at least one book on the subject."

***

Erin went to the cavern to search for information, but Mac stayed on the patio to enjoy the peacefulness and to say another prayer, thanking God for his family and friends. He kept thinking how blessed he was to know people who were willing to help others, and who would even take an armed stand against evil. Tanner came out the back door and took a seat beside him. The two men looked at each other, smiling, then sat for several minutes and listened to the quiet sounds of the forest.

"Mac, I need to talk to you about something." Tanner spoke quietly, looking apologetic at interrupting their reverie. "We have a problem and I need your input."

"Okay. What's on your mind?"

Tanner took a long, deep breath. "Charlie made a discovery right after he shot that pig yesterday. He went to the creek to wash up, and found the bodies of the cops from town."

"Wha-…uh…*all three* of them?" Mac looked horrified.

"Yes. They'd been shot multiple times. The men want to give them a proper burial, but we don't know where to bury them."

Mac gave him a confused look. "The obvious place is the town cemetery."

"Well, that's the problem. We aren't sure we have enough gas to get to town and back. We've siphoned all we could from the extra vehicles already, and used up a lot making runs into town in Ian's truck, getting supplies from my kennel and Ernie's house. Do you know of anywhere nearby that would be suitable to bury them?"

"It's too rocky. You planning on digging graves by hand?"

"We'll have to. Isn't there somewhere close that isn't so rocky?"

Mac took a long, deep breath. "Tanner, I haven't said anything because the supply is not infinite, and I would appreciate it if you kept it quiet, even among the group members. I'm afraid that BJ will insist on going after his boys when he finds out where they are, and right now, that's a fool's errand. And some might want to use it up running around the area scavenging. I also don't want any bad guys to find out about it, and if they see or hear a vehicle, they might come looking."

"For what? Mac, what in the world are you talking about?"

"I'm saying that I have fuel. A tanker load. I was supposed to deliver it to McAlester, but I kept hearing on my CB that there was trouble all over. When I heard about the refineries getting blown up, I just brought the tanker on home. It's hidden over at our place. I put stabilizer in it and haven't said a word to anyone, but I have gasoline, about 9,000 gallons of it. I know that sounds like a lot, but we can't afford to waste it."

"I understand your reasoning, but I also think you should have trusted someone with the information. If something happened to you and you hadn't told anyone, we'd never have guessed it. Too many secrets can be dangerous."

"I know. It isn't that I don't trust you. It's that the fewer people who know about it, the less chance that it'll become known outside the group. Anyway, we have plenty to take our police officers into town. Maybe that builder, Brian, is still around and can dig the graves for us."

"I'll contact Ken and ask him. He'll probably want to do a graveside service. That'd be good, I think."

"Yeah. I hate this whole thing. Three good men. The chief was married, and barely in his fifties. I think the other two were single men. They were both nice fellas. What a terrible waste, dying like that."

Tanner shook his head, then stood. "I need to climb the mountain and try to raise Ken on the radio. It's a sad day."

Tanner went back into the lodge to tell Erin where he was going and why. Shane came in while they were talking and offered to go along, so he and Tanner grabbed rifles and headed toward the spot on the mountain where radio reception was best.

The two friends didn't talk much on the hike. Both of them were too busy keeping an eye on their surroundings, watching for danger. What would have seemed paranoid just a few months earlier had become routine and necessary since the collapse. They were careful to go a slightly different way when they traveled anywhere in the woods, so they wouldn't leave a trail that might lead strangers to the lodge. They also scanned for signs that others had been in the area.

Shane kept going when Tanner stopped to use his radio. He went about fifty yards further up the hill, stopping in a cluster of trees so he could stand guard while Tanner talked.

Tanner only spoke once on his handheld before he got an answer. Terri Abbott told him that Ken was in the basement fellowship hall at the church building, so he probably hadn't heard the radio. Tanner debated briefly about waiting while Terri went to get Ken, but decided that she would learn the terrible news soon anyway.

"We have some sad business to take care of, Terri. Charlie was out hunting yesterday, and found

Chief Johnson and both of our police officers. They were murdered. We need to get them buried, and wondered if Ken would do a service at the cemetery. And if he's still around, maybe Brian Powell could use his Bobcat to prepare the graves."

There was a long pause. "Oh, I hate hearing this." Terri sounded like she was crying. "Of course, we'll help in any way we can. I'll go tell Ken and we'll get back to you shortly."

Only about ten minutes passed before Ken's voice came over the radio.

"Tanner? You there?"

"Yeah, Ken. Sorry to bear such bad news."

"We have Yvonne Johnson here. She's been staying with us since the prison riots, because her husband didn't come home. We just told her. She took it like she was expecting it, but she's still pretty broken up. Terri and the other ladies are with her."

"Do you know if Brian is still around?"

"Haven't seen him in town, but I've already sent two of the men out to his place to see if he's there. If he's not, we'll use shovels, but we'll get the graves dug somehow. The funeral home is abandoned, but of course, they left all the caskets that were stored in the back. If you can get the bodies to town, we'll take care of getting everything ready here."

***

One of the men who had gone to see Brian knocked on the door of the Powell residence just outside

Kanichi Springs. Brian peeked out, recognized the men, and opened the door. He listened, then promised to be in town early the next morning to dig the graves with his equipment.

"Fortunately, I still have a little fuel stored in the back. Not a lot, but for this, I'll use it. See you tomorrow."

***

It was a beautiful, bright day with only a few white puffs of clouds in an azure sky. Tanner, Ian, and Shane used Talako's game cart to move the bodies one at a time to Ian's truck at the lodge. Mac brought over a few cans of gasoline and poured some into the tanks of the furniture truck and Erin's green Expedition. Ian drove his vehicle and Tanner drove Erin's. The people at the lodge who had known the officers went into town, but several who were not acquainted with them stayed behind to guard the lodge.

Ian drove straight to the funeral home, where Ken and a couple of men from the church had three caskets waiting. The men took on the gruesome job of placing the bodies as respectfully as they could, considering the deteriorated condition of the remains.

"This definitely needs to be a closed casket service," Ken sighed. "I've already spoken with Mrs. Johnson. She understands that she's better off remembering him the way he was. She won't ask to see her husband. The other men didn't have any relatives in town. I don't know if they have any family anywhere, I'm ashamed to say."

Ian drove the truck slowly to the cemetery, which was an easy walk from the church, and most of the people who were staying there attended the service. Ken spoke briefly about how the officers had served the town faithfully, and about salvation and eternal life. He said a prayer, and a small group sang "It Is Well with My Soul" while the caskets were lowered using ropes.

Brian waited patiently until the mourners were back inside the church building before starting up his Bobcat and filling in the triple-sized grave. Tanner stood to the side, watching the area while Brian worked.

Brian loaded the Bobcat onto its trailer and climbed into his truck, then motioned for Tanner to hop in.

"Brian, thank you. You saved us from some back-breaking work today. How have you been?"

"I manage. Ernie got me to thinking about prepping, but I left it too late. I didn't get a lot done before the collapse, but with fishing, I get by. Some days, when the fish are really biting, I bring the extra ones to the church. I don't have any way to keep it from spoiling, and it gives me a chance to help out some. You still out at your place?"

"No, I moved out to my grandparents' house, then into the lodge that Ernie left to Erin. There's quite a group there now. We had a meeting last night, and they were all in agreement that if you need help, or have to leave your place, you're welcome to join us."

"Are you sure you want to take on another mouth to feed?"

"We are. It takes a lot of adults to do all the work that needs to be done, and stand watch, too. Some people think Erin is crazy to take in so many people, but I think Ernie would approve. There's strength in numbers, and people who are alone or with only a few others can't keep up the pace over time, doing all the work by hand and staying alert for trouble, too. We have good folks who contribute plenty to the group, more than compensating for the supplies they use up. Ernie used to say that if you're staying in one place, you need a minimum of sixteen adults just to cover the necessary everyday jobs. There's lots of room, and Erin has quite the green thumb. She grew a lot of food over the summer, and the women canned it to add to the food storage. Charlie and I have kept the group and the folks at the church supplied with venison and wild hog, and Ian fishes in the creek. We're doing well, considering."

"Wow. It's good to hear that someone is doing well, and it's kind of you to help the town folk so much. I wasn't expecting this invitation. I truly do appreciate it. Could I have some time to think about it?"

"Sure." Tanner handed Brian a radio and a solar charger. "If you need to get hold of us or Ken, we all carry these. Just let us know if you need us, buddy. Now, would you come inside with me for a few minutes? There's some information I've been asked to share, and you need to hear it, too."

Tanner and Brian entered the church foyer, then descended the stairs to the basement, where Ken had gathered everyone except for those on guard duty.

"Friends, it's been a sad day for what's left of our town," Tanner began. "I need to tell you that our officers and Chief Johnson were shot several times each, by someone who lured them or forced them out into the wilderness area. Charlie discovered them when he was hunting, or no telling how long it would have been before they were found. We don't know who fired the shots, or when, but we know that it wasn't real recent. There was only a single piece of evidence found at the scene."

Every eye was on Tanner and silence filled the room. Tanner pulled his hand out of his pocket and held up the lighter. Several people gasped.

"We all know who this belongs to. We do *not* know that he pulled the trigger, but we can be pretty sure he was there. This means that if you see him anywhere, avoid contact. Stay away from him. Hide, if you have to, but remember that Barry Kline cannot be trusted. Please let Terri or Ken know if you see Kline, so they can let us know. From now on, consider Deputy Kline to be armed and dangerous, and don't let him convince you otherwise."

***

Tanner's grandparents had stayed home, reluctantly missing the brief service. Talako and Julia had been friends with Chief Johnson and his wife, but they couldn't leave their daughters and sons-in-law shorthanded. With only six adults to stand watch and care for five active children, plus do the work required to survive, they were already struggling to cover all the bases.

Julia dusted flour from her hands, took off her apron, and left Rose to finish the batch of tortillas they were making. She found Talako sitting on the sofa in the living room, where he had gun parts and his cleaning kit laid out on old newspapers that covered the coffee table.

She slipped in beside him and kissed his weathered cheek, smiling at the man she had called "husband" for over fifty years. They had known each other since they were both too young to remember, and had grown up on neighboring farms. Their friendship as children had blossomed into a deep and abiding love, rooted in their Choctaw heritage. Talako had a Scottish ancestor, a trader several generations back, who had married a Choctaw woman, and while Julia's family was proud of their pure-blood status, her parents didn't object to her marriage to a man who obviously loved their daughter, and who was so knowledgeable about the Choctaw culture and language.

Their lives had been blessed with children, grandchildren, and great grandchildren. When trouble came, as it does in every life, they had weathered it together, as a team. Hard work and frugality had allowed them to prosper, and Julia believed that every single thing they had was a heavenly gift, that God's hand had guided them through making every decision along the way.

"Do you think that we should consider moving to the lodge?" she quietly asked. "All of us are exhausted, and we're spread too thin to adequately guard this place. If just one of us gets hurt or sick, we won't be able to manage."

"I've been thinking about it, and praying, too. It seems to me that it's inevitable that those of us who live in the area will eventually have to deal with refugees from the cities, gangs of thugs, or both. They'll gradually work their way to our area. If we stay here until they come, we may be driven from our home and have to leave most of our supplies behind. I don't want to be a burden to Erin by arriving empty-handed, but I'm also not quite ready to leave our home."

"So, why don't we go ahead and move the bulk of our preps into the caves? Our children and grandchildren played around here for years and never found the entrance, so I don't think the bad guys will find it, either. We can go ahead and move most of our supplies, maybe keep a few weeks' worth of supplies here, then when we have to bug out, we won't have to worry about anything except getting the children to safety. If we run out of something here, we can easily go to the caves to get more."

"My *ohoyo¹,* that's an excellent idea. You're still one very smart gal. Let's ask Erin and Tanner to come over, and we'll discuss the best way to do it."

Talako pulled the radio from his belt and went outside, walking east about a hundred yards to get better reception. After a brief conversation with Tanner, Talako returned to the house.

"Tanner and Erin will be here in about thirty minutes. They're bringing Micah, too, so he can visit with the boys."

Julia made tea and set out some sugar cookies that Dana had made the day before. She caught Talako's grin and demanded, "What?"

"Oh, nothing."

"Don't give me 'oh, nothing,'" she warned.

"You're just a very special woman. Here we are, in the middle of a collapse, with the whole country falling apart, but you're thoughtful and generous enough to offer our guests refreshments. I am so proud to be married to a woman who has the class to observe a few social graces at a time like this."

"If we forget the things that set us apart from the animals, we'll lose our humanity. I refuse to let this family sink to that level."

"Have I told you today that I love you with all my heart?"

"You just did. I love you, too."

***

Tanner, Erin, and Micah slipped quietly through the back door of the McNeil home. Tanner patted Micah

---

[1] Wise woman

on the shoulder and told him, "Good job. You're learning to move more quietly." Talako and Julia hugged them all and invited them into the living room. Dana and John were on guard duty, but Rose and Will joined the other adults after getting the older children settled down with a board game in the dining room. Little Wyatt was asleep in his crib, so for the moment, it was fairly quiet.

"Julia and I think that it's time to move most of our supplies into the cave. We'll only keep enough food for a couple of weeks. If we have to leave here, we don't want to leave our preps behind. Where do you want us to store them?"

Erin looked at Tanner, then turned back to Talako. "The cache cavern has a little room, but we'll probably need to put some things in another cavern. We can get you a lot of help for the move, and we should probably post extra guards during the transfer. I think you're wise to plan ahead like this. Your supplies will be safer in the caves and it'll make it much easier on you when you decide to bug out. When do you want to do it?"

"Soon. Maybe in a few days, a week at the most," Julia said.

They chatted for a while, catching up on what news they had, then Rose and Will went to relieve Dana and John so they could spend a little time with the guests. Wyatt woke from his nap and snuggled into Erin's lap to eat a cookie.

"I'll be glad to have you all come stay at the lodge; it'll just be nice to have you with us. Maybe you should just go ahead and come now," Erin pleaded, "although I hate to think about you being driven from your home.

"We'll stay here for a while, but it'll be a relief to know that our supplies are secure. I guess we need to inventory what's here. I'll plan a menu for two weeks, and get busy sorting out what to move." Julia nodded thoughtfully. "Yes, this is the right decision. It's the best possible thing we can do right now."

Talako offered them more cookies, but they declined, wanting to leave the rest for the children.

"So, what have you heard on Mac's radio lately? Anything interesting?" Talako asked.

"Well, things are really bad in Detroit. That's no surprise, of course. There is basically a war going on there between Muslims and everyone else. Lots of deaths, from what Mac heard. There's a crazy cult in California, and what sounds like cholera is still spreading in several areas, along with a few other diseases. The cities are not a healthy place to be.

"Oh! I almost forgot," Erin added. "He heard from Jen's brothers. David and Price, better known as the 'Martin Menaces.' They've been working for NREC, a branch of FEMA, at some camp in Colorado. They're doing okay, although one of them sent a message to BJ and Francis, hinting that maybe there are problems. David told Mac to tell his dad that they are thinking a lot about old times, especially the pranks they used to pull. He specifically mentioned a stunt at summer camp, back in 2007. He said that it was the best one they ever did, and he thought they might try it again real soon."

"What does that mean?" Julia frowned.

"That's exactly what we asked BJ. It seems that the boys decided that they didn't like the routine at the camp, so they stole some food and ran away. Search parties looked for them for three days. They were almost back home when some of the searchers found them. BJ is convinced that David was trying to tell him that they don't like what's going on where they are, and are preparing to desert, if you can call leaving coerced duty 'desertion'. He wanted to take one of the cars and go after them, but Frances put her foot down. She insisted that their chances coming here would be better than the chances of him making it there alone, finding them, and all of them making it back. I think she's as worried about the boys as she can stand, and adding the worry of BJ being out there would be too much. And she's right; BJ probably wouldn't make it by himself. David and Price know the general location of Kanichi Springs, and they're two resourceful young men, so we may be seeing them soon. We're all praying for their safety."

***

When the children's game was over, Tanner, Erin, and Micah headed back to the cave entrance. Tanner nudged Erin and pointed at Micah's clothes.

"There are holes in his jeans and the back pocket is torn almost off. He's grown some since he came to us, and those britches are about two inches too short. His shirt has a rip, too, and the sole of his left shoe is coming loose. We need to see about finding something for him to wear besides those rags," Tanner murmured.

"Micah!" Erin called in a loud whisper. "Wait up."

The boy stopped, looking sheepish. "Uh, I guess I forgot what Tanner taught me. I did good going, but I'm doing a terrible job going back." He began to count his own transgressions on his fingers. "One, I forgot to move silently, and two, I wasn't watching my surroundings, and three, I didn't use cover, did I? I could have led a bad guy right to the cave. I'm sorry."

"We all need to look around carefully before approaching any cave entrance," Erin explained. "We'd have a very hard time surviving without our supplies, Let's try to do better, until caution becomes a habit, okay?"

"Okay."

Tanner was looking into the forest, carefully scrutinizing the area. Erin and Micah both began searching the woods for anything unusual. Finally, Tanner signaled for them to keep moving, but silently. Just a few feet from the concealed entrance, they scanned the area once again, then quickly slipped through a gap between a large boulder and a stand of birch saplings.

The temperature dropped several degrees as they stepped into the dark cave. Picking up the flashlights they had left there when they came through earlier, they turned them on and walked single file, remaining quiet until they reached the cavern that Erin had nicknamed "the cabana." They stopped briefly to admire the pretty pool of clear spring water, then continued toward the lodge.

"Micah, how many sets of clothes did you have when we brought you here from Gus's?" Erin asked.

"Three. That is, two pairs of shorts, one pair of jeans, and three tee shirts. Oh, and my hoodie and some underwear. Why?"

"Did you leave more clothes at your house?"

"Sure. But when my foster parents died, I just took what I could fit into my backpack and went to stay with Gus. I was scared to stay at the house by myself. My foster parents got money from the state to buy stuff for me, and sometimes they spent their own money on me, too. They were real nice people, treated me like I was really their kid. I miss them." Micah blinked back tears.

"I know you do. I'm sorry that you've had to go through all this at such a young age. I hope you know that you're welcome to stay with us as long as you want." She ruffled his hair and smiled. "We kinda like having you around."

Micah's expression brightened. "I really like it here. I'm learning a lot from you and from Gus and Charlie. Shane is going to teach me how to kick bu-...uh, how to kick. Ian said I could go fishing with him, and Charlie's going to take me hunting."

"Well, we're going to have to do something about clothes for you, and soon. What you're wearing is about to fall apart. We'll go to town and get your things from your house, but as fast as you're growing, we'll need to get larger sizes soon. Maybe Frances can make you some longer pants for winter. I don't know what we'll do about shoes."

"My grandmother has some hides she tanned, and she knows how to make moccasins. Or maybe we can locate some shoes in town. All the children will probably need shoes eventually, and that's something none of us thought of when we planned our preps."

"Ernie had some extra shoes and boots for me in the cavern, but I'm not growing anymore. How do you figure out what sizes you'll need when there are growing children involved?"

***

Gus dropped into one of the old chairs on the patio behind the lodge. The deck above provided deep shade and made the patio a favorite spot to rest and cool off. Charlie sat in the chair next to Gus, with Shane and Vince on the other side of the glass-topped table, Blitz and Major at their sides.

"I been thinkin'," Charlie began, but Gus cut him off.

"That can't be good."

Charlie glared at him while the others chuckled, then Charlie grinned. "Always the smart mouth, ain'tcha? Well, as I was sayin' before I was so rudely interrupted, I think we need to set up some kinda warnin' system near the cave entrances. Mac said refugees would be in the area soon, and we don't need 'em stumblin' onto our cache."

"What do you have in mind?" Vince asked.

"Well, this here old man," Charlie smirked as he jerked a thumb toward Gus, "is supposed to be a mechanical genius. He oughta be able to figger sumpin' out."

Gus ignored Charlie's jibe, narrowing his eyes as he thought about the problem. Moments of silence passed, as the others quietly watched Gus think.

"Doorbells," was all he said.

"Ah. Doorbells. Got it," Shane agreed, nodding solemnly.

"Huh? What're ya talkin' about?" Charlie demanded, his head pivoting back and forth between Gus and Shane, like he was watching a tennis match.

Vince grinned. "I think they might be talking about, uh, doorbells."

"Dang it! Y'all cut it out and answer the question!"

Gus tried unsuccessfully to smother a huge smile. "We can solve the need for an alarm with doorbells. They hardly use any electricity at all, so they won't drain the solar batteries. The old hardware store got broken into, but I doubt that anyone took doorbells. If they don't have any, we'll get some from abandoned houses in town. All we need is enough wire to run from the cave entrances to the lodge, and three doorbells. I bet I could even hook up some lights in the lodge to show which entrance has intruders. We'll need to bring it into the pantry somehow so it doesn't show or give away the secret door, but we'll figure something out on that. Yeah, three doorbells, and hopefully we can find ones that sound different. And a small light under each one, mounted on the wall in the lodge. A button to push, or a tripwire near each cave entrance. It'll work, I'm sure."

"I bet that once we get the wire and such, we could have it done pretty quick," Vince added. "We need to step it off and get an idea of how much wire we'll need. It's gonna be a lot of wire to string. I hope we can find enough."

***

When Tanner, Erin, and Micah got back to the lodge, the men were just coming in from the patio, and a few of the women came down the spiral stairs at the same time, and everyone started talking at once.

"Hold it!" Erin demanded, holding her hands up to stop the deluge of words. "Please. Just let us sit down, and then we can all take turns."

Most of the group gathered in the living room, finding seats anywhere they could. Richie and BJ were on guard at the doors, but could hear what was being said. Tanner sent the dogs to assist them.

"Okay. Who wants to go first?" Erin asked.

Charlie cleared his throat. "I reckon ol' Gus had a fairly decent idea. Let him tell about it."

Gus shared his plan to set up an alarm system to protect the caves and the supplies, then Frances mentioned that she thought she could make hanging partitions for the caverns to provide privacy and warmth through the winter for any additional people who came to join the group, if only she had some extra blankets. She added that she could make summer clothes for the children from sheets, if there were any left behind in abandoned houses. She also wanted quilts to cut up and make winter jackets and hats.

Then Erin told about their visit with the McNeils and the plan to move their things into the caverns, and how Tanner had noticed that Micah needed clothes from his house in town.

Erin propped her elbows on her knees. "Okay, we have several ideas for improvements, and they all require a trip to town. I guess we'll have to make plans to go soon. Anybody else?"

Lydia raised her hand. "I could sure use some more clothes, too. When I left, I only had what I could carry in a small bag. There's a lot left at my house, if it hasn't been looted already. Frances and I are about the same size, and I'm sure I have some things she can use, too."

"I've been worrying a little about the septic system here." BJ shook his head. "It is handling a lot of waste, with so many of us here. Have we thought of adding some Rid-X or a similar product to the tank?"

"That's something I haven't seen in the cavern, or even under any of the sinks. Uncle Ernie didn't think of everything, after all. Maybe we could find some Rid-X in town," Erin offered.

"I doubt it, unless there's some left in the grocery store or maybe the hardware store. Folks in town didn't need it because they were on the town's sewage system, not septic tanks. We'll look, though. If we don't find any, we can sacrifice some of our sugar and yeast keep it going," BJ offered.

"We have quite a bit of sugar, but not enough yeast to spare, if we want bread to eat," Francis argued.

"Then we'll have to make our own. I saw something in one of Uncle Ernie's books about how to make yeast. We'll make some, and use it for the septic. But we can sure look for Rid-X in town, just in case there's some stashed somewhere. I hope everyone is remembering not to flush toilet paper. We all need to remember to use as little as possible, and put it in the trash basket. Wads of toilet paper are a major cause of septic problems, not that we have much paper left to use, anyway."

"What'll we do when it runs out?" Lydia wanted to know.

"Ever heard of 'family cloths'? We'll be doing a lot more laundry, and finally using up some of the swimming pool chlorine that's stored in the cavern. Ernie once told me that liquid chlorine loses its effectiveness as a disinfectant over time, but the dry stuff will last for ages, as long as it stays dry. We'll put a little in a five-gallon bucket in each bathroom, with some water, and we'll use the cheap washcloths that we found in the cavern to clean ourselves, then drop the dirty ones in the chlorine solution. They'll have to be washed in really hot water, separate from our other laundry. It's not ideal, but it sure beats not being able to wipe at all," Erin explained.

"Let's contact the McCoys, the Gibbses, and the Fosters and see if they need anything. We'll plan on going in the morning, and we can take some food to the folks at the church at the same time. While we're out, we should go by the kennel and pick up the rest of Tanner's supplies. How about we let Ian, Lydia, and Gus plan the trip? Tomorrow might be a good day to go." Erin yawned. "Now, it's been a busy, tiring day. I'm going to rest for a bit. Somebody wake me up in about an hour."

***

Erin, Jen, Sarah, and Val all had a little free time that evening, so they took a couple of crank-up flashlights, and wearing swimsuits under their clothes, went to the little pool in the northernmost cavern. The spring that fed the pool was warm, so the four friends lowered themselves into the water with sighs and moans of pleasure.

"Being able to shower and wash my hair every day is something I really miss," Val groaned. "Erin, are you sure it's okay for us to use this water for bathing? I mean, won't we get it dirty?"

"Tanner said that it must have an outlet somewhere, since there's water coming in, but it doesn't overflow. That should make it sort of self-cleaning."

"It feels great to just sit here," Jen sighed. "I miss daily showers, too, but mostly, I miss eating out and going dancing. I don't miss work, though, not at all. I was good at selling cars, but that's a man's world. No way would I ever have made sales manager, and the routine was getting old. I didn't even realize I was in such as rut."

"I miss my job." Sarah frowned and shook her head. "It may sound corny, but I loved teaching, having an impact on young people, knowing that they were about to go off to college or to work. I really, really miss that. What do you miss, Erin?"

Erin looked thoughtful. "I don't. Truly, I just don't miss much of anything. Yes, there were conveniences and fun things to do, but my life was actually pretty shallow. Most of the books I edited were good reads, but very little of the fiction I edited had much real impact on people's lives. I guess Uncle Ernie's books at least made people think. I know they influenced lots of people to prepare for emergencies and crises, but most of the rest were just stories, enjoyable stories, to let people escape from their lives.

"Here, I've found a place to call home, with people who need me. I am in a position to help people and I have a purpose. I'm the one with the most gardening skill, and I can pass that on to others. I've made new friends and deepened my relationship with each of you, and I've found a man to love, trust, and admire. I'm more content than I've ever been, and every day is both a blessing and a challenge."

"Speaking of men…is it just me, or does it seem like Richie kinda likes Lydia?" Val's eyebrows emphasized the question, arching over sparkling eyes.

"If she volunteers or is asked to do something, he offers to help, and I've noticed that they sit together for most meals, and it isn't always Richie who makes that happen," Jen mused. "I think there's interest on both sides."

"Richie's a nice guy, really sweet, and good-looking now that he's toned up a little, and he must be pretty smart, too. Pharmacy school isn't easy. There's a lot of upper-level science involved, like organic chemistry." Sarah rolled her eyes. "Trust me, that's a tough course."

"So Sarah, what's new with you and Ian?" Val inquired.

"Things are developing, I think. Ian and I are moving in that direction, but we're in no hurry."

"Seriously? It looks to me like he's a goner. He can't keep his eyes off you and I think you'd be crazy to let him slip away. He's smart, kind, funny…not to mention *hot*!" Jen poked Sarah with an elbow. "If I hadn't fallen for Shane the day I met him, I'd be giving Ian a second look, for sure."

"Hey, hands off my man," Sarah warned, giving Jen a mock evil eye. "So, Shane, huh? You think he's 'The One'?"

"I do, but I don't think it's mutual." Jen gaped as her friends burst into laughter. "What? It's not funny."

"Yes, it is, Jen. Oh, man," Val gasped. "I can't believe you don't realize that the man is nuts about you. *We've* all known it for weeks."

"No, what? Really?" Jen sputtered.

"Really. No doubt about it," Erin assured her.

Jen shook her head. "I don't understand how a man who can kick several butts at once without even breaking a sweat can't seem to let a woman, one he's supposedly head-over-heels for, know that he's interested. Yeah, he flirts with me, but he does that with every female here, even with Kyra and the twins. I don't think he singles me out, not at all."

"Jen, when you're not looking, he's watching you. He flirts, yes, but mostly when you *are* looking. I think he's trying to get your attention, or make you jealous, maybe. He's super protective toward you. Anytime there's a possibility of danger, he's within striking distance of any threat to you, and he's on guard. His demeanor, his stance, his awareness of everything goes on high alert. Like when we've gone to town, he's watching out for all of us, but especially you. I don't know how to explain it, but keeping you safe is his 'Prime Directive'."

"So, why hasn't he said anything?"

The other women looked at each other and shrugged, just as baffled as Jen.

"Maybe he's thinking that he lost his means of making a living, or maybe he's hoping things will return to normal soon. Who knows what a man is thinking? Shane might be one of those old-fashioned men who wants to be the provider, or at least financially secure before making a commitment." Erin thought for a moment, considering her next words. "I don't know, but I do know that if he's not already in love, he's well on his way."

"Hey, I'm turning into a wrinkled prune here. Besides, I'm the only one whose love life we haven't examined, and that's because I don't have one." Val started climbing out of the pool. "And that's fine by me. I'll be happy to wait until this mess is over, if it ever is. And if true love comes knocking on my door before then, I'm not answering."

"Yeah, right!" Sarah teased. 'You'll fall just as hard as any of us, maybe harder, since you're not expecting it."

***

Vince was sitting in a rocking chair on the front porch late that evening when Erin came outside. She had just finished cleaning up the kitchen following a dinner of deer steaks with carrots and peas. She smiled and took a seat in the rocker next to Vince's.

"Erin, I've been hoping to have a chance to visit with you. I want to tell you how much I appreciate it that you let me stay here and be a part of the group. I didn't have anywhere to go, anything to live for except to hunt Ollie Simmons down, but now I feel like I have friends and a home. I know that the group has gotten pretty big, and you might have even more people who need to come, so please understand that I'll be happy to move into a cavern or take on extra duties if necessary."

"You're most welcome, Vince. You've been a real asset to the group. I edited books about prepping, and I know that other than Uncle Ernie, most of them advised against taking people in, but I believe that there's strength in numbers. Look at how exhausted Tanner's family is, with six adults. They're spread too thin, trying to get everything done, take care of the children, and guard the house. Mac and Claire are even worse off, with only two adults. But we're stronger with more people. We share the work, and there are enough of us that we can each occasionally have a day off from standing guard. We each have a little free time during the day, too, and that's important for our sanity. And if bad guys come around, we'll be glad for every adult we have. I think things are a lot easier with more people, and I know it's safer."

"I agree. It's a real blessing that your uncle had the foresight to stockpile supplies, too."

"Yes, it sure is. He was really into prepping, and because of the success of his books, he had the money to do it right. I am just sorry that he didn't live to give us advice and see how good his planning really was." Erin looked away, sad for a moment, then turned back to look at him.

"I am curious about something, Vince. What was it like, working at the prison, being around all those criminals so much?"

"Well, it wasn't easy." Vince pushed his brown hair back out of his eyes.. "A guard there had to be on alert all the time, because the inmates were just waiting for a chance to cause trouble. They would fight with each other, or attack a guard if they thought they could get in a few hits before more guards came. They said and did things that I wouldn't even try to describe in mixed company. And they used the foulest language you can imagine, dropping f-bombs and taking God's name in vain constantly. That was one thing that I hated most about it.

"Most of the other guards picked up the habit of talking back to them in the same kind of language. I made a promise to myself that I wouldn't sink that low. My parents raised me to believe that an intelligent, classy person can express strong emotion without being vulgar, and I decided to honor them by not picking up the really bad stuff. One time, when I was about eight, I said 'hell' in front of my mom, not as a place, but as a cuss word. She made me apologize, then washed my mouth out with Dial soap. That stuff tasted awful, let me tell you. I was real careful to watch my mouth after that! I think it's disrespectful to talk filth, especially around ladies and children, so I was always determined not to let myself get that habit. Oh, I slip with a milder curse occasionally, but I don't use the Lord's name in vain, and I don't use the f-word at all."

"Thank you for that. I'm glad that we don't have anyone in the group who likes to cuss, at least I don't think we do. I haven't heard any bad language, at any rate. Maybe the men talk worse when the women aren't around; I don't know, and I don't want to know. I'm just glad I don't have to listen to it."

"There's been a little of that, but like me, the guys here only use milder words. I haven't heard any really nasty words from anyone. One of my guards told me once that everyone uses that kind of language. I told him that wasn't true, because I don't. He didn't believe me, but after a while, he learned that I meant it. It isn't necessary, and it's not going to come out of my mouth.

"Now, I'd like to ask you a question, just between us. I've noticed that Richie and Lydia seem to be, uh, close. Are they a couple?"

"I think it's headed in that direction. Why?"

Vince frowned and stared off into the distance for a moment before answering. "I just think she's a really special lady, but I don't want to cause any tensions in the group. I'll just be honest: I'm attracted to her, but I'd never do anything to hurt her, or Richie, either. I really like and respect him, and I wouldn't even try to cut him out if they've got something going, so let's just pretend I never brought it up, okay?"

Erin gave him a serious look. "Okay. The last thing we need is a rivalry getting started. I won't say a word to anyone."

Chapter 3 – The Next Morning

Ollie Simmons parked the rusty old van and looked around carefully before getting out. The old farmhouse looked abandoned, but Ollie and the gang of convicts he had recruited had been using it for a few months. He had killed the old couple who lived there, dragged the bodies out into the forest, and moved in.

But now Ollie's gang was dead, killed by people in that stinking excuse for a town. He didn't really care about the gang members dying; he didn't care about anything except himself and his desire for liquor, women, and power, not necessarily in that order. It just angered him that the townspeople had the gall to stand up to *his* gang. That was a direct challenge that he would not allow to go unpunished.

He was actually a little bit pleased that Weasel was dead. The scrawny runt had started acting like he was Ollie's second-in-command. Ollie snorted in disgust. He didn't need a lieutenant. Just because Weasel had followed him around when they were kids, and covered for him a few times when he needed an alibi, didn't mean that they were *friends*. Ollie didn't want friends; he wanted -- no, he *deserved,* followers, men who would accept his rule and do as they were told. Nobody was going to get by with usurping Ollie's power.

What he wanted now was a new gang. He planned to go round up some of the boys from the prison, and he figured he knew some places to look. When he got a new gang put together, they would pay a visit to the town of Kanichi Springs and show the people there who was really in charge.

The old farmer who had lived in the house hadn't had much, but he did keep a big tank of gasoline behind the barn, for his ancient Ford tractor and beat-up farm truck. The tank wasn't full, but Ollie figured it would last long enough to get his immediate plans accomplished, then he'd have to find more gas somewhere, maybe on another farm in the area. They had tried to start the old truck, but the battery was dead, and jumping it didn't work. The gang had wanted to have another vehicle, but while he pretended to be frustrated about it, Ollie was secretly happy that it wouldn't start. He'd figured that having a additional vehicle could start trouble in the gang, maybe even give some of them a means to go off on their own. If they found some loot on their own, it might weaken Ollie's grip on them.

Ollie entered the house, letting the screen door slam behind him, and went to the kitchen to see what he could find to eat. Most of the food that his gang had stolen was gone already, but with them dead, what was left would last a while.

***

Barry Kline pulled his shiny black Toyota truck up to the door of the barn and climbed out. His squad car was inside the barn, out of sight, and he was wearing civilian clothes. People would notice a deputy in uniform, or anyone driving a car with a light bar and "Sheriff" painted on the sides; Kline didn't want to be noticed.

He went up the steps of his uncle's old farmhouse and stuck his head in, calling, "It's me. Don't shoot!" before entering. He tossed his cap on the ugly green sofa and went through to the kitchen, where Ollie sat, eating cold pinto beans, right out of the can.

***

The next morning, Kline and Ollie climbed into the old van and took the backroads to a couple of towns south of Kanichi Springs. When it was just the two of them, Kline drove because it gave Ollie a feeling of authority to have a chauffeur. Kline went wherever Ollie told him to, and by the time they drove out of the second town, three men had joined them. Two of them were escapees from the prison, and one was just a desperate young fellow with nothing better to do.

Ollie explained to them that he was the boss and they would do as they were told, but in return, they would have a place to stay, and a share of all the food, booze, and women that they could find. As soon as they got a few more men, they'd start raiding homes in the area.

Kline just smiled and went along with whatever Ollie said. He obeyed without question, seemingly accepting Ollie's leadership without hesitation, but he was really only biding his time. Kline had nothing against Ollie; it wasn't personal. Kline believed that he was the true brains of the gang and should be the one calling the shots. His opportunity would come. In the meantime, he pretended to kowtow to Ollie, while slyly and subtly planting ideas in Ollie's head, making Ollie think they were his own. Kline wasn't quite as stupid as people believed, and he planned to help Ollie rebuild the gang. Ollie might be the public face of violence in the area, but Kline knew in his heart that *he* was the real leader, the behind-the-scenes puppeteer who was smart enough to let the others take the major risks while he stayed safely out of sight, just as he had done for years, running a drug-smuggling ring right under the noses of the other law enforcement officials in the area.

The members of the old gang had thought that Kline was a wimp, a servant to Ollie, and he was content to let them think that. He never went on raids; instead, he volunteered to stay behind and guard their lair. He didn't care that he never got a turn at the women they caught. Kline didn't like women; he didn't like men, either. He was completely asexual, totally lacking any drive to have sex with anyone. He didn't drink, and he didn't do drugs. He only wanted power. Power to control people, to be able to tell them what to do and have them obey without questioning his authority. He didn't even mind the position he had assumed, pretending to be subservient to Ollie. In fact, it fed his sense of power to know that he had them all fooled, that he could manipulate those hardened criminals so easily, making them believe the act that he had perfected. Inside, he laughed at them.

They were idiots, and he felt superior knowing that none of them suspected a thing.

He would get rid of Ollie when the time was right. He could wait and pretend. Barry Kline was a patient man.

Chapter 4 – Second Week of September

Erin decided they'd need to take two vehicles to town, Ian's truck and Erin's Expedition, and at the last minute, added two dogs, Blitz and Flash. The first stop was the church, where they caught up on news from the folks staying there. Two of the young families had left to return to their own homes nearby, thinking that it was safe now that the gang was gone. This meant that it was mostly women and children living in the basement fellowship hall, with only Ken and two other men. Erin brought them several jars each of green beans, tomatoes, carrots, and peas that she had grown and canned, plus big baggies of dehydrated onions and celery.

Ken and Terri Abbott both looked pale and gaunt. None of the townspeople had been able to bathe in many weeks. Terri's hair, always neatly groomed before the collapse, was longer and stringy with oil and dirt. She wore it tied back with a piece of twine. The stress of caring for the townspeople was taking an obvious toll on them, but Erin was at a loss as to how she could help alleviate the strain. *I'll think about it and do some praying,* she decided. Promising to be in touch soon, Erin couldn't help worrying that with winter on the way, it would become harder to provide food and other supplies for everyone.

Gus and Vince took the big truck to the hardware store. The others circled around to Lydia's house and the home of Micah's foster parents, which was just three doors south. Tanner and Erin left the dogs to guard the Expedition, then went to retrieve Micah's things, and

Richie helped Lydia gather her belongings. Both houses had been looted, but only food, liquor, and jewelry had been taken.

Tanner looked around the kitchen of Micah's house. "I think the gang did this. Whoever it was left a mess, but didn't go out of their way to trash the place. They weren't interested in much besides booze, drugs, and food. I bet Micah's foster dad's clothing was taken, if it fit any of the looters, but I'm not going into that bedroom in there to prove that theory," he promised. "Even with the time that's passed, and with the door closed, the smell is pretty bad."

"I wish we could properly bury all the people who've died in town, but that's going to have to wait. I'm sure that a search of all the houses would result in finding several bodies. It's just a bigger job than we can handle right now. Tanner, did you find any toys, sports equipment, or such in Micah's room? Anything sentimental?"

"I got his baseball glove and ball, a football, and an electronic game device, too. There were some board games, Monopoly and Clue, I think. I found his Bible, as well. Inside, it says that it was presented to him when he was baptized about eight months ago. I got a picture of him with his foster parents that was hanging on the wall in his room. There weren't any pictures or other mementoes that I could find."

"I wonder what happened to his biological parents. I heard they were both in prison."

"Yeah, for dealing drugs. They weren't even married. I don't know where they were sent, but I doubt they'll come back here. In case they do, would you like to leave a note?"

"I think we should." Erin looked around, spotting a memo pad beside the phone. She wrote, "Micah is well and safe with friends," and put the note on his dresser. "I don't want them to come around, so I didn't say where. Is that wrong?"

"No, I don't think it is. If they really cared about the kid, they wouldn't have been using and selling drugs. He's much better off with our group, and we sure don't need druggies coming to the lodge. That note may ease their minds, if they come by here, but like I said, I doubt they care enough to look for him, if they're still alive. They're probably not even together, since they were in different prisons."

"You ready? Let's get this stuff loaded, and go help at Lydia's house."

***

Vince stared at the pile in front of the hardware store. "Gus, if you get any more stuff from here, we won't be able to haul it all. Why do you want all this?"

"I had more ideas when I saw some of this. We'll be able to set up a system that will keep us secure and make life easier, too. I want to add some more latches to the back side of the cave door. It'll make it stronger, just in case. I found a few boxes of septic tank treatment, too.

"I knew the guy who owned this store. Benson was a paranoid old coot, but that's good, because he stocked lots of gadgets. I got a couple of security cameras. They're white, but I found camo duct tape to cover that up. I think I can wire them to Erin's old computer and fix us up some eyes on the end of the driveway. And I think I can rig up some kind of antenna so we'll be able to talk to our friends in town without climbing the mountain.

"Someday when we have time, I'd like to go check out ol' Benson's house for more ideas." Gus paused. "I wonder what happened to him."

"Maybe he's at his house, barricaded in with lots of food and supplies, waiting to shoot you if you get too close," Vince teased.

"He might at that," Gus mused.

***

Lydia asked Richie to look around her kitchen and living room for anything that might be useful, while she quickly gathered clothing and shoes from the closet and dresser. He found a few odds and ends in the kitchen drawers, then spotted some legal pads and pens on the desk. Picking up one of the pens, he hefted it in his hand, looking at it with curiosity.

"Hey, Lydia. What kind of pen is this? I've never seen one like it before. It sure is heavy."

Lydia came from the bedroom and looked at the pen that Richie held out. "Yeah, it's different, all right. I had forgotten I had that. My dad bought it for me when I moved here from Paris. It's a good pen, writes really smooth, but it's more than just a pen. I think he called it a tactical pen or something like that. Here, I'll show you," she said, holding out her hand to take the pen.

Richie gave it to her, and she removed the cap, placing it on the butt end of the pen. "See, it's got a really fine, sharp point, and it's made of strong steel, which is why it's so heavy. I can use it to stab an assailant." She grinned as she enacted a mock attack on Richie, making repeated stabbing motions toward him, stopping just short of his neck and chest.

"Okay, I get the idea," he laughed as he pulled her close. "That's kinda cool. But I'd rather kiss you than get poked full of holes."

A few minutes later, breathless, Lydia put the pen into the front pocket of her ragged jeans, and motioned toward the growing heap beside the door. "We'd better get this stuff ready to load."

She had gathered clothes, linens, two picture albums, a tent, two cots, and a couple of sleeping bags. She also had five jumbo packs of toilet paper and three of paper towels.

"Hey, I had coupons," she protested when she saw Richie's raised eyebrow.

"Anything else?" Richie asked, grinning.

"I don't think so. Did we get the pillows?"

Richie glanced at the huge pile. "Yep, got 'em."

They carried their haul out to the front yard and Lydia suddenly remembered that she might have left some clothes in the laundry room.

"Would you wait here and tell the others that I'll be right back? I'm tired of wearing rags, and I think I'll just go ahead and change while I'm in there. It'll only take a few minutes. I'm pretty sure there's a load of jeans and dark shirts that I left in the dryer when I bugged out. Here, hold my gun for me; I'll be right back."

Richie nodded, and sat down on the steps to wait. Lydia went inside and to the back of the little house to get her clothes. She opened the dryer door and pulled out a clean shirt, then started to unbutton the ratty-looking blouse she was wearing, when a hand suddenly closed over her mouth and she felt a knife against her throat.

"One little sound, and I'll slit your throat," a gravelly voice said in her ear.

Lydia froze, terrified. The man was thin, but strong, and held her in a vise-like grip, pulling her toward the back door. Lydia tried to resist, until she felt a stinging, shallow cut on her throat, and a warm trickle of blood running down to her collarbone. He forced her down the back steps and across the yard, through a gate and into a storage building behind a neighbor's house. Lydia was almost petrified with fear; she knew that she had to start thinking, and quickly, but her brain just wouldn't work. The thug shoved her down on the floor of the shed, and gave her an evil smile.

"Now, let's you and me get to know each other better."

Richie was just beginning to wonder what was taking everyone so long, when he saw Tanner and Erin come out of Micah's house and begin loading the boy's things in the back of Ian's truck.

He stood and stretched, then went back into the house. "Lydia? You ready? Let's go, honey," he called. His query was answered by silence. He hurried to the laundry room, and seeing the open back door, knew that something was wrong. He looked out, but saw no sign of Lydia, so he stepped out, listening. Then he noticed a trail where the tall grass had been trampled.

A soft *thump* and a cry came from a small garden shed across the fence. Richie rushed across the knee-high lawn, threw the gate open, and burst into the building. He barely had time to register that Lydia knelt on the floor with her shirt ripped down the front, struggling to escape a filthy beast of a man who stood leaning over her, one hand grasping a fistful of her hair, the other unzipping his jeans. Richie had his Glock out, but couldn't risk hitting Lydia, so he lashed out hard at the man, using one of the kicks that he had learned from Shane. The kick went a couple of inches low, missing the man's knee and hitting him in the calf muscle. The man howled and staggered, but didn't fall; instead, he whirled around, slashing at Richie with the knife. A long, bleeding, red line appeared across Richie's chest.

Richie jumped back, but tripped on a rake that was leaning in one corner and fell against the wall, dropping his gun. The man took immediate advantage by stepping forward and stabbing Richie in the stomach. Blood ran crimson all over Richie's abdomen as the man shoved him away and turned back to Lydia, the knife held low at his side. She had risen to a crouching position, facing him.

He opened his mouth to say something, but only got out, "Now, where ..." when Lydia sprang toward him, jabbing hard with her steel pen, stabbing him first in the throat, then over and over and over, wherever she could reach, while screaming Richie's name.

Erin and Tanner heard her cries; Tanner signaled Flash to stay, and called Blitz to find Lydia. They rushed through the house and across the backyard to the old shed. They found Lydia standing over a dead stranger, her eyes wild, almost crazed, both of them covered with blood splatters, and Richie barely breathing on the other side of the shed. Tanner darted over to check on him, while Erin guided Lydia away from the dead man.

Tanner ripped off his shirt and pressed it against Richie's deep wound. He could see that the cut across Richie's chest was shallow, but the lower one was serious. He placed Richie's hand against the folded shirt.

"Richie, hey, buddy, hold this tight, okay? Stay with me now. Stay with me."

Erin got on the radio and alerted Angie to meet them at the lodge, then she contacted the men at the hardware store.

"Gus, we've got a problem! Richie's hurt bad. We need to take him to Angie right now. You and Vince come by Lydia's and pick up the stuff in the front yard, and we'll see you back home. And Gus? Pray. Pray real hard."

Gus and Vince had gathered a treasure trove of items that would enhance security at the lodge: rolls of wire, motion detectors, doorbells, solar garden lights, tools. They threw the last of their haul into the truck, then rushed over to Lydia's house to grab her things.

"Hurry, Gus! Let's get this stuff loaded! I wonder what happened to Richie."

"Yeah, me, too. Erin sounded pretty shook up, so we'd better get a move on."

"I sure hope he'll will be okay. He's been a good member of the team. That's the last of the load. Let's get home as fast as this old truck will go."

***

Angie arrived at the lodge within minutes of getting the alert from Erin, and quickly set up her supplies. She told Frances to boil water to sterilize the instruments and got Val busy covering the table with a sheet, asked BJ to find a TV tray or some small table where she could lay out her instruments, then told everyone else to clear out so she would have room to work. She washed her hands and arms, then grabbed a pair of sterile gloves, and was just pulling the second one on when Tanner came through the door carrying an unconscious Richie.

As an experienced ER nurse, Angie had seen a lot of serious injuries, including more than a few knife wounds. She quickly assessed the shallow cut on Richie's chest as being less serious, and concentrated on the stab wound. It appeared that the assailant had stabbed

Richie right under his sternum, with the angle of the knife slightly toward the right. She cleaned the blood away so she could see better, frowned, and poured QuikClot into the narrow hole.

Then she cleaned the long slash across his chest and used steri-strips bandages to close it.

When she turned to the others, who stood watching from the living room, she shook her head. "Without the proper equipment, I have no way of knowing whether the knife nicked his intestines or liver. How long was the blade?"

"It was about five inches," Tanner answered.

Angie frowned. "Not good. We have no anesthetic, so I can't open him up to look. I'm sorry. There's not much we can do for him now, except wait and pray."

Lydia looked like she was about to faint, but pushed away the hands that reached out to help her and staggered over to Richie's side, taking his hand in hers and looking down at the man she had just begun to love.

"You have to help him. You have to find a way. Do something! You have to *do something!*" she cried.

"I don't know what to do. I'm a nurse; if he came into the ER, a doctor would order a CT and we'd have a whole team working on him. I'm not a doctor and I don't have the proper equipment. I can't see inside him. I can't cut him open without anesthetic. Maybe if we could find something to use, like from a dentist's office or a veterinarian, I could try to help him, but right now, there's nothing I can do. I'm *not a doctor.*"

"No, but you're the closest thing we have," Lydia pleaded.

"Should we try to find something like that? There was a vet clinic on this side of McAlester. If the druggies didn't already think of it, we could try to locate some kind of drugs to put him under," Tanner offered.

"Yes. If you could find some Halothane or Isoflurane, I could use that. Isoflurane is a gas commonly used for small animals, and also for oral surgeries. I have a mask to administer it if you find some. I wish I had a pulse-ox." At Tanner's puzzled expression, she explained, "One of those clips we use on your finger to monitor pulse and oxygen levels. But grab whatever you can find. Many drugs that are used in veterinary medicine can also be used by humans. Be careful, but hurry. He may not have much time. And everyone needs to understand that even if I can get in there to look, I may not be able to repair the damage. It all depends on what the damage is, but maybe.... Maybe."

She jotted down the names of the drugs on a slip of paper, and handed it to Tanner, who pointed at Vince and Ian, motioning for them to go with him.

***

The three men ran to the Expedition, AR15s in hand. Tanner drove, taking the quickest route to McAlester. It was the first time any of the group had gone into the city since the collapse, and they knew the trip could be dangerous, but felt that it was worth the risk if it might help their friend.

"The closest possibility is the vet's office. If we don't find anything there, I know of an oral surgeon whose office is on the third floor of a building downtown. That may be our best bet, because he didn't have a sign out front, just his name on the building directory in the lobby," Ian explained. "Most people probably wouldn't think of a surgical clinic being there, since the other offices in the building were leased to lawyers, accountants, and such, so maybe it hasn't been looted. It's an odd place to have your wisdom teeth out, but the guy's brother owns the building.

"Okay, in the next block, that's the vet's office, that one with the green awning. Should one of us stay here as a guard?"

"Yeah. I'll stay," Vince volunteered as Tanner pulled up and turned the motor off.

Ian led Tanner to the door, where they could see that the lock was broken. Someone had already been there, but they went in anyway, and searched each examination room.

"I think he did surgeries back here," Ian said, gesturing toward the last room. Inside, they saw a large cabinet. The door had been pried open, and it looked like, from the empty spaces, that some of the bottles had been taken. They dumped the contents of a wastebasket on the floor, then used it to carry all of the remaining bottles, but none of the drugs were the anesthetic that Angie needed.

"Okay, let's try that office downtown. I hate to even go into that area," Tanner complained. "I have a feeling that if there are any lowlifes left in town, that's where they'll be."

Tanner drove cautiously toward central McAlester, with the windows down. Vince sat in the back, watching the left side of the street, while Ian concentrated on the right side. They saw only a few people, and most of them scurried away as soon as they saw the SUV coming, fear in their eyes. A couple of the men they passed turned to watch the SUV until it was out of sight, staring hard at the first moving vehicle they had seen in quite a while.

"Okay, it's that building up there on the right. Maybe two of us should stay here this time. The Expedition drew some attention on these empty streets, and it's our only way to get home in time to help Richie," Vince suggested.

"I'll go," Ian offered. "I know where it is. You two can wait here and guard our ride. I won't be long."

Ian strode across the sidewalk and through the broken glass of the front door. His long legs took two steps at a time up to the third floor; he didn't see a soul on his way to the surgeon's office. Slowly opening the door to the hallway, he peered out and listened intently, then hurried to office 3C. Surprisingly, the door was intact and still locked. Ian pulled a set of lock picks out of his pocket and went to work. *Finally, working for my uncle pays off*, he thought. *I didn't follow my uncle into the locksmith business, but he did teach me some useful skills.* It took him less than two minutes to open the door, cross the lobby, and pick the lock on the door that separated the waiting room from the doctor's work area. He quickly located the room off the surgery suite where the oral surgeon stored his supplies.

The drug cabinet was locked, but once again, the lock picks and Ian's nimble fingers did the trick. *Yes! There's that stuff Angie wanted, and there's some Fentanyl, too!* Ian looked around for something to carry the drugs in, but as he searched, he heard a noise out in the hallway. He froze, listening and wishing that he had closed the door to the hallway behind him. He moved back out of sight, but where he could see a reflection of the hallway in a decorative mirror.

A short wiry fellow crept in, eyes darting from side to side as he nervously glanced around the waiting room. *I left that door open, too. Dumb move, but lesson learned.* Ian grimaced as he realized that he had been careless, not once, but twice.

The stranger shuffled down the hall, looking into the surgeon's private office and the three exam rooms. Then, as he stepped into the surgery suite, he jerked to the left when something clattered against the wall in the corner. Ian had placed his lock pick set on the floor and kicked it across the room to distract the man. It worked, and when the man turned toward the sound, Ian stepped forward, and his hand chopped down on the side of the man's neck. He fell, hitting his head on the edge of a counter. Ian leaned over and checked his pulse. The man was alive, but unconscious and bleeding from a gash on his forehead.

Hurrying, Ian found a sturdy box in the storage closet and quickly emptied the cabinet's contents into it. There were several drugs he had never heard of, but some he recognized as antibiotics and pain relievers. He took them all, and also a couple of boxes of syringes and needles, and a small tank of nitrous oxide. With the tank under his arm, he lifted the box and headed for the stairwell. *This will be the dangerous part. Going down three flights of stairs loaded down like this – not the smartest thing I ever did.*

Ian made it down to the street level without incident, and when Vince saw the load he was carrying, he ran over to help.

"Any luck?"

"Yep! Exactly what Angie said to get, plus a lot of other stuff. I'll tell you all about it later, but right now, I believe I see company coming," Ian gestured toward an alley across from the office building.

Vince grabbed the tank of laughing gas and put it on the floor in the back of the SUV, then relieved Ian of the box, sliding it across the back seat and scooting in beside it, just as a group of about ten young men emerged from the alley, spotted them, and charged forward, brandishing baseball bats and tire irons. Tanner had started the SUV just as Ian jumped into the front seat. They were about to pull away from the curb when one of the punks swung his bat and put a dent in the right rear fender. Vince and Ian leaned out of their respective windows and aimed their AR15s at the teens, who promptly backed off, arms raised, when faced with superior weapons. Tanner raced down the street, speeding away from the small gang.

Once they were out of town, Ian related what he called his "little adventure" in the surgeon's office. "I left the guy there, lying on the floor. I think he'll live, but he'll have a whopper of a headache. Don't tell Shane, but his kenpo lessons came in handy and kept me from having to use my gun, which could have drawn unwanted attention."

Tanner drove fast up the turnpike, in a race against time. The big SUV was powerful, and capable of high speeds, so Tanner opened it up. They passed a few people walking on the shoulder; some tried to flag them down, but Tanner never slowed. They were making good time, until they topped a hill and could see a large group of refugees coming toward them. The people moved slowly, heads down and feet dragging, until they noticed the Expedition. At that point, they began to run toward it, waving their arms.

Tanner could see that they were going to block the road and force the SUV to stop, so he slammed on the brakes, made a fast U-turn, and sped back to the last exit they had passed. Exits in that section of the turnpike are miles apart, and the delay frustrated the three friends, but there was nothing else they could have done. Tanner sped down the exit ramp, turned left, and wound his way through the backroads the rest of the way to the lodge.

"It's a good thing you grew up around here and know the roads. I'd be lost by now if you weren't here," Vince said. "What lousy timing, meeting that mob of refugees, today of all days."

***

The trip back took three times as long as the trip into McAlester. When they finally got back to the lodge, Ian grabbed the tank of Isoflurane and ran to deliver it to Angie. Vince and Tanner followed with the rest of the items they had found. Richie was conscious, so Angie spoke softly to him, explaining what she would do, with his permission, in an attempt to determine if the internal injuries he had sustained were something she could repair.

"I'm going to be upfront with you, Richie. I may get in there and find out that the knife perforated your intestines. If so, I'll do my best to clean it up and repair it, but peritonitis is a very serious possibility. If the knife hit your liver or an artery, I may not be able to do anything for you. There may be internal bleeding that I can't stop, and further blood loss from the incision may be too much. I just need you to tell me if you want to try this, or do you want to just wait and see. I can't make any guarantees either way, but there is a slight possibility that the damage is something that can be repaired. I just can't know without going in. I've also never done this before, although I've assisted with similar surgeries many times. It's up to you. I'll do whatever you decide, but you need to decide soon."

"Where's Lydia? I want Lydia."

"I'm here, Richie," Lydia responded from a few feet away. "I won't leave you. I'll be right here, no matter what you decide."

"What do you think I should do?"

"I think it's your decision, but if there's any chance that Angie could stop the bleeding or sew up your stomach, or whatever, maybe you should consider it. I just want you to stay with me."

"You know I love you, Lydia. I've never been in love before, but … I know that this is real. I've tried to show you, rather than just saying words, so you would know, really *know*, that I mean it."

He turned his head to look at Angie. "Okay, I'm willing to try it if you are. And I want everyone to know that if it goes wrong, it's not your fault. Let's do it."

"I'm going to try to put some fluids in you first. The guys found some Ringer's lactate at the vet's office. It'll replenish your electrolytes, too. While that's going in you, I'll be studying up on the rest. I'll do what I can; I just hope it's enough."

Angie asked for lamps to be placed where they would provide light for the surgery, then had everyone except Sarah, Tanner, and Lydia leave the room to minimize distractions. Scrubbing again at the kitchen sink, she allowed her hands to air dry, then slipped on gloves. She catheterized Richie, started a line in a vein in his arm, and got Gus to put a nail in the wall to hold the bag of fluids, then stripped off the gloves, got out her medical book and refreshed her memory on how to administer the anesthetic. She checked over her instruments and made sure she had sutures ready, then showed Sarah which instruments were which. She had chosen Sarah to assist because Sarah had a background in science and was accustomed to doing dissections, so hopefully she wouldn't be squeamish about the surgery.

She checked the catheter bag for urine, but there was very little. *With fluids going in, he should have some coming out…unless he's got internal bleeding. This isn't looking good.*

Using the mask, she administered the Isoflorane and monitored Richie carefully as he went under. She and Sarah both scrubbed and put on fresh gloves. *Pulse and oxygen are good. In a few minutes, I'll prick his toes with a needle and see if he shows any response. Lord, please guide me. I've seen this done, but I need your help to save our friend. Your will be done.*

Once she was convinced that Richie was completely out, she carefully used a scalpel to open the wound, clamping bleeders as she explored the damage.

"Tanner, shine that light right into the incision. Sarah, I need you to use those gauze 4x4s to sop up some of the blood so I can see better. I wish we had suction. Yes, right there. Good job."

Examining the depths of the wound, what Angie saw filled her with dread. Not only was Richie bleeding internally, but he also had a small nick in his intestine in addition to the cut in his stomach. She could see that there had been some leakage, and that meant that the danger of infection was exponentially higher.

She cleaned it up as much as possible under the circumstances, stitched the perforations with absorbable sutures, and did what she could to stop the bleeding, praying the whole time. Then she closed the incision, mentally reminding herself to close all three layers: the peritoneal cavity, the muscle, and the skin. Then she bandaged it, before changing the depleted bag of Ringer's for a new one. She wearily pulled off her gloves, and sat down on one of the chairs where she could watch him.

With the worst of the bleeding stopped, Richie's urine output increased somewhat. He was still extremely pale, but that was to be expected. He would wake up soon, and she needed to get him started on pain medication before he did. The bottle of Fentanyl from the surgeon's office was almost full, and when she saw that her patient was beginning to stir, she injected some into the port on the tubing, and hooked the nitrous oxide to the mask and started the flow.

***

Lydia sat beside the table, holding Richie's hand with both of hers. *I'm just beginning to love you, and I think we could have something very special together. Please don't die. Please, live and let me love you until we're both old and wrinkled.*

Angie came over to check the fluids, and noted that the urine bag was starting to fill up. *Well, at least that's better. We'll just have to wait and see on the rest.* She pulled Richie's eyelid up to check his pupil, and when she did, he mumbled something and moved his leg a little.

"He's waking up now. I'll do my best to keep the pain level down where it's bearable, but he needs rest most of all. Reassure him, but don't tire him out, okay?"

"Do you think he'll be alright?" Lydia begged.

"I hope so, but I can't say for sure. Keep praying, and keep him calm. We'll know more soon. I'm going to sit out on the porch and relax for a few minutes. Call me if you need me."

Lydia bowed her head, praying with all her heart, as tears streamed down her face. She straightened up, and was startled to see that Richie was looking at her.

"You're awake! How bad is the pain? Should I get Angie?" she blurted.

Richie's lips and mouth were so dry that he had trouble speaking. "Thirsty. Water"

"I'll ask Angie. Don't move."

Lydia darted to the door and told Angie that Richie was awake and thirsty. Angie came in and checked his vitals, noted that there was only a little blood on the bandage, and that his eyes were clearing.

"You may have a few ice chips. Lydia, crush an ice cube in the blender. He can only have a little, maybe about a teaspoon, and if he keeps that down okay, he can have a little more in a while. Richie, you need to stay as still as possible. We'll lift your head for you, so don't try to raise up on your own. Your muscles will hurt like the dickens around the incision if you try to move. Just let us do the work, and just let those chips melt in your mouth. I'll put some balm on your lips so they won't be so dry."

***

By using the Fentanyl solution and the nitrous oxide, Angie managed Richie's pain enough that he slept for a few hours at a time through most of the night. The next morning, he asked her to reduce the dose just a bit so he could stay awake for brief visits from the other members of the group. Under strict orders from Angie, they came by a few at a time, and only stayed long enough to encourage him or say a brief prayer with him. He seemed to be in good spirits, and the hope that he might recover began to grow.

By late afternoon, however, Angie noticed that his abdomen was becoming swollen and hard, so she checked his temperature, blood pressure and heart rate. *Temp 102, BP 100/60, and heart rate 120. That's not good. I need intravenous antibiotics! Lord, what should I do?*

By dusk, it was becoming obvious that Richie was not doing well. His blood pressure dropped to 92/56, and his heart was beating much too fast. His abdomen was distended and he was exceptionally pale, with a temperature of 105, and he complained of pain in spite of the Fentanyl. Angie knew, with very little room for doubt, that she had failed to prevent the worst-case scenario, peritonitis.

"Richie, I need to test something, and I'm afraid it's going to hurt. I'm going to push down on your belly, and then release it. Tell me if you have increased pain."

She pressed down, then released, causing Richie to cry out. "I'm sorry. Was the pain when I pushed down, or when I released?"

"Release," Richie gasped.

Angie's eyes filled with tears, but she refused to let them spill over. "You have all of the symptoms of peritonitis, which is inflammation of the peritoneum, the lining of the inner wall of the abdomen. It can be caused by infection from a perforation of the stomach or intestines, both of which you had. If the infection gets into the blood stream, it's called sepsis, and will cause internal organs to shut down. I tried to prevent it, but I failed. I just don't have the equipment that would be available in a modern ER, and I don't have the skills, either.

"I'm so very sorry to have to say this." Angie paused, looking defeated, then spoke slowly. "Untreated peritonitis is almost always fatal. It doesn't respond to oral antibiotics, and that's all we have. I don't know of any treatment for it that I can try."

"How long?"

"Not long. The pain will become excruciating. I can give you more medication, or even put you under again, if you want, so you won't feel the pain."

"No!" he whispered. "No, I want to stay awake and spend what time I can with Lydia. And you said 'almost always'. I might be the exception; it could happen. No, I don't want to go under."

"If you change your mind, or if the pain becomes unbearable, just tell me. I'll be right here with you. I'm sorry I can't do more."

"It's not your fault. You did your best, and I appreciate it. I'm not giving up yet. Don't you give up, either."

"I'll get Lydia. I made her lie down for a bit, but I'll get her."

***

Angie found Lydia on her bunk, staring at the wall and crying softly. She sat down on the edge of the nearest bed and leaned over to put her hand on Lydia's shoulder. "Richie is asking for you, dear. I need to tell you that he has apparently developed peritonitis, and the prognosis is not good at all. He probably doesn't have long. He knows, and he wants to spend the time with you," she said gently. "Go to him."

Lydia rose and ran down the stairs. Angie went to tell the others the sad news.

Richie lingered for almost ten hours, and Lydia never left his side. At the end, he smiled at Angie, thanked her again for trying, and told Lydia not to give up on love, that she was too special to be lonely, and that he loved her and wanted her to be happy. Then, surrounded by the friends who had become his family, he quietly left the pain behind.

Chapter 5 – The Next Day

Richie was buried in the town cemetery early the next morning. Lydia picked out the casket, and Tanner did the eulogy, mentioning Richie's unselfish character and willingness to help others. He told how, before the collapse, Richie had helped people in the town who couldn't afford their prescription medicines, and how he had become a valued member of the group at the lodge, and how he worked hard, always volunteering to do the tough jobs. Tanner praised his friend's integrity, positive attitude, and gentle sense of humor. Some of the attendees tried to sing "How Great Thou Art", but one by one, they broke down in tears. Everyone in town had known Richie; he had been respected and loved, a friend to each of them.

Lydia stood between Erin and Frances, a stunned, vacant look on her face. She had truly believed that he would survive in spite of everything; his passing was a terrible shock. It had all happened so fast that she just couldn't process it yet. It was like a nightmare that refused to end, and it left her feeling devastated and lost.

When the service ended, Lydia asked Terri and Ken if she could speak with them privately.

"I need to get away for a while. I can't go back there and look at the table where he died. I just can't, not yet. May I stay with you for a week or so? I'll work hard and help with the children. Maybe that will keep my mind occupied and keep me from thinking about Richie constantly."

"Of course you may, Lydia. Ken has training and experience with grief counseling, too, if you want someone to talk to. You're welcome to stay for as long as you need us," Terri assured her. "Do you want me to tell Erin?"

"No, I'll do it. I think she'll understand. It's just for a while, until I can get my mind around it."

Erin came over, and the two friends clung to each other while they talked. Erin asked, "How are you holding up?"

"It's hard, Erin. Richie and I were just friendly acquaintances when we lived in town, each too busy trying to run our businesses to take much notice of the other. Then we were thrown together at the lodge, and I realized what a great guy he was. We were on the verge of something wonderful, then he died to save me from that monster. He loved me so much that he died because of it. And I loved him, more than I thought was possible, more than I even realized, but I wish he hadn't loved me. I wish he hadn't been a hero, that he hadn't come after me. I would rather have suffered through a rape than lose Richie. If I hadn't remembered those clothes … if I hadn't left my gun with Richie. If this collapse had never happened, I wonder if we ---- well, it doesn't matter now. It just doesn't matter now."

Erin understood, and promised to bring some of Lydia's clothing and more food to the church soon. Every member of the group, and all the people from town felt the sense of loss, but they all knew that Lydia felt it most deeply.

***

Although a sense of sadness hung over the group, there was still work to do so they would be ready for winter. Erin felt that staying busy would help everyone deal with the grief, so she came up with several projects that they could tackle. The first one was getting the McNeil family's supplies moved to the caves.

Julia had already gotten to work on an inventory of their preps, which was made more difficult by the fact that their storage space was limited, and therefore packed full. The pantry was crammed with buckets stacked almost to the ceiling. She and Talako had stored cases of food under beds, in closets, and behind the sofa even before their grandchildren had arrived with their own supplies.

Bulk storage of non-temperature-sensitive items, such as bandages, duct tape, flashlights, and tarps, was in the garage and a small storage building east of the house. Julia was assisted by whoever was not on guard duty or watching the children. They went through it all, and stacked most of it along the walls of the house so it could be moved to the caves. It took almost three days to sort it all out, but the family was finally left with food for about two weeks and a first aid kit. They could go to the caves to replenish their food stock when they ran low.

Dana and Rose packed the children's summer clothing and most of the linens, which wouldn't be needed in the coming weeks. All of the camping gear would go, too, as would photo albums and special family keepsakes. They kept out enough dog food for the three shepherds to eat in the next few weeks, and stacked the rest to be taken to the caves.

"I have a strong feeling that we need to get this done quickly. Just a premonition that we should hurry." Julia gave Talako a worried look. "Would you get Tanner on the radio and let him know that we're ready for that help he offered?"

Talako agreed, and immediately went to the spot in the woods where he got the best reception. Tanner assured him that the people at the lodge were ready to help.

"Grandfather, we've worked out a plan, and if you'll corral the kids, and post two guards about halfway up your driveway, we'll take care of the rest. Erin and Gus have it all figured out. We'll be there within the hour."

With Rose keeping the children occupied in the back bedroom, Will and Talako grabbed rifles and took up positions on either side of the long, curving driveway. Will's bullet wound from the fight in town was healing well, but he wasn't ready to lug boxes and buckets yet. Julia stayed in the house so she was available to point out what needed to be carried to the caves. John was ready to help with the heavy lifting, and Dana would carry lighter items. At the lodge, Gus, BJ, and Frances stayed behind as guards. Frances's proficiency with a rifle had improved considerably, and she was ready and eager to help protect the group. Micah had grown enough to be able to help carry boxes, at least the smaller ones, so Tanner took him along.

With almost military precision, the rest of the group moved in near-silence through the cave. Tanner raised a fist to stop everyone a few yards from the exit, then slipped forward and listened, watching the area carefully. Blitz sat beside Tanner's leg, relaxed and calm, so Tanner knew that no dangers lurked close by. He stepped out, still observing, then signaled for the others to come out.

As soon as they emerged, Erin took Blitz toward the west side of the mountain, where she would have a view of a portion of the road, while Ian took Major east, and Jen accompanied Flash uphill to the south. Jen had developed an interest in working with the dogs and knew enough of their commands to handle the job. Charlie set up just yards from the cave entrance. That left Tanner, Shane, Valerie, Micah, and Vince to help John and Dana carry the supplies. They moved toward the house, maintaining silence.

The move went like clockwork; they grabbed whatever Julia pointed at, carried it to just inside the cave, and stacked it against the wall. The plan was to get everything inside the cave quickly, then move it the rest of the way to the caverns when those guarding the area were no longer needed outside, giving them several more strong backs for the trek through the caves.

Suddenly, they heard a loud racket, the sound of something crashing through the woods northeast of the house. A yell went up, in a voice that none of the group recognized. The sounds grew fainter, then died away. Ian gave a loud whistle, and Major came running back.

Tanner appeared beside Ian, who continued to stare north.

"What?" Tanner murmured softly.

"Guy in a white tee, spying on us."

"He see anything?"

"I doubt it. Major heard him and bristled up, then I saw him and sent Major to chase him away. The house is between him and the cave. I don't think he could see what was going on back there."

"Okay. Talk to you more later. Good job."

They finished the move, then Tanner slipped off into the woods, circling around to let the guards know that they could come in. Most of the lodge group left to start moving the preps further into the caves, but Tanner, Erin, and Ian stayed behind. They went into the house with Talako and Julia, and told them about the intruder.

"We had a visitor. Ian sicced Major on him to run him off, but he was spying on the house. I don't like it. Ian, did you get a good look?"

"Not really, but he was young, wearing a white tee, and he was skinny. Not that that's any help. There's a lot of skinny people around these days."

"Grandmother, grandfather, I think the time is close, very close, for you to come to the lodge. That guy might be alone, but he might also have friends. There's not enough of you to effectively guard this place."

"Can you spare a couple of people to help us, at least part of the day? If we had just two more guards, it would be a lot better." Talako's stubborn reluctance to accept help was subordinate to his aversion to leaving their home.

Tanner smiled. "We'd already decided to make the offer. You'll have two extra pairs of guards staying here this evening, and they'll be happy to take whatever shifts you assign, day or night. But I still think you should be thinking seriously about coming to the lodge. The children would have more people to look after them, and it would give all of you a break. By the way, all the extra guards are volunteers. Everyone at the lodge understands that you need some help."

Julia put her hand on Talako's arm. "We should go soon. Remember my premonition?"

Talako nodded, then looked at his wife. "I learned a long time ago to listen to you, *ohoyo.* You know things before they happen, so we'll go as soon as we can get ready. Tanner, we accept the help. With a few more to stand guard, we can start packing up the rest of our things."

Julia chuckled softly. "Wow. If I had realized that you'd agree so readily, I could have skipped a lot of work, sorting through it all."

Chapter 6 – Third Week of September

"We're going to have to come up with a way to grow more food next year. Pots on the deck work great, but we'll have more people than we can feed if more families show up. I don't want to dig into what's stored in the cache cavern unless we have to." Erin stood, hands on her hips, surveying the rows of planters filled with vegetables.

Sarah nodded. "You're right. And we have folks at the church building depending on us, too. They have a few backyard gardens in town, but no way to preserve food for the winter. If we don't help them, they'll starve."

Tanner and Ian came out and offered to help. Erin pointed at two tubs of veggies that she and Sarah had picked.

"Those need to go to the kitchen, please. Can you guys think of a way we can grow more next year?"

"Didn't you buy some fencing to go around the yard or something? If we could find a place that gets enough sun, and isn't too rocky, we could have a garden," Tanner offered. "I just don't know where. It would need to be close so we could water the plants. Let us have a little time to think about it. We'll talk to Gus and Charlie, too. There's got to be a way."

***

Tanner found Gus and Charlie playing checkers on the patio. The two had been friends for decades, and were good company for each other. He sat down and watched as they finished the game.

"Dang it, Gus! Cain't you let me win ever' now and then?"

"What would be the fun in that? You won almost every time we played last week, so quit your complaining. Tanner, you look like a man with something on his mind. Spit it out, boy, and give that cantankerous old geezer something to do besides cheat at checkers."

Charlie sputtered and glared at Gus while Tanner laughed.

"Do you two ever actually come to blows?"

Charlie grinned. "When we was younger, we sure did, more'n once. But now we just fight with words. I used to whup Gus on a reg'ler basis, but now it takes him too long to heal. Who would I play checkers with if Gus was laid up?"

"You and I remember those fights very differently, old man." Gus's eyes narrowed. "I seem to recall that you had two black eyes in your senior picture."

"Who you callin' old? I'm less'n a year older than you. I think you held off bein' born on purpose, just so's you could avoid the draft. Six months older, and you'd've been in 'Nam with me."

Tanner held up a hand to stop the argument. "You two sure do like to yammer at each other. Thanks for the chuckle, but I do have something serious to discuss with you. Erin needs more space to grow food next year. We have fencing to keep critters out, but the ground here is too rocky, so where could we put a garden that we could water it easily?"

Charlie glanced at him. "You know where we could get some more flower pots?"

Tanner interrupted. "There's no room on the deck for more pots."

"Who said anythin' about the deck? We can fence in an area in front of the lodge. Growin' in pots'll eliminate the need to dig through rock. If we can find enough big pots and some soil from somewhere, we could put a fence around 'em so Erin could grow a lot more food."

"I got it!" I know where we can get pots." Gus paused, looking thoughtful. "They're big and heavy, but remember those square planters on all the corners downtown? And some of the stores had round or rectangular ones out front. There's two in front of Lydia's shop. They're already full of dirt, too. I bet there's at least twenty huge planters just on Main Street, and more over in front of the school. We just need to load 'em up and bring 'em out here, if you young bucks can lift something that big, that is. You should do it when it hasn't rained in a while, because dry dirt isn't nearly as heavy as wet dirt.

"Maybe we can get Brian Powell to load 'em for us. I'm pretty sure he has a front-end loader. We should start a compost pile, too, to enrich the soil in those planters. Erin is going to love this idea."

***

Tanner grabbed Shane and Ian, and the three of them climbed the mountain behind the lodge. While the other two concentrated on watching the forest for danger, Tanner contacted Mac with his radio. Mac agreed to bring some gas over and help get the fence up.

Then Tanner switched to the channel he had told Brian to monitor. The builder volunteered to help before Tanner even finished telling him what they wanted to do. Tanner asked Brian if he had given any more thought to joining the group at the lodge.

"I'm leaning that way, if you are sure you have room for me. In fact, I know I have to do something before it turns cold, so I might as well go ahead and move. I'm pretty much out of everything, and I've been living on fish from the river. This winter, that won't be feasible. Once it turns cold, I won't be able to walk all the way to the river every day to fish, so yeah, I'll come."

"What will you do with your equipment?"

"I don't know. I'd like to bring the Bobcat with me, it that's okay. It's handy for a lot of things."

"Sounds good. I'll get back to you with a time for loading those planters."

***

Mac kissed Claire and reminded her to lock the door behind him, then he drove his pickup around to the back of their property. He had several fuel cans, which he filled from the big tank truck hidden in the trees under camo netting. *It's a good thing I happened to have the right connectors and a hose with a nozzle, so we could get the gas out of the tanker and into cans or cars without it spewing all over everywhere*, he thought. He put the full cans in the bed of his pickup and headed over to the lodge. The men had already started on the fence, but Ian came over to help Mac pour the gas into the delivery truck from Ian's furniture store. They then poured some into Tanner's pickup.

"Man, driving T-posts into the ground around here is a royal pain. We go down a few inches and hit solid rock, then move over a bit and try again, and again, until we can sink one far enough." Ian wiped the sweat from his forehead. "The posts are certainly not evenly spaced, and the enclosure has a funny shape, but it'll work."

"Where are you going to put the gate?"

"Gate? Crap! I don't think we even have a gate."

"I have a four-footer in my barn. I bought it for the fence I never got done. You guys are welcome to it." Mac stared at the men who were working on the posts. "You might want to wait to put up this side of the fencing. Brian needs to be able to get in there with his Bobcat."

Tanner came over to the trucks. "Are we ready to go?"

"I guess. Who's going to help in town?" Mac inquired.

"All the guys except BJ, Gus, and Charlie. They'll stay here with the gals."

***

Claire read a story to Kyra and left her napping in her room, then fed little Ford. Holding him up against her chest and patting him lightly on the back, she heard a satisfying burp, then placed him gently into his crib. Looking at herself in a mirror, she considered cutting her hair short. It was impossible to keep clean, but maybe if it was short, it would be easier. *I look a lot older than I am,* she admitted to herself. *Bags under my eyes, scraggly hair, and way too thin. My eyelids are puffy, too. I used to be kinda pretty, but not anymore.*

She was so very, very tired. Trying to keep up with Kyra, breast-feeding the baby, cooking, tending the little garden, doing laundry – the chores never ended. Mac helped out a lot, but he couldn't get up every couple of hours in the night to feed Ford. They had to go outside and use a hand pump to get water, wash clothes by hand, and hang them on the sun porch to dry. She cooked over a campfire in the backyard, or used their sun oven when it wasn't too cloudy. Then they had to pump more water and heat it over the fire to wash the dishes. Everything was so much harder these days. She knew that they were better off than most people, and was thankful for the canned and freeze-dried foods that Ernie had talked Mac into purchasing with the last of their savings, but she was just so tired.

The sun had moved since she had opened the red-checked curtains in the kitchen early that morning, so she went over to close them, hoping to keep some of the heat at bay. She caught sight of movement near the road, and ducked to the side, out of sight, then cautiously peeked out.

Two scruffy, mean-looking men were standing beside the mailbox at the end of the gravel driveway, quietly arguing about something. One was a barrel-chested bald man with tattoos all over his arms and neck. His shirt wasn't buttoned, and when he turned, she could see more tattoos on his chest. His face was round, with a bulbous nose and fat lips. The other was tall, but scrawny. His clothes hung on him like hand-me-downs from a much older brother. His dark blonde hair was long and greasy, and looked like it didn't have even a passing acquaintance with a comb. He had a large, hooked nose in the middle of a long, narrow face.

Claire was sure that they couldn't see her staring through the narrow gap in the curtains. The sun would be glaring off the window glass and there were no lights behind her. She reached into an upper cabinet and lifted out a cereal box. It was empty, except for a Glock 9mm that Mac had hidden there. He had chosen a type of cereal that Kyra hated, and put the box up high where she couldn't reach it, but where Claire could get it in a hurry if she needed to. This was the first time Claire had ever needed it, and she prayed that she wouldn't have to use the gun. Then she waited.

Tattoo Man pointed at the house and said something that caused Greasy Hair to shake his head in protest. Finally, after more arguing, they turned and walked away.

Claire started to breathe again. *Dear Father, thank You. Please keep them walking until they're far away from here.*

Then she went to the closet and got out a set of suitcases. She filled the biggest one with clothes for her and Mac, and the smaller ones with things for the children. *This is it. I can't take this anymore. We're going to Erin's and that's final. For the children, we have to go to Erin's.*

***

They took the delivery van and Tanner's pickup, pulling Mac's flatbed trailer. The men met Brian downtown and started loading planters and pots into the trucks. Gus had decided to come along for the ride, and walked to the hardware store to look around again. He made a big pile of items near the front door, an assortment of things that made perfect sense to him, even if not to anyone else. Two garden hoses, PVC pipes and connectors, nozzles, a couple of droplights, buckets, more wire, masonry screws, nails, a rake and two hoes, garden trowels, a wheelbarrow, plastic sheeting, a roll of tarpaper, and lightbulbs. He was excited about his finds, and went back through every aisle, asking himself which items might be handy to have someday. When he was finished, the store was practically stripped bare. The others finished loading the planters and the truck pulled up in front of the store. All the guys pitched in to load the treasures Gus had found, piling it on top of the planters.

"We need to go by the grocery store," Gus informed them.

"What for? The food disappeared a long time ago," Shane said, puzzled.

"Ah, but I'm not after food. Seems to me that they had a small floral department that sold both cut flowers and live plants. Live plants need to be fed, so they probably sold plant food. I bet we can find some smaller pots there, too, and if I'm remembering correctly, they had tomato plants and such for sale, all in pots. The plants will have died, but the pots are full of dirt, and they had some bags of potting soil stacked up out front, too. They also had a few of those plastic wading pools for little kids." Gus raised one eyebrow. "Erin mentioned growing herbs and dehydrating them to season our food. Those smaller pots will be perfect, and I can think of at least a dozen uses for wading pools."

"Gus, I'm glad you're on our side. I'd sure hate to have you for an enemy. I never would've thought of any of that," Shane admitted. "I sure hope that stuff is still there."

Most of it was. Gus reminded them not to dump the dead plants, since Erin could reuse the soil. There were four of the colorful wading pools, which were only about five feet in diameter, but they would work for growing some things, like lettuce and beans.

"One of these pools is our future compost bin. It'll be easier to turn the compost if it's contained in something," Gus explained.

There were a few other items that Gus grabbed from the store, like flyswatters and plastic spray bottles. The rest of the store's merchandise was pretty much gone, but Gus cruised through, latching onto anything that might prove useful, such a few rolls of plastic bags from the produce department.

***

Brian carefully angled the Bobcat so that Shane and Vince could wrestle the last concrete planter into place. They had brought a total of twenty-four to the lodge, and there were still several left in town that they couldn't fit on the trailer or in the truck.

"Let's call it a day, guys. You can finish the fence tomorrow or even next week, but you've put in a lot of hard work today. Frances and Val have a fantastic dinner almost ready." Erin turned her smile on Mac. "Why don't you go home and bring Claire and the kids over to eat. If she already has dinner prepared, just bring it and add to the bounty."

When Mac got home, he found Claire and the kids waiting on the sofa beside a pile of suitcases, boxes, and sacks. Kyra huddled beside her mom, clutching her stuffed giraffe, and Claire held the baby in her arms. It was obvious that she'd been crying.

"What's wrong, Claire? What's happened?"

She told him about the two strangers, then stood up.

"Let's get this stuff into the truck. We're going to the lodge. Tonight. We can't do everything that needs to be done and keep our children safe, too. Now, Mac. It's time, *past* time. I have a feeling that those men will be back, probably with reinforcements, and I'm at the end of my rope, physically, mentally, and emotionally."

"Okay. You're right, as usual. I'm so sorry, honey. My stubborn pride has put us both through hell, but I'm not leaving our preps. Let me get Tanner on the radio. We're gonna need a bigger truck."

***

Mac's radio message put an end to Erin's plan for getting showers taken and putting their feet up until dinner was ready. They took Ian's truck over to the McCoy home, and while Ian, Tanner, and Vince helped Mac load supplies into the big delivery truck, Jen and Sarah stayed at the lodge to help Erin move her things upstairs to the room where the single women bunked. With ten beds in the room, it wasn't crowded yet, but the rest of the people who might join them were married couples with children. Erin worried about how they would manage when the McNeils came, or if the Foster or Gibbs families needed to bug out to the lodge.

Doing some figuring in her head, she realized that there were five in the Foster family and five in the Gibbs family who might need to come, plus eleven in the

McNeil family who *would* be coming soon. The McCoys would add another four to the twelve who were already living at the lodge.

It's a good thing that Ian brought all those mattresses from his store, and his truck has been a blessing several times already, Erin mused. *Am I crazy to take in all these people? No, I don't think so. Every one of them has been an asset, and I truly believe we're better off with them, than without them. With the lodge and three cave entrances to guard, we need the help.*

"What are you frowning about?" Frances's voice made Erin jump.

"Oh! You startled me! I was just trying to figure out what we'll do if more people come, which they probably will. The cache cavern is pretty full, so we'll have to put Mac and Claire's preps in one of the other caverns. When Tanner's family comes, there will be three more married couples, plus five children. I wish we had more rooms where couples could stay together. And I don't know if you've noticed, but we also have some single folks who are starting to show an interest in *becoming* couples. Ian and Sarah are spending a lot of time together, and Shane can't keep his eyes off Jen."

"Not to mention you and Tanner, huh? Has he popped the question yet?"

"No, and I don't expect that he will, under the circumstances. There's too much turmoil right now, and we've hardly had any time together lately. Our relationship is on hold due to conditions we can't control."

"A wise woman once told me that if we wait until the perfect time to do the important things in life, we'll never do any of them. There will always be some crisis or some obstacle to overcome, so we just have to step out there sometimes and take a chance. You and Tanner are special together. You'll make it work somehow. Don't wait to be happy."

Erin hugged her, then sighed. "You're right. Now if I could just catch him in a free moment and convince him. He's needed by so many people and does so much for us all. What would we do without him?"

"Or without you. The two of you have become our safe harbor, our problem solvers, our leaders. There's not a person here who isn't grateful for everything you've done for us, Erin."

"We're in this together. Everyone contributes to the group. Having you all here makes survival possible, because I couldn't do it all alone, or even with Tanner. We need you *all*, every one of you." Erin touched Frances's arm. "You've been a tremendous help to us by doing most of the cooking and BJ helps with all sorts of chores. I'm so glad you're here."

***

By the time the trucks returned with the McCoys and their supplies, dinner had been on hold for quite a while, but Frances supervised rewarming the food, and everyone was relieved to be able to finally sit down and eat. Claire hadn't had time to prepare a meal, but there was still enough for everyone.

When Sarah and Erin had finished the dishes, Tanner stood up and stretched. "I vote that we just leave all that stuff in the trucks until morning. We're all beat, so let's get our new folks settled in for the night and worry about the rest tomorrow."

"Brian, you'll be upstairs in the men's dorm, and Micah can show you where everything is. Short showers, everyone, and you'll have to take turns. The ladies can wait until morning, but you men are really dirty, and I don't want to have all those sheets to wash, so clean up before you even *think* about sitting on a bunk." Erin grinned at Mac, Clair, and Brian. "Welcome to the lodge, friends. I hope you sleep well."

Chapter 7 – End of September

Charlie, Tanner, and Vince set out early, leaving with Flash and Major out the front door of the lodge, to pay a little visit to Charlie's garden patch. The marijuana plants should be just about ready, since there had been no rain for several days. Charlie had checked on them every other day for two weeks, whenever he could get someone to accompany him. He knew better than to go alone; Erin's number one rule was that nobody got out of sight of the lodge alone, *ever*.

The men eased through the trees, traveling about twenty yards apart, rather than together. They not only didn't want to leave a worn path, they needed to make themselves into a less conspicuous target. Tanner and Vince each walked with a dog, and they kept Charlie in the middle.

They came together at the small clearing where the marijuana grew. Charlie examined the plants' flowers, grinning happily.

"See that? The trichomes look just like sugar crystals, a nice creamy white. That's perfect. The days gettin' shorter after the fall equinox is what makes 'em flower, and no rain means they'll dry quick. I'm gonna use these here pruners to remove the bigger leaves, then I'll cut the stalks. You boys can move out a ways and stand watch. I only have this small patch, so I can handle it by myself. Might need some help carryin' the bags back to the lodge, though."

Tanner took Flash uphill about fifty yards to the west, and Vince moved almost as far east with Major. They stayed alert, because in the spring, Charlie had been beaten by some punks who knew he had weed growing somewhere in the area. Any pothead would be aware that it was time for the harvest, and there could be druggies out in the woods, hoping to stumble onto somebody's hidden garden. The smell might even be enough to lead someone to them, if they happened to be downwind.

Charlie worked quickly, cutting with the expertise of an experienced grower of pot. He filled three big bags, then signaled to the others with a low whistle. Just as Tanner and Vince started to move toward Charlie, Major tensed up and growled at something to the north. All three men immediately took cover in the trees and watched the area that Major's stance indicated.

Nothing moved for several minutes, then Tanner caught a glimpse of white. A young, emaciated man peeked around a tree, and not noticing the danger, sniffed the air, then sauntered toward the clearing.

Tanner gave Major and Flash the verbal signal to chase, and the two big dogs charged forward. The look on the stranger's face was almost comical as he skidded to a stop, turned, and sprinted as hard as he could in the opposite direction. Tanner waited until he could no longer hear the sounds of the kid crashing through the woods, then gave a shrill whistle, recalling the dogs.

"Let's go, quickly! I don't think he would dare come back, but if he does, I don't want him to see which way we went. I bet that was the same guy who showed up near my grandparents' place the day we moved their supplies. If so, he's hanging around the area, and I don't like that one bit."

"The dogs didn't hurt him?" Vince wanted to know.

"Nah. I gave the signal to chase, not to attack. It's a useful little trick when you just want to scare somebody away. They would have chased him as long and as far as he could run if I hadn't called them off, and when he stopped, they would have held him until I told them to release. Here they come. Spread out, and let's move."

They took a very different route back to the lodge, one that left them out in the open for a much shorter time, going well to the west, then a little north before stopping to observe. There was no sign of the stranger, and no noises; the dogs were relaxed, so Tanner waved them all around a boulder, and then into the cave. Once inside, they watched for almost fifteen minutes to see if they had been followed. Nothing stirred outside the cave entrance except birds and squirrels, and neither of the dogs went on alert, so Tanner signaled the others to move on.

As the three quietly made their way through the cave, Vince had his first chance to really look around. Days earlier, when they moved the McNeils' supplies, they had been in a hurry and also maintaining silence, so he couldn't ask questions. He was particularly impressed with the "cabana" cavern.

"This is wonderful. We could use this for laundry or bathing. To have a source of water without having to go outside into the open . . . this is a real asset."

"There are more caves to the west, with more caverns, and two more entrances. One of them is near a stream and a small pool just a little way outside. We may need to use those caverns for sleeping if our group keeps growing, which I am sure it will."

Chapter 8 – Early October

Barry Kline smiled inside as he turned away from Ollie Simmons. Once again, he had maneuvered Simmons into doing something, and had him thinking that it was all his idea. The new gang had grown to eleven, which was about all they could fit in the van; Kline wanted them to return to Kanichi Springs and finish clearing out the town, and Ollie had finally agreed to go soon.

Kline hated the people who lived in that town, even the ones he didn't know. Childhood there had been hell for him; his mother had died, his dad was the town drunk, and the kids at school didn't like him, often making fun of his chubby body and ragged clothes. They never knew that he always wore long pants and long sleeves to hide the scars and bruises. Barry had been burned with cigarettes and beaten every time his daddy got drunk, which was almost every day. His daddy was from Kanichi Springs, and any town that could spawn someone that mean was a town that needed to be destroyed.

He didn't want to burn it down; he just wanted to see it empty, deserted, and dead. It would be a ghost town, a place that held no appeal for anyone. The stores whose owners had turned him in for shoplifting would burn, though. He only stole food and shoes when his old man drank up every dime he earned and left his son to go hungry and barefoot, but he had repaid his dad for that already. Barry had stolen some whisky, and for once, gotten away with it. He gave it to his daddy, and once the old man was passed-out drunk and darkness had fallen, Barry dragged him out to the garage and shoved him into the truck, then drove him out deep into the woods and tied him tightly to a tree. And Barry, at age seventeen, calmly drove home in his daddy's old pickup. He parked the truck behind the grocery store, which had closed a few hours earlier, and walked home.

The only thing he kept was an old silver lighter, etched with a scorpion, that his daddy had used to light the cigarettes he used to make blisters on his only child. It reminded him that he had been strong enough to put an end to the torture, and that he could do whatever he had to do to survive. He told anyone who asked that his dad had gone out for smokes and never came home. So far, the body had not been found. Barry figured that after so much time had passed, it never would.

No one in the town had helped Barry, and he hated them for it. That he had carefully kept the abuse secret, that he had lied for years about broken bones and bruises to cover for his daddy, that he had kept to himself and never once asked for help, didn't matter. In his warped mind, the town was to blame, and the people there would pay.

***

"Vince and Shane are up to something," Erin whispered to Jen. "They're always off somewhere talking, but they clam up if anyone approaches."

"I think they're planning to go after Ollie Simmons. Vince has a score to settle, and if you're going after a bad guy, Shane's the best partner you could get. Frankly, I'll feel a lot better when Simmons is dead. I know I shouldn't wish anyone dead, but I can't help it. That man is evil."

"Ollie hasn't been seen lately, at least around here, but Mac talked to some guy he knows, another ham radio operator, who lives southwest of town, and he said that a guy who sounds a lot like Ollie had been seen in that area, driving an old van. The bad part is that he had a load of passengers riding with him who looked like thugs. If he has a new gang, it'll be 'same song, second verse' coming up. I doubt we'll be able to repeat our last little surprise. They'll be more careful the next time."

***

Dinner that night was vegetable soup, and everyone who wasn't on watch found a seat wherever there was a space, to eat and visit. Vince finished and took his empty bowl to the kitchen, rinsed it, then stood by the fireplace and cleared his throat.

"Could I say something, please?"

The room grew quiet. Vince seldom spoke out, so everyone was curious to hear what he had on his mind.

"I made a vow to find Ollie Simmons and take him down. Some of you may know that he was in Cell Block A and made threats against my family. After the prison riots, I went straight to my sister's house and ..." Vince blinked back tears. "I found her and my little nephew. They had both been raped and their throats were cut. What had been done to them was exactly what Simmons had said he would do.

"Shane and I are going hunting. We plan to locate Simmons and see what the situation is. If he has a new gang around him, we promise not to go in with guns blazing, but if he's alone, or with just a few others, we're going to eliminate the threat. And believe me, his continued existence is a threat to all of us."

"What will you do if there's a gang?" Valerie asked.

"We'll come back here and discuss it with the group. If we find their hideout, maybe we'll take the fight to them. But we'll need help from all of you. Right now what we're looking for is information. We need to know where and how many before we start anything, so this is a fact-finding mission, just a recon, so we can plan our next move," Shane explained.

"But if he's alone or with only one or two others, he's mine," Vince added. "I hope nobody has a problem with that, but that's just the way it's going to be."

***

Vince and Shane planned to travel on foot and carry only what was absolutely necessary. They hoped to find abandoned barns or houses to sleep in. At Tanner's insistence, Major would accompany them. Having the dog along meant taking food for him, but he was exceptionally alert and would save them from having to stand watch at night.

Each man took an AR15 and two handguns. They carried as much ammo as they could without weighing themselves down, and enough MREs for four days. They dressed in camo and wore sturdy, comfortable boots. Checking their gear one last time, they loaded up and said their farewells.

Erin hugged each of them and told them to be careful and come back in one piece. Jen hugged them, too, staying in Shane's arms considerably longer than necessary. *Uh-huh*, Erin thought, *there's definitely something developing between those two.*

Micah solemnly shook their hands, telling Shane that he'd better come back so they could continue their kenpo lessons.

"Good hunting, my friends. Be safe, and we'll see you soon," Tanner patted Vince on the back and shook his hand, then gave Shane a fist bump.

They exited through the pantry and used the caves that curved around the west side of the mountain, silently emerging near the stream. Clambering down the mountainside, they made their way to the road, staying in the trees to observe for several minutes. Deciding that it was safe, Shane crossed, then covered while Vince crossed. They had agreed that they would not relax their vigilance and would take their time, rather than take chances. They would also keep an eye on Major's posture and reactions.

They bypassed the town, working their way west and slightly south, and staying in the forest whenever possible. Developers hadn't yet turned this part of the

Kiamichis into one-acre lots with paved roads and luxury "cabins". Much of the land remained vacant, some of it accessible only with a four-wheel drive or an ATV. Houses were few and scattered; most were small homesteads with working-class owners.

Shane stopped, peering through the trees. A small house was just visible in a clearing directly ahead of them. There was a faint aroma of meat cooking, and as they edged closer, they could see clothes hanging on a line. There was a child's bike, still with training wheels, lying in the dirt near the porch. Several wooden planters held the homestead's raised-bed vegetable garden.

Vince and Shane had discussed whether to approach homes that were obviously not places that Ollie and his gang controlled. Going up on somebody's porch these days was a good way to get shot, but on the other hand, good folks needed to be warned about the gang and the dangers they presented. They decided that if they could safely let people know, they would, but going to the door and knocking was too risky. They watched this house for a while, trying to decide on the best course of action to take.

A screen door at the back of the house banged shut, then a woman who looked to be about thirty carried a laundry basket over to the line and began to take down the clothes. A little boy ran over and got on the bike, riding it clumsily around the yard. A calico cat perched on a short stump and licked her paws. Shane glanced at Vince, eyebrows raised.

Vince shrugged, handed his AR15 to Shane, and said. "Cover me. I hope I don't give her a heart attack," before carefully stepping into the open, both hands spread and out to his sides.

"Ma'am?" Vince called from about thirty yards away.

The woman whirled around, pulling a small pistol out of her hip pocket and pointing it at Vince.

"Ma'am, I mean you no harm. I'm Vince Sullivan. I used to work at the prison and I'm just out checking on folks and passing on some information."

"What information?"

"There's a man named Ollie Simmons who escaped. I believe he has a gang and is in the area. I just want to warn you to be on the lookout and be careful. Simmons is tall and very skinny, with thin, greasy hair and really bad teeth. He's a rapist and a murderer. I also want to say that the church in Kanichi Springs is helping folks. Lots of ladies and children are staying there, so if you need help, you can go there. That's all. I'll just be on my way now. Take care, ma'am, and God bless."

The woman just stared at him, but when he turned to leave, she called out, "Thank you."

***

Before darkness fell, the two men had found three more houses. The first was abandoned. The second was a rundown little cabin. There were small signs that someone was living there, but nobody came outside, so they moved on. At the third house, which was way back in the woods and far from any roads, there was a big mongrel dog gnawing on a fresh bone. It sensed their presence and stood up, staring intently in their direction. Major went on alert, as well, sensing the other dog's hostility. Vince and Shane eased back into the forest, then turned and went due west to skirt the property.

"Let's move on. We need to find a spot to spend the night. Anyone who has a dog that alert probably also has a few guns. This place may be isolated enough that they'll be okay. For some reason, that looked like a place where a man lives alone." Vince glanced back toward the house.

"Yeah, it did. No flowers, no decorations like wind chimes or such, and just one chair on the porch. The bone that dog was chewing looked like the leg bone of a deer. The curtains were plain brown, with no ruffles. Must be a guy."

The two friends climbed an old fence and continued walking for about half a mile. Large rocks and fallen trees littered the ground, They traveled as quietly as possible, surveying their surroundings, and finally found an old homestead where the house had burned, leaving a brick chimney standing like a sentinel. Nearby, the barn still stood, the doors hanging open. They entered cautiously, and found only a few bales of old hay stacked in a corner.

"Well, it isn't the Ritz, but it'll do. The sun will be gone in ten minutes or so. Let's just spend the night here. This hay doesn't look or smell moldy. We can break a few bales and make our beds." Shane dropped his pack and stretched, rolling his head to relieve his tight neck muscles.

***

Ian put his hands on his hips and smiled at Gus and Charlie, They had been working on and off for several days, using whatever time they could manage away from hunting, fishing, and working on Erin's new garden. Now they stood just inside the northern entrance, and they were finished, except for testing their new security system.

"Are we ready?" he asked.

"Yeah. We'll test this one first, then go to the other entrances and test them. Too bad the radios don't work in the caves." Gus frowned slightly. "They're pretty much line-of-sight, and the caves aren't straight, but of course, if the radios worked in here, we wouldn't need this alarm system."

The alarm system consisted of three very different doorbells, each with a light right under it, mounted on the wall in the lodge's living room. One doorbell, the one for the north entrance, played the ubiquitous Westminster chimes. The button for the second one was located at the entrance near the little stream, west of the lodge. It played a simple "ding-dong".

The third was for the entrance closest to the lodge, which was toward the southwest side of the mountain. It made a loud, ugly, buzzer sound; Gus had chosen that one on purpose, because whether they were inside the caves or outside, if intruders were in the vicinity of that cave, they were really close to finding the cache cavern and the secret way into the lodge. He wanted an alarm for that entrance that would get everyone's attention.

"We need to work out what we'll do for each bell and have some drills, get our reaction time down and everyone in the right position to defend the place. I hated drills in the military, until I saw how they saved lives in an emergency. With children to protect, the last thing we need is a panic caused by people not knowing what to do." Charlie scratched his chin. ""We'll have to drill the kids, too, at least the ones that are old enough."

It took over an hour to complete the testing, but the system worked. Ian had prepared a new duty roster, so the cave entrances would have guards to push the buttons. Each guard would be paired with one of the dogs. If strangers came near the caves, the guard would push the alarm button and use his or her best judgment on whether to confront the intruders or retreat and wait for reinforcements, depending on the number of people sighted and how close they were to the cave.

Chapter 9 – The Next Day

Shane crept forward, crouching low. An old one-story farmhouse stood across a pasture, about a hundred yards ahead, with a dilapidated old barn about thirty yards east of it. Vince edged around to the west, way back in the trees, hoping to find a spot where he could see into the barn.

They could both hear voices. Male voices. From the tone, it sounded like an argument, with others egging it on. Vince signaled for Shane to come to him, and they slipped further back into the woods, then circled around to a spot where the trees were much closer to the house. The voices got louder, the anger more obvious, then they heard a crash, and a man came flying out the screen door, landing on his back in the dirt. The door slapped back against the side of the house, bounced off, then slammed shut. The man rose quickly, just as another man pushed through the door and jumped down the two steps from the porch. Fists flew, with several other men yelling encouragement. Then two more men stepped out onto the tiny back porch, where they stood silently watching.

Shane grabbed Vince's arm and pulled him away, back into heavier cover.

"That was Simmons! I guess he did gather a new gang. How many did you count?" Vince demanded.

"Seven, I think, but there may be more in the house. The guy with the big belly who stepped out with Simmons was Deputy Kline. They sure looked friendly."

"We need to go back to the lodge and decide how to handle this. As much as I would love to put a bullet in his brain, we gave our word that we wouldn't take him on if he had more men. Besides, we'd be stupid to start anything, not knowing the exact number of men he has. They haven't been hitting Kanichi Springs, or we would have heard about it from Ken. So where are they getting their supplies?"

"There are two or three smaller communities not far from here, but that means the gang has access to fuel. Come on. I have an idea."

Signing for Major to come, Shane led the way, circling around to the west, where they could see the other side of the barn. Clearly visible in the waning light was a large tank with a long hose and a nozzle.

"There's the fuel, I bet. Most farmers around here have a tank. Sometimes they have one for gasoline and another one for diesel. Okay. Here's the plan...."

***

Finishing off a couple of MRE's, Vince and Shane cleaned up the area and removed any obvious signs that they had been there. They had already fed Major, who lay snoozing near Shane's feet.

"Time to go. I'm ready." Vince checked his gear one more time.

"Me, too. I'm glad it's clear and there's a full moon. It's hard to be quiet when you can't see where you're stepping."

Slowly making their way through the forest, the two men cautiously approached the old farmstead. Shane veered south, staying in the trees, and took up a position where he had a clear view of the back of the house and the barn, including the fuel tank.

Vince waited, watching and listening. There were no sounds other than natural night noises. If any guards stood watch, they weren't visible. Finally, Vince emerged from cover, crouched as low as he could, and made his way to the fuel tank. Just as he reached for the nozzle, the back door of the house squeaked open. Vince froze.

A short, muscular man with a gleaming, bald head descended the steps and walked out into the middle of the yard. Vince heard the sound of a zipper, then the splatter of urine hitting the ground. The man finished, zipped his jeans, and went back into the house.

Dang. If he had turned the other way, he'd have seen me. If he had been a few seconds later coming out, he'd have smelled the gasoline. That was too close. Vince wiped the sweat from his forehead.

He waited a couple of minutes, then carefully lowered the nozzle so that gravity could do its job, and started the flow. Gas poured onto the dirt, soaking in immediately. When the flow stopped, Vince eased back into the trees.

***

The next morning, Ollie Simmons and his gang piled into the beat-up old van. Barry Kline was the only one who stayed at the house, supposedly to guard it, but in reality, to minimize his risks. Ollie started the van and drove between the house and the barn, stopping next to the fuel tank. That's when he noticed the dangling nozzle and the smell of gasoline.

"Which of you fools did that?" he screamed. "Who filled the van up yesterday?"

The others turned to look at a young black kid. He immediately began denying that he had spilled the fuel.

"Get your ass out there and see if there's enough to fill up for today," Simmons hissed.

The kid scrambled over two other guys and ran around the back of the van. He grasped the nozzle, took off the gas cap with his other hand, and shoved the nozzle in. Nothing. Not even a dribble.

Simmons came around to glare at the young man, who began backing up, hands raised to ward off what he knew was coming. As he opened his mouth to plead, Simmons pulled a pistol and calmly shot the kid, then looked at the others.

"Somebody take out the trash," he snarled, as he kicked the body.

Chapter 10 – The Next Day

Vince, Shane, and Major returned to the lodge by a different route, stopping only to warn one elderly couple about the gang, and to eat. They were careful, but moved quickly, staying in the forest as much as possible. They arrived just in time to clean up and have dinner with the group.

Vince explained what they had found, and everyone enjoyed a chuckle over the gasoline. Micah asked why they didn't just use the gasoline to burn the place down.

"There's too much danger of the fire getting out of control and spreading to the forest. Who would come and help if it became a wildfire? And besides, we didn't know if they had any captives in there. They seem to like women, you know."

"Oh. I didn't think about that," Micah mumbled.

"When you have choices to make, you have to ask yourself 'what if' and realize what the consequences could be," Shane explained. "We wouldn't want to start a wildfire that would burn down the homes of innocent people, or even burn the lodge."

"So what are we going to do about this? Of course, we need to warn the folks at the church building, but then what?" Erin looked around the room. "And do we want to ask for help from the other families in the area, or can we handle it alone this time?"

"I'd feel better about it if we consulted the others," Tanner mused. "Somehow, it just seems like we shouldn't take unilateral action on something that affects us all."

"Tanner's right." Shane glanced at the others. "We need a plan, and the families should be involved. Besides, we may need their help."

"Okay. In other news, you two weren't here for the grand inauguration of the new cave alarm system. We have three alarms, and the lights and different bells will alert us to where any uninvited guests are. Also, we expect Tanner's family to finish their move in a day or so. They'll take over guarding one of the entrances, and plan to take turns sleeping in one of the caverns west of the lodge, but I hope to talk them into sleeping in the lodge. We'll still be doing all the cooking here, and after they eat, they'll deliver meals to the guards at all the cave entrances.

"Gus is working on some type of removable way to block the little opening in the smaller east cave, so people can sleep there without the cold wind freezing them out. Then in the summer months, we can take it off so there'll be some air circulating. We'll see how it goes, how bad the winter is, but we plan to have guards on the entrances all the time."

Erin paused, then added, "Mac and Gus are going to rig some type of antenna up on the mountain so we can use the handheld radios without having to climb up there every time. I don't understand all the technical terms, but they say they can do it if they can find a solar panel and a battery. Now, let's contact the other families and see what they want to do."

***

Nolan and Angie agreed to meet with everyone. Jimmy Gibbs said that his mother was very ill and he would go along with whatever the group decided to do, but his family couldn't be at the meeting. Talako and Will said that they would represent the McNeil household, so a meeting was held the next morning.

"We know that these are bad men who have committed crimes, and now they're desperate. The way I see it, we have two choices: hit them where they live, or set up in town to ambush them again." Nolan scanned the room. "The second choice means waiting for them in town, when they haven't even shown their faces in Kanichi Springs lately. They may be hitting other towns, or just raiding homes in the country, and we have no way of knowing where they'll go next. Plus, they'll be more careful when and if they come back to town, and I really don't want to leave my place unguarded while we hang around waiting for them."

Gus stood up. "You're right, Nolan. I say we hit their base. We have to use what we know. We don't know where they'll go next, but we do know where they'll be holed up between raids."

"Okay," Tanner interjected. "Any new ideas? Any suggestions? Then let's vote. All in favor of going after the gang at their base, raise your hand."

Every hand went up, so Tanner asked for volunteers to come up with a plan. Talako, Nolan, Vince, Shane, and Charlie moved out to the patio to figure out the best way to get the thugs out of the house and into the open.

The handheld radios that almost all of them carried crackled suddenly, but the words were incomprehensible. Tanner and Erin headed up the mountain to see who was trying to get through.

It was Jimmy. Naomi Gibbs had passed away, her damaged heart finally giving out. Jimmy had already contacted the Abbotts, and they would hold a small service in town the next morning.

Another good soul, gone home, Erin thought. *How many more will die because we lost our medical services, our supply chain, our ability to just run to town when we need something? Oh, Lord, when will this end? And this is also going to delay whatever plans we have for stopping Ollie Simmons and his new gang.*

When Tanner broke the news to the others, Angie and Nolan left to go help the Gibbs family, their longtime friends and neighbors. Frances and Val got busy preparing a meal to take to them.

Just because our society has collapsed doesn't mean we can't still help our friends, Erin thought sadly. *I really liked that sweet old lady. May she rest in peace.*

The meal was simple, consisting of a casserole made with some of Charlie's wild pig and noodles from the cache, accompanied by green beans and slices of tomatoes. Since Mac's disclosure of his gasoline stash, they had gas in Erin's Expedition, so Tanner and Erin took the hot meal to the Gibbs home and offered their condolences. Lee Gibbs was sad to lose his lifelong companion, but relieved that she was no longer suffering.

"She was a good woman. We met in elementary school, when she was in the fourth grade and I was in sixth. Her family had just moved here from Arkansas. Some boys were teasing her about her size, picking on her. She was so little. I had a reputation as a fighter and I ran those boys off pronto. Naomi and I were friends after that. We dated a little in high school, but mostly just went around in the same group. When I got back from a stint in the Mekong Delta, she was all grown up and so pretty. I was tongue-tied the first time I tried to talk to her, but she was just like always, and that helped me relax. I fell hard for her, and I was blessed beyond measure when she agreed to marry me. I've been blessed every day since, too. I'm sure gonna miss her."

Erin hugged him, tears in her eyes, and whispered, "I will, too. She was an example to me of what it is to be a real lady, and a good woman."

Tanner made arrangements with Jimmy to pick the family up the next morning around ten. They would transport the body in Tanner's pickup; the family would ride in the Expedition, and they would all stop by the funeral home for a casket. A few members of the group from the lodge would come over to guard the Gibbs house while they were at the service.

***

The day was gray, and thunder rumbled off in the distance as Naomi Gibbs was laid to rest. She had been a member of the church in town since childhood; doing the service was hard for Ken, who was close to the whole family, but in spite of getting choked up several times, he managed to get through it. After the brief funeral, Tanner and Erin gave the Gibbs family a ride back to their house and picked up the volunteers who had stood watch for them.

As they continued north on the old dirt road, Tanner noticed smoke in the direction of the lodge. He sped up, but as they got closer, it became obvious that the smoke was further way than the lodge, so he drove past the lodge driveway and went on to the next corner. From there, it was easy to see what was burning.

"Oh, Lord, no!" Erin cried, seeing flames in the windows of Mac and Claire's house. Tanner turned the Expedition around and raised a cloud of dust getting back to the lodge, while Erin got on the radio to alert the group.

Most of the men were waiting with shovels when Tanner slammed on the brakes near the front steps. Erin got out, a worried look on her face, and the men piled in. Gus ran up with Tanner's chainsaw and squeezed in last.

"All gassed up. I sharpened the chain yesterday, getting ready to cut some wood for winter."

When they got close to the house, Shane spotted a bald man and a skinny fellow fleeing into the trees.

"Hold your ears! I'm going to give them a reason to keep running," he shouted, then leaned out the window and fired three shots at the men.

"We can't save the house. It's too far gone, but we can try to save the tanker. Tanner, turn in the second drive...right there. Now, follow it back to the clearing." Mac glanced back at the little house that he and his trucker friends had built before he asked Claire to be his wife. He had proposed in the kitchen, after giving her a tour. So many memories, so much love, in such a small home.

Tanner stopped and all the men jumped out, determined to keep the fire off the tanker long enough for Mac to move it to safety. Ian and Shane pulled the camo netting off and rolled it up in a big wad.

Charlie took his rifle and kept his eyes on the woods where those two strangers were last seen. Gus and BJ got Mac's old Ford tractor and put the blade on the front, then BJ started it up and began scraping a firebreak across the clearing.

"BJ on a tractor?" Tanner shouted to Gus.

"He said he grew up on a farm! He sure seems to know what he's doing," Gus yelled back.

Mac started his big truck and brought it around to the tanker. The blue paint on the right side was bubbled and scorched, but the tires held so far. He drove around and lined it up, not bothering to jump out to check the height of the fifth-wheel plate. He backed under the trailer and did a quick tug test to confirm that the fifth wheel jaws were locked to the kingpin, then hopped back out to wind up the landing gear and attach the air lines.

By the time Mac had his rig ready, the fire had spread. Trees on the other side of the drive were burning, and the hip-high weeds and grass that had almost taken over the driveway were ablaze. Tanner had cut down several cedar trees around the clearing, and Shane helped Ian drag them away from the tanker. They had seen how fast a cedar could virtually explode into flames, often sending burning branches several feet away, causing fires to spread more rapidly. Mac's barn was already engulfed in flames and the roof of the house had fallen in.

"You can't drive through that, sitting on a gasoline bomb!" Gus pulled on Mac's arm, but Mac jerked away.

"I'm going to park it in the middle of the patch that BJ scraped off!" Mac bellowed. Indeed, BJ had used the blade on the tractor to clear off the brush and weeds, starting in the center and circling the clearing in a widening oval, leaving bare dirt behind.

"Tanner!" Mac yelled, then gestured toward a tree, making cutting motions. Tanner ran over and revved up the chainsaw, felling the tree as quickly as possible and as low as he could get.

Mac jumped in behind the wheel of his rig, then turned as sharply left as he could manage, running over stumps to center the tanker on the bare ground. Trees burned all around, but none were big enough to hit the truck if they fell. Mac climbed down and stood, hands on his hips, staring at the fire. It was too big for so few to fight, but the forest was still damp and green from recent rains. All they could do was hope that it wouldn't burn out any occupied homes.

BJ parked the tractor near the tanker and turned it off.

Shane slapped him on the back, and asked, "BJ, where did you learn to do that?" and pointed at the cleared area.

"I grew up in Creek County, on a farm. I was there visiting my folks in 2012 when a huge fire came through and burned up half the county. I watched their neighbor do this, scraping around his new log cabin. Over four hundred homes burned, but not his."

The fire crackled and roared, and thunder rumbled. Then, it started to rain.

Mac stood with the other men, exhausted, as they watched the fire die. The rain was saving other homes in the area, but his home was gone. The house, the barn, the pump house, Claire's little garden, and the tool shed, burned to the ground. He stared at the steaming ashes for several long moments, then shook his head and started to walk away. Tanner stopped him.

"I'm sorry, Mac. I wish there was something we could have done."

"At least Claire and the children were at the lodge. My family is safe, and the rest is just stuff. Meaningful stuff, but still, what's really important to me is my wife and kids. We'll be okay.

"Now, what are we going to do with this tanker? We can't leave it here, because those two men may have seen it. I can get it into the clearing at Erin's, but not with all those cars parked there. We need to get rid of most of the cars, anyway. They'll provide cover for bad guys if we get attacked."

"Let's see: we have Erin's Expedition, Sarah's Explorer, Ian's big truck, plus two pickups, Richie's and mine. I've been meaning to find a place to put those. I think we should keep the Expedition, and maybe Sarah's Explorer, but the rest should be moved elsewhere. Ian's truck has been a lifesaver for hauling things from town and from my kennel, but we've already gotten pretty much all the stuff we needed to get. I'd like to keep it nearby, though, just in case. You know, there's a pretty big space in a clearing past my grandparents' house, and since I'm sure that just as soon as they hear about this fire, they'll be moving into the lodge, we could probably park the extra vehicles there, along with Rose and Will's mini-van, and John and Dana's SUV. My grandparents can just leave their vehicles in the garage."

"Sounds good, but let's take all the batteries out and store them in the cave," Mac suggested. "They might have nearly empty gas tanks, but we don't want to make it easy for thieves to steal them. Someday, when there's gas again, those cars will be needed.

***

Claire took the news about the house like the strong woman she was. She knew that it bothered Mac more than he would admit, even more than it bothered her; after all, he had built it with his own hands and the help of his friends.

"Honey, don't fret about the house. We'll be fine, and we'll have another house someday."

"Claire, it's all gone. Our family photos, our mementos. It's gone."

"Oh, no, it's not, Mac McCoy! Do you really think I would leave our photo albums behind? Your grandpa's shotgun? My mom's quilt and my dad's Stetson? No! I would never do that. They're in tubs in the cavern, except for the shotgun, which is under the bed over there. We left the furniture behind, but I brought all the things that had sentimental value. Our real treasures are our kids, but I wouldn't leave the little we have to remember our families by."

Mac looked both surprised and happy. "Have I ever told you that you are the best, the smartest, the strongest, the most beautiful woman I know?"

Claire smiled, and hugged him. "Not nearly often enough."

***

Tanner was right in his prediction that his family would move to the lodge immediately when they heard about the fire. The thought that ruffians might set their home on fire, placing the children's lives in danger, was the deciding factor. Even Talako's reluctance to leave the house where they had raised their children was overshadowed by the fear of possibly subjecting the little ones to a fiery death. They agreed that the extra vehicles at Erin's could be parked on their property, and made the final preparations to relocate.

Ian, Shane, and Vince went out on foot to scout the two roads that the cars would use to get to the McNeil's. They used the radios to let the drivers know when it was clear. The little convoy moved carefully. Ian, in his big delivery truck, and Erin, in the Expedition, brought up the rear.

They loaded the family's clothing, the children's toys, some very nice paintings by a Choctaw artist friend of Talako's, plus the few supplies they had left into Ian's truck. The family piled into the SUV and the drivers of the other vehicles rode with Sarah in her Explorer.

Once they got the trucks unloaded at the lodge, Erin and Tanner took the Expedition, and Ian and Shane took the delivery truck back to the McNeil's house. They parked Ian's truck facing outward in case it was needed, then removed the batteries from each car and pickup and loaded them in the back of the Expedition.

Erin gave everyone a ride back to the lodge. By the time they got there, Mac had the tanker wedged into a corner of the yard and covered once again with the camo netting. All of those who had been outside were soaked to the skin. The rain continued to fall steadily, if not hard, and lightning ripped white-hot lines from sky to earth.

"Okay, everyone who is wet, go change into dry clothes. With the humidity as high as it is, it'll take the wet stuff forever to dry, but hang it up so it can start.

Frances and Val have something cooking that smells good, so hop to it." Erin smiled, then headed upstairs to follow her own advice.

The rain continued for three days, accompanied by unusually warm temperatures. The air felt heavy and thick, almost oppressive. Close quarters and the weather combined to make the members of the group irritable. Even the children were fussy and whined constantly.

Getting everyone settled at the lodge proved to be a much bigger challenge than Erin had anticipated. The original plan had been for the McNeils to stay in the caverns on the west side of the lodge, but BJ and Frances volunteered to give up the bedroom downstairs. That meant deciding which of the three married couples from the McNeil family would get the room. Rose and Dana insisted that their grandparents should have it, but Talako and Julia insisted just as strongly that one of the young couples with children should take it. They all said they would be happy staying full time in one of the caverns, but Erin worried that with winter coming, it would be too hard on the children, and the older folks, too. Finally, they decided that Rose and Will would have the bedroom, since they had more children, and those children were younger.

Erin still didn't want Talako and Julia to stay in a cavern where the temperature was cool all the time; their arthritis might be aggravated by the low temperatures. They finally agreed that Talako and John would sleep in the men's dorm, and Julia and Dana would bunk with the women. They discussed moving one set of bunks from the women's side to the men's, so that Zeke and Tucker would have their own beds, but decided that it would make the men's side too crowded, and with the adults all having guard duty at various times, the boys could just "hot rack" wherever they could find an empty bunk.

Rose and Will's twins, Gina and Isabelle, would sleep on a twin mattress on the floor in their parents' room, and for the time being, Wyatt would have to sleep between them, at least until other arrangements could be made.

The McNeils would take over the guard duties for the northern entrance, but suggested that when spring arrived, they could probably sleep in the caverns. They would figure out whether to make any changes once the weather warmed up..

Erin was worried about more people coming, so the first chance she got, she grabbed Tanner's hand and practically dragged him to the cache cavern, intending to discuss the problem with him. But as soon as she stopped, he spun her around to face him, wrapped his arms around her, and kissed her, hard. When they ran out of air, Erin's eyes were glazed.

"Wow," she whispered. "Remind me to drag you into a cave more often."

"I've wanted to do that for weeks, but things have been too hectic. Sometimes, I wish we could escape all of this and go lie on a beach or something. Just relaxing and not being constantly surrounded by people sounds like heaven. I love them all, but sometimes I just need you and some *quiet*."

"We may have a little free time now that we have extra people to help out. Ian is working out a new schedule for guard duty, so everyone will get a day each week without standing watch. I told him that if he made it where he and Sarah had the same day off, he darn sure better give other couples equal treatment."

"Erin." Tanner kissed her again, softly this time, then held her face in his big hands, gazing into her eyes. "I know the timing stinks, but I love you so much. Will you marry me?"

Erin's heart pounded at those words, ones that she hadn't expected to hear under the current circumstances. The love she saw shining in Tanner's eyes made her answer easy.

"Yes, of course I will."

They never did get around to discussing the problem of overcrowding in the lodge.

***

Most of the group members were worried about what the "Simmons Gang", as they had begun calling them, might be doing. Tanner thought they would be looking for a new source of fuel. Shane figured that they would split up, traveling on foot to scour the area for supplies. Either way, that put people in jeopardy.

"We need to hit them soon," Vince insisted, as Shane nodded in agreement. "We've been delayed by the weather, but it's clearing off. The gang may have already relocated, but if they haven't, they soon will. I guess the fuel tank was the reason they stayed at that farm, but with the gas gone, they'll move on. Now that I've had time to think about it, I wish that we hadn't dumped that gas. We always preach at Micah to think about consequences before making decisions, but I sure didn't stop to think. If we'd thought it through, we'd have known that it might make them go elsewhere. At least before, we knew where to find them."

"Hey, you did what most of us would have done," Ian assured him. "We all need to start thinking more about long-term consequences and overall strategy. It's done now, anyway, and you can't change it. We just need to figure out what to do next. I can't help wondering if the guys who burned Mac's house are part of that gang, or just two drifters."

"Yeah, me , too. And it matters, because they may have seen the tanker," Vince interjected. "If they did, they'll be looking for it. What we need is another scouting expedition to see if they're still at the same spot. If they aren't, we sure do need to find them before they find us."

"True. Let's get ready to go out again as soon as the weather clears. Dang, but I miss checking the forecast on my phone. Now, we just have to wait and see what the weather is when it happens, with no warning that it might turn bad." Shane shook his head. "We'll have to watch the sky and take our chances."

***

The sun came out at last, about three days later, so Vince and Shane slipped on their backpacks and headed out through the west caves. They would stay out this time until they found the gang or ran out of food, whichever came first. They took Blitz this time, to give the young dog some experience. Once again, they would warn others if they could do so safely, and would travel through the forest to avoid roads.

The first two days went much like their previous trip, even though their route was different. They spoke to one old fellow who lived alone and had been off the grid even before the collapse. His tiny cabin was nestled back in the forest so far that nobody would ever find it except by accident. He told them his name was Jeb, and he hadn't seen anyone lurking around when he went out to fish or check his traps, but would keep an eye out, then he invited them to come back by on their return trip if they had time.

They slept that night in an old loafing shed, and just before sunrise, the rain started again, promising a miserable day. Erin had thoughtfully tucked plastic rain suits into their packs, olive green ones with pants and a hooded jacket, which the two men put on over their clothes. They decided to move out, going slower because of the weather, but feeling a strong, urgent need to find out where the gang was hiding.

That afternoon, they reached the gang's old farmhouse and saw that the van was gone. Watching carefully for any sign of movement, they saw and heard nothing except normal forest sounds, even after the rain stopped. Finally, late in the evening, Shane slipped up to the house, and crouching under a window, peeked in, then moved to the next window. Vince sneaked around to the back and noticed the door standing open. There was no sign of anyone, so he drew his handgun and entered. Clearing each of the five rooms, he stuck his head out the front door and motioned to Shane.

"Ain't nobody home," he drawled, trying to mimic Charlie. "Them punks musta lit outta here already."

"Looks like they aren't planning on coming back, either. They sure didn't leave anything behind. Let's go check the barn."

All they found in the barn was some old hay and some rusty farm implements, plus one fairly new patrol car with "Sheriff "on the sides. The keys were in it, and the gas cap was hanging on its plastic strap. When Shane turned the key, the gas gauge read empty.

"I bet they siphoned whatever gas was in this so they could all ride in the van. Say, do you smell something? I get a whiff of some rotten smell every so often. It's like something dead." Vince went around the outside of the barn, following the scent across a pasture to the edge of the woods. There he found the young black man. Vince turned the body over, and recognized him immediately from the tattoos on his face and arms.

When Shane came up beside him, Vince gestured toward the corpse. "That was one of the inmates at the prison, one who had gotten fifteen years for armed robbery. He wasn't a bad kid, really. He just got in with the wrong crowd and made some really stupid decisions."

"Looks like he made one too many poor choices. So what do we do now? Which way should we go?"

"We go south, maybe a little west. The closest towns are in that direction. The thugs are probably getting desperate for fuel, so we'll check farms for tanks. Let's go. We might make another mile or two before we have to find shelter for the night."

***

Sarah and Erin pulled another plastic tub off the stack in the cache cavern, and looked over the list taped to the top of the box. This one contained packages of socks and underwear in a variety of sizes.

"Okay, let's put this one over there with the other clothing items," Erin suggested. "We've gotten a little disorganized lately, going through boxes and not putting them back where they belong. Writing a general description of what's in each one on the end of the box will make it easier to locate what we're looking for."

"How many more are there? Here, use the marker and write 'socks and undies' on that tub, and I'll get the next one down." Sarah reached up and grabbed another tub, easily lifting it down.

"Girl, you've always been strong and athletic, but all the work we do around here has grown some muscles on you," Erin remarked. "I guess we're all probably in the best shape we've ever been in."

"True." A new voice commented as Jen and Val entered the cavern. "We've been on duty at the north entrance," Jen said. "What are you doing?"

"Trying to organize these tubs better, and marking the contents on the end instead of just on the top. When they're stacked, we can't see the labels Uncle Ernie put on them," Sarah explained.

"Do you realize that this is the first time we four have been together, without others around, in quite a while? I've been meaning to tell you something, and I guess now's my chance."

The other three turned to stare expectantly at Erin, waiting to hear her news.

"So Erin, what's your news?" Val inquired.

"I have an announcement. I wanted to tell you three first, since you're practically my sisters." She smiled. "Tanner and I are engaged."

Silence reigned for about a millisecond before pandemonium erupted. Laughter, congratulations, and best wishes mingled with hugs and tears. Calm finally found its way back, amid smiles and giggles.

"And just when did this happen," Jen demanded.

"Yesterday, I dragged him in here to talk to him about something. I can't even remember now what it was. And he just asked me. It was a total surprise, under the circumstances. I figured he'd wait until things get back to normal, but he wants to get married right away." Erin beamed. "And so do I. so I guess that when we've taken care of the Simmons gang, we'll be planning a wedding."

Chapter 12 – The Next Day

Shane crept through the trees, staring intently at a house outside a tiny community about seven miles from Kanichi Springs. The house was old, but larger than most of those they had seen in the area. Two stories tall with white siding, it stood about forty yards from a huge red barn, the kind with a hayloft. An old stock trailer sat rusting beside the barn, and behind it were two fuel-storage tanks of the type commonly seen on farms.

Vince circled around, slipping through a wide gate that separated the homestead from a huge hay meadow. The grass was high enough that he could crouch down and scramble his way across, unseen by any eyes that might be watching from the house. He found a small cluster of trees and stood up in the shadows where he could observe the house. Using his binoculars, he scanned the area. Nothing moved, but Vince sensed that there was someone inside. He couldn't explain it, but he had spent too many years around criminals to ignore his hunches.

He shifted slightly and looked over the area again.

There! What was that? I saw movement. Yeah, there he is, Vince thought.

Shane had already seen the man, who was doing something in the trees on the other side of the yard. The man squatted down near the base of a tree and seemed to be pulling on something, then he said something, and a male voice answered from Shane's left.

Uh-oh. There's at least two, and I almost walked right into one of them. What are they doing?

Shane held perfectly still, knowing that moving might draw their attention. Standing in the trees, he was glad that he was wearing camo and had the training to remain still for long periods, for hours, if necessary. The voice from his left said something, then its owner emerged from the woods. Shane recognized him on sight; it was the bald man they'd seen fleeing from Mac's place the day of the fire.

Baldy joined the other man as he looked over whatever they had been doing, then the door of the house opened, and Ollie Simmons stuck his head out.

"You finished out there? It better work!" he yelled.

"It'll work! We got two more to set, and we'll be done. Nobody will be sneakin' up on us without makin' a lot of noise," Baldy shouted back.

Ah. Tripwires, attached to something that will make a racket. They're more cautious now, unfortunately. Shane remained motionless. Until the two thugs completed their work, he and Vince were pretty much stuck. It was too risky to move out, and somewhere nearby could be a strand of wire or fishing line that could bring the whole gang down on them. Vince was quite a bit further away, and might be able to withdraw safely, but Shane was much too close. He was fairly certain that there were only two men outside, but five minutes ago, he'd thought that there weren't any, so he waited.

It took about forty-five minutes for the two thugs to finish, but once they went inside, Shane was finally free to move. He took his time retreating, watching for the tripwires, and eventually located one, which he carefully stepped over. He followed the wire and found a bundle of beer and soda cans tied together, and the lid off a metal barrel nailed to a tree a few feet away. It was obvious that if he had hit the wire, the cans would have swung free and collided with the lid, making a racket that would alert the men in the house. *They think this will protect them, but now that we know about it, and they don't know that we know, we'll have a slight advantage. If we had come an hour later, we wouldn't have a clue these traps were here. Now to figure out what to do about it.*

***

That evening, Shane and Vince dined on MREs in a barn about three-fourths of a mile from the farmhouse, and tried to formulate a plan. The tripwires that the gang had installed added a whole new level of danger to a direct attack on the farmhouse.

"We know where a couple of tripwires are, but trying to find the others without setting one off or being seen is out of the question." Shane pulled his boot off and scratched his foot.

Vince had already heard all about the fight against Ollie's first gang. "Do you think that the same rules apply this time? When you hit them before, in town, you waited until you saw them commit a crime, but we all know what these animals are capable of, so do we wait this time, or just go after them?"

"I'd say we go after them. The last time, all we *knew* that they were guilty of was looting and vandalism, until they caught that girl and one of them raped her before we could stop him. This time, we know that at least one of the guys who burned Mac and Claire out is in that house. The skinny one probably is, too. Barry Kline is at the very least an accessory to a triple homicide, and may be the shooter. Simmons is a convicted rapist and thief. All the others are hanging around with them, so it's fairly safe to assume they aren't choir boys. I think the gang will stay there for a while, if there's fuel in that tank. We should head back to the lodge and come up with a strategy of some kind."

"I have an idea. It's dirty and underhanded, and in normal times, it would even be illegal, but these guys don't play by any rules, so I think we can break a few to stop them. My idea is sneaky enough that it just might work, but I need to think through the details," Vince replied. "It was awfully hot today, for mid-October, and all that rain we got has made it humid. My grandpa used to say that hot and humid equaled storm weather, and I don't like the looks of that sky. We could probably make a mile tonight, but we might not find shelter, so I vote that we stay here tonight. It's still a little daylight left, but I'm tired, so let's get some sleep. We've got a long walk tomorrow."

***

"I wonder why they haven't hit us here," Terri mused, as she and two other ladies prepared a meager lunch for those who were living in the church fellowship hall.

"They probably figure that there's no liquor or drugs in a church, so it's not worth their time. Or they have no idea that this basement is even here," Yvonne Johnson replied. Widow of the police chief, the middle-aged woman was renowned in the area for her cooking skills. Even with the few supplies they were able to get, she managed to turn out tasty meals for the townspeople who had been living in the basement for many weeks, with only a few excursions outside.

"They're after women, too, if their past behavior is any indication. I hope and pray that they never find us here," she continued.

"That's why Ken is upstairs, keeping a watch for them, and that's why I have a kitchen knife in my pocket. If they get past the men, I don't plan on making it easy for them. In fact, if it looks like they're coming this way, I think we should pass out all the sharp knives we have. They'll pay in blood for trying to rape us. There's no commandment that says we can't defend ourselves from a rapist. A steak knife or a utility knife is better than nothing, I guess."

Ken came down the stairs just then, looking tired. "I think maybe that Simmons fellow is through with Kanichi Springs. Hopefully, they won't come back again since they've pretty much cleaned out everything they wanted."

Chapter 13 – That Same Day

"You four clear that warehouse, and meet me back here in thirty minutes," Sergeant Lopez ordered. "And no goofing off!"

Price and David Martin looked so much alike that many people thought they were twins. Only eleven months older, David had just scheduled the classes for his senior year at Northeastern State University in Tahlequah when the economy collapsed. Price had been ready to start his junior year. The two were best friends as well as brothers, and had planned to go into business together. Being conscripted into a so-called security force by the government had taken the pair far away from their family; they wound up in Pueblo, Colorado after completing their training at a camp near Denver. Their parents, Frances and BJ, had made it to Erin's lodge, and reunited with their sister, Jen. Their only means of communication was by radio, and that was rarely allowed and carefully monitored.

The two young men agreed on the first day of basic that they would stop the practical jokes that had earned them the moniker "the Martin Menaces" and do their best to avoid drawing attention to themselves. That turned out to be the hardest part of their adjustment to their new lives. They were veteran pranksters, but somehow they managed to curb their impulses and stay out of trouble.

While making a point of being friendly and cooperative with the other young "recruits", they were always careful about getting too chummy with anyone in particular. They were assigned to the National Emergency Recovery Corps (NERC), and received food, shelter, and medical care, as well as uniforms and boots, for their service. Each member of the Corps got two days off per week, but the two days were never back-to-back, and the five days when they did work were always at least twelve hours long. Price and David had worked extra hard to keep the sergeant happy and to gain his trust. As a result, he wrote the schedule so they would have their days off together.

Some of the other NERC soldiers had discovered a park in town, right on the river, where people used to rent kayaks and canoes to use on the Arkansas River. Spending their days off riding the rapids had become a favorite pastime for many of them, and the Martin brothers had been invited to join in, but Price pretended to be terrified of the water as an excuse to decline the invitation. David confided in some of them that Price had almost drowned as a young boy, and had feared the water ever since.

The duties they performed when they first arrived in Pueblo consisted of setting up huge tents where food and water were distributed, taking down information about people who came for help, and patrolling the streets to prevent looting and vandalism. David volunteered them both for the latter, then explained to

Price that it would allow them more freedom of movement and a better chance to check things out.

Over a period of several weeks, their assignment gradually changed from protecting people and passing out supplies to rounding people up and taking them to a camp at the west edge of the city. The tall, barbed-wire-topped cyclone fence surrounding the camp was supposed to keep the "refugees" safe, but Price had taken one look at it, and whispered to his brother, "If they're trying to keep the bad guys *out*, why are the guards facing *in*?"

That question created a new urgency for the Martin brothers. They began that afternoon to plan an escape, preparing to travel the hundreds of miles to the lodge near Kanichi Springs, a place they had never been. Every day off from that point forward was spent thinking about and getting ready for desertion from NERC and a journey to a home they had not even seen.

The dangers of the trip they planned were multiplied by the fact that only twice had anyone tried to leave NERC in Pueblo. Both times, the deserters were ruthlessly hunted down, captured, and beaten. They were then separated and sent to remote places much further from their homes.

In front of the warehouse, their team, which consisted of three young men and one young woman, opened the double doors to the large metal building, and weapons drawn, entered the gloomy interior. The only light came from dirty windows set high above their heads. The place had obviously been a target of expectant looters, but the crates of plumbing supplies held little appeal to the hungry people in a city where the water and sewage plants had shut down months earlier. Pueblo was connected to the nation's electrical grid, which terrorists had severely damaged. Some cities had the power back on, but Pueblo wasn't a priority for whoever decided where repairs took place, and water systems required electricity to work.

Splitting into pairs and clearing the four long aisles in leap-frog fashion, the NERC team found nothing of interest. When they reached the far end of the building, they could see metal stairs leading up to offices whose windows overlooked the warehouse floor. There were three offices: one for accounting, one for shipping, and at the far end of the catwalk, one that said "Manager" on the door. The team split up to clear the offices, with David staying downstairs as a guard. The first two were vacant, but in the third, Price found three teenagers huddled behind the desk.

"We have to take you to the camp, kids," he said resignedly.

A girl, who looked to be about sixteen and would have been pretty if she had a bath and her hair combed, scooted back like a crawfish, scowling at him. "You can't make us go there. We won't go," she hissed.

"They'll feed you, and you'll be safer," Price insisted.

"They'll separate us. We're family, but they'll keep us apart," the older boy pleaded softly, his eyes begging for mercy. "Mister, please! Don't make us go."

Just then, David yelled, "Hey, Price! We're waitin' on you. You find anything?"

Price hesitated, then put a finger to his lips and whispered, "Stay quiet. And plan to move immediately to somewhere safer. Good luck."

Turning, he shouted, "No, all clear in this one."

***

Late that night, David stood with Price outside the fence around the refugee camp. Nearby were three long rows of tents for the NERC soldiers, each tent large enough to sleep six. David pretended to smoke a cigarette, which gave them an excuse to avoid entering the tent they shared with four other young men. The brothers spoke quietly and there was plenty of noise from inside the tent to cover their voices.

"I managed to swipe two more MREs from the cook tent this afternoon when I took out the trash. You get anything?" Price asked.

"Three boxes of raisins. They're not very big, but I had to be able to hide them in my pockets. I grabbed some chocolate bars, too, and a pack of smokes we can use for barter. I'm ready to get out of here."

"Not yet. We need to be sure we can get far enough away in one day. When we don't report for duty after our day off, they'll be after us. We have to have a real plan before we take off, if we want a reasonable chance at making it out of here. Say, what took you so long in that warehouse today?"

Price casually looked around before he answered. "There were three kids in that office. Looked to be late teens, maybe. They didn't want to be separated, and I'm tired of forcing people to go to a place where they don't want to be. I told them to move out, get somewhere safer."

"Dang. If Sarge finds out, we'll be cleaning latrines forever, or worse, get sent out west somewhere. We'd never get home from there. Speaking of Sarge, I heard him talking to the helicopter pilot today. He asked about some new thermal-imaging equipment they expect to be delivered in a couple of weeks. It'll be installed in the chopper."

"Blast it all! That'll make it even harder to escape," Price complained.

"Yeah." David took another fake drag on his cigarette. "They can use it to find deserters, and people like those kids you neglected to round up today. You better hope those three don't talk when they finally get caught."

"I hope we're gone by then."

"Me, too. Ya know, something strange was going on with Sarge today. I was just cleaning up around the grounds this afternoon, acting like I wasn't listening to them, but Sarge knew I was there. I glanced up, and he was looking right over that pilot's shoulder, straight at me, when he asked when that equipment would be in. It was almost like he wanted me to know."

Price's frown was emphasized by his lowered eyebrows. "You think he knows?"

"Nah. I doubt it. He'd be on us like a duck on a June bug if he even suspected."

"Well, either way, it means we better prepare to leave soon. We want to be far away from here when they get that imaging stuff installed."

***

Near the entrance to the cave west of the lodge, Sarah sat on a plastic lawn chair, about three yards back from the cave's opening, absently scratching Flash's head, watching, and listening. She was bored and just about to doze off when she felt the dog stiffen slightly. He stood, hackles raised, staring out at the sunlit forest. Sarah gave him the hand signal to stay, then slipped silently closer to the entrance.

Crunch. Crack! The sound of a muttered curse followed the sound of a foot stepping on leaves and the snap of a fallen tree limb breaking. Sarah backed up slowly, just a few feet, and pressed the button that would alert her friends back at the lodge. There was someone out there making a lot of noise and not far at all from her position, and she knew the dangers of anyone discovering the caves.

In the lodge, a doorbell sounded a loud "DING-DONG", and a light came on under a hand-written sign that read, "WEST CAVE". Everyone in the group knew what to do; twice-daily drills had made their responses automatic and swift. Guards on the doors doubled, as seven people grabbed their AR15s and headed out through the pantry to help Sarah. About halfway to

Sarah's position, Tanner and Charlie split off and took the cave branch that went more to the south. Ian was on duty at the south opening, and knew when he saw them coming that there was trouble.

"Charlie's here to relieve you, Ian. Come on; we've got company." Tanner signaled for Blitz to come, then led the way, quietly circling around the curve of the mountain to intercept the intruder.

It took them nearly ten minutes to reach a spot where they could hear a male voice muttering something as whoever was approaching tramped through the woods. Tanner motioned for Ian and Blitz to wait as the unknown visitor came closer.

A kid about eighteen or so came into view, dusting leaves and dirt off his ragged clothing. As he neared their position, Tanner stepped out into the open, holding his weapon at the ready. The kid almost walked into him before realizing that Tanner was there. The shock and fear on the young man's face only increased when Blitz growled threateningly.

"Don't shoot! Please, don't kill me!" The cry dwindled to a whimper as the kid scrambled back, hands raised in front of himself as if to deflect bullets.

"Stand still and be quiet, and I won't shoot. What are you doing on this property?" Tanner asked, wearing his meanest expression.

"Just hangin," the kid began, but Ian stepped out and cut him off.

"Cut the crap. Who's with you? Where'd you come from? Talk, or I'll sic the dog on you."

"Please, no! I've been chased by dogs too many times lately. I'm alone, just me. Nobody else, I swear."

"Keep talking. Name, address, what you're doing here. Talk!" Tanner ordered.

"My name is Noah Thomason. I was looking for work in Okmulgee, and planning to go to the tech school there, but my girlfriend kicked me out. I was going to study culinary arts to be a chef. Then things went sour. I was making my way home to Mena, Arkansas, but I got lost and gave up. My mom and stepdad prolly aren't there anymore, anyway. I've been, uh, scavenging in empty houses and cabins around the area, fishing a little. I never hurt anybody or took anything unless a house looked abandoned. I'm just trying to survive, man."

Tanner looked skeptically at Ian, who shrugged.

"Stay put, kid. If you try to run, the dog will get you, I promise. Blitz, hold!" Tanner led Ian a few yards away, then got on the radio to let the others know that they had a prisoner.

"What're we gonna do with him? We can't let him stay at the lodge, since we don't know what kind of guy he is, but I hate to turn him away with winter coming. Any suggestions?"

Ian thought for a minute, then asked, "What about town? Maybe there's someplace he could stay there."

"Ken and Terri are having a tough time feeding the folks who are already there. Plus, if we don't want him, we can't justify pawning him off on them."

"Charlie's shack?" Ian offered.

"Maybe. Would you go relieve Charlie and send him to me?"

Ian nodded and took off running toward the south cave. Fifteen minutes later, Charlie appeared.

"Ian said you needed to talk to me. What's up?"

"That kid over there." Tanner tipped his head toward Noah. "He says he from Mena, got lost trying to get home, and has just been scavenging and fishing to survive. We don't want to take him to town or the lodge, but it'll be cold soon, and he'll need shelter."

"I ain't usin' my shack, if that's what you're gettin' at. It's right cozy, even got a little wood stove. The druggies from town are likely gone, but anyhow, this late in the year, they'd know that I done harvested my weed, so I doubt they'll be comin' around. I don't reckon I'll be needin' the shack, 'less ya'll decide to kick me out."

Tanner slapped him on the back. "No chance of that, Charlie. We gotta keep you and Gus around for some comic relief. You know, that kid's shirt used to be white, and he's terrified of Blitz. I wonder.... We may have seen him around before."

"Yeah, I was thinkin' the same thing. Both times the dogs chased somebody off, they was wearin' a white tee shirt. Let's ask him, see how he reacts."

The two friends strode over to where Blitz sat staring at the boy. Tanner gave a slight signal with his hand, and the big pup relaxed.

"Noah, how long have you been in this area? I'm thinking maybe I've seen you before."

"Could be, sir. I've lost track of the days, but prolly about a month, I think. I prolly should head south where it's warmer. I don't have anywhere to stay around here, and it's already getting' cooler. Do you have another dog? I got chased by German shepherds a couple of times, but they weren't the same color as this one. Scared me pretty bad, too, but then they just stopped, turned around, and left. Were they yours?"

"Yes, they were. We have several, and they're all trained protection dogs. You were lucky we didn't tell them to attack." Tanner gave him a stern look, then sighed. "We've got an offer for you. There's an old hunting shack not too far from here. It has a cot and a wood stove, and sort of belongs to Charlie, here. You can either leave the area now, or you can spend the winter in the shack by yourself. If you choose to stay, you'll be near a stream where you can fish and maybe do some trapping. We can spare some food, I guess, and we'll let you have a radio so you can contact us. In exchange, you'll keep an eye out for strangers and let us know if you see anything suspicious. Think about it."

"Could I borrow a blanket or a sleeping bag? I don't even have a pan to cook in, or a pillow. Just my pocketknife, some fishing line and hooks, and the clothes I'm wearing."

"We'll get you fixed up with necessities, but we'd better not see you snooping around or scavenging from our neighbors." Tanner's eyes narrowed. "If we do, we won't call the dogs off. You understand what I'm telling you? We don't trust you, but we're willing to give you a chance. Don't mess up, because one chance is all you get."

"Charlie, would you radio the lodge and ask someone to put together some supplies for Noah, and bring them to the shack? We'll take him, and whoever brings the stuff can meet us there."

Charlie and Tanner took Noah on a winding, confusing trip, carefully keeping him from seeing the lodge or any of the cave entrances and taking more than twice as long as a direct trip would take. When they arrived at the shack, Charlie showed him the wood stacked behind the shack and pointed out a faint trail that led to the stream.

"This here place don't have a bathroom. You can just pee anywhere outside. There's a chamber pot in the corner for bigger jobs, and there's a spade by the woodpile so's you can bury yer poop. Don't just dump it; it'll wash into the creek, and you're gonna be getting' yer water and eatin' fish outta that stream. I'm sure Erin'll be bringin' you a water filter, but still, you don't want your poop in the creek. Now, let's go inside." Charlie led them inside the cramped, one-room hut. "There's a cot and a little table. You can hang yer duds on them pegs over there, and do yer cookin' on the wood stove. If yer still here come summer, you'll wanna cook outside. Best stay inside at night. There's big cats and bears around here, not to mention our local Bigfoot."

Noah's head snapped around, his eyes huge. "Bigfoot? He comes this far? I know folks who've spotted him down around Clayton and Honobia, but I never heard of him comin' up this way."

"Well, he's been known to travel 'round a bit when the seasons change. Just keep an eye out. He's not 'xactly sociable. You ain't gonna see him if'n he sees you first."

Sarah and Erin arrived with a duffle bag, a bedroll, and a backpack. The duffle contained a set of clothes, a jacket, a LifeStraw, and other supplies, including a small skillet and a saucepan. The backpack was full of bagged rice and beans, and a few cans of veggies.

When he saw the women headed toward the shack carrying AR15s, Noah looked at Tanner and asked, "Your ladies carry guns?"

Tanner kept his poker face with difficulty. "Yes, and those two are both crack shots. I wouldn't mess with them if I were you."

Erin walked right up to Noah and looked him in the eye. "I'm Erin, and I'm the boss around here. Don't make me mad. You really don't want to be around when I'm mad."

Charlie was standing back where Noah couldn't see him, and didn't bother to hide his grin. Tanner coughed to hide his chuckle.

Sarah tossed a sleeping bag and a pillow on the cot and gave Noah a handheld radio and a crank/solar charger. "Keep this charged, and use it if you need help or see anybody snooping around. I already set it on the proper channel to reach us. We'll be checking on you periodically, but there's no need to talk unless there's a major problem. Two clicks, pause, then three clicks, so you'll know it's us. Click twice if you're okay, three times if you need help. Got it?" Sarah explained.

"Yes, ma'am. I appreciate all this, and I'll be a good neighbor, I promise. Having a roof over my head and a cot sure beats sleeping on the ground. Thank you."

***

Once they were out of Noah's sight and hearing, Tanner began to mimic Erin. "I'm the boss around here," he said in a mean voice, making the others laugh. "Girl, you put some *fear* into that poor kid. He really thinks you're the meanest woman God ever created."

"Well, I didn't want him to think that we have any weak spots. He needs to be a little afraid of the consequences of not keeping his end of the bargain."

"Oh, he's afraid, fer sure. More of you than of Tanner, and he's plumb terrified of Tanner. That young man ain't gonna be any trouble. He's just a kid without nowhere to go. He'll mind his manners, I betcha," Charlie grinned. "That was pretty durn funny. You sure can sound tough when you wanna."

Chapter 14 – The Next Day

Vince and Shane arrived back at the lodge, exhausted, but satisfied that they had found the gang's new hideout. They told the group about their excursion, about meeting Jeb, and about the tripwire system that the gang had installed.

"We should just burn the house with 'em in it," Charlie insisted. "That'd be safer for us than a shootout."

"Charlie, what if the fire spreads? We got lucky when Mac's place burned, but we can't count on rain saving the day again. We need a way to lure those scumbags away from the house. Even if we got close without catching a tripwire, they'd still have the advantage over us. They'd hold the high ground from the upstairs windows, and we'd be out in the open part of the way to the house to set a fire. We need to dangle something they want in front of them so they come to a location of our choosing," Tanner explained.

"If we went in at night, straight up the driveway where there ain't no tripwires, we could use the gas in the tank to burn that house down. We'd pick a still night, right after a rain, so the woods'll be too wet to catch."

"Somebody owns that house, Charlie. They may have bugged out, but what right do we have to destroy their home?" Erin sighed. "They might come back some day, only to find that their house is gone. I'd hate to be part of doing that to someone, like those guys did to Mac and Claire."

"Okay. No burning," Vince agreed. "I have a better idea. The house is fairly close to the road, and the driveway is straight. I think I know a way to entice them to come out the front of the house and down the road a little ways. We'll set up an ambush out there, early. Before daylight, maybe, then nail those punks. But to make it work, we need a motorcycle."

***

The next morning brought another unseasonably hot day. The humidity level was in the unbearable range, and the wind blew incessantly until early afternoon, when it suddenly got eerily still and quiet. The sky turned a sickly shade of green, and lightning flickered to the southwest. Erin was on the deck, cleaning up the plants that had reached the end of their season, and the children were playing a rowdy game on the patio beneath.

Talako came out on the deck and looked up at the sky. "I don't like this. It's too still. We need to get everyone inside right now. That sky looks just like it did when they got baseball-sized hail in Wilburton. Come on, Erin, inside the lodge." He held the door open for her as she picked up a basket containing a few tomatoes.

Erin hurried down the spiral stairs, followed more slowly by Talako. She stuck her head out the back door to call the kids to come in.

"Aw, do we have to? My turn's coming up," Zeke complained.

"Yes, right now. There's a big storm coming. I think we might find some snacks to make up for having to stop your game," Erin hinted with a smile.

Talako called out the front door to the men who were finishing the fencing around the new garden. "It's time to come in. Storm's brewing, and I heard Erin mention snacks."

Before the men could reach the door, the still, heavy air was stirred by a strong gust of cooler wind. "Temperature's changing. This is going to be a big one, I think," Mac groaned. "Just what we need, and no weather service to give us any details. I'd sure like to see one of those computerized weather maps that tells the direction and speed of storms, with radar to show us what to expect."

"We'll have to rely on my grandfather for weather forecasts, but he's good at it. If he says we should go inside, I'm heading that way," Tanner replied, as he held the door open for the others to enter the lodge.

Just minutes later, the wind was howling through the forest, causing trees to thrash violently, then the rain and hail started. The hail wasn't very big at first, but quickly changed to golf-ball size. The racket was deafening as the white lumps of ice hit the metal roof of the lodge. Erin suggested that the children take their cookies and Koolaid into the cave, with the adults to supervise. It was the first time they had all gone into the cave at the same time, leaving the lodge doors unguarded, but it was much quieter once they pulled secret the door closed.

***

In town, the handful of people who were still living in their own houses went to their basements or ran to the church building; people in Oklahoma learn early to watch for signs of severe storms, and they had seen enough to know that this one could be a real doozy. They had also been through too much in recent months to take life and safety for granted. The hail started just as Ken closed the door at the base of the stairwell. They could barely hear it in the basement, but the children had picked up on the nervousness of the adults, and some were crying. Others just clung to their mothers, or stared with huge eyes at the ceiling.

The combination of cool, dry air from the northwest and hot, humid air from the south and southeast had combined to create a supercell capable of wreaking havoc on the area. Unseen by those who had taken shelter from the storm, a huge wall cloud formed and began to rotate. Weather radar would have shown a distinct hook in the cell, and if electrical power had still been available, sirens would have been blaring in every town across at least six counties. Cell phones would have beeped an alert, and radios in cars would have warned people to take shelter immediately. But none of those alarms were sounded, because of the collapse. People had to rely on their own experiences and common sense; those who weren't paying attention, or who had no personal memories of supercell storms to serve notice that this storm would be violent, were about to learn a hard lesson.

Ken and Terri gathered their children together in a corner of the church basement and prayed together as a family for the safety of everyone who might be in danger. Others joined them, and lifted their pleas to heaven. As they held hands and asked for God's protection, the wall cloud circled itself into a descending funnel, which would have been almost transparent if anyone had been looking for it. It lowered itself to the ground, and as it began to pick up debris and dirt, finally became fully visible as the monster that it was. It touched down in the wooded area at the southwest corner of town, tearing at trees and sharpening limbs into lethal missiles; it wasn't very broad at the base, just moderately thick. The roaring that many people likened to a freight train was loud, but few people could hear it until it was right on top of them, because they had already taken shelter.

The twister hit the trailer park with tremendous force, shattering the first mobile home like a glass ball dropped on concrete. Other trailers pulled loose from their tie-downs, and were thrown against the backs of the stores across the alleyway. One rolled toward the southeast several times, knocking down a fence and some small trees before coming to rest against the monument that dedicated the park to the town's war heroes. The brick wall of Gus's mechanic shop caved in when hit by one of the flying trailers, which punched through and stopped several feet into Gus's backroom.

The end that was still outside continued to thrash as it disintegrated, causing extensive damage to the business on the west side of the shop, and ultimately, causing the storage loft above Gus's back room to fall. Dumpsters from the alley flew up, circling the twister before being flung outward, striking homes and businesses hard enough to break through walls.

The tornado destroyed virtually every one of the mobile homes, then angled across Bailey Street, crushing a small house before it slammed into a row of stores, two of which were vacant; it tossed bricks and awnings, breaking storefront windows as it angled across Main Street. Richie's Drug lost every window, but sustained no serious structural damage. The shops on the north side of the street were not so lucky: they took a direct hit. Bricks flew in every direction, with shards of glass, signs, and pieces of shelving units becoming deadly projectiles, as well. Two stores were completely leveled, while only one wall of the third remained standing. Strangely, a paper calendar still hung from a small nail on that wall, flapping wildly until the storm passed, then dangling limply in the pouring rain.

The two houses between those shops and the church never had a chance. Both were constructed of wood; one was a large two-story home with white aluminum siding, and the other, a smaller house with tan vinyl siding. The larger house was empty, but unbeknownst to any of the townspeople, the little one was occupied. Two of the people in town that day were strangers. They were travelling together, trying to get to their families in Henryetta, and had spent the night in the smaller house. They had planned to see if there was any food left in any of the abandoned homes or any businesses in town, but never got the chance.

One of them was cowering on the floor, crying. The other one sat on the sofa, watching the storm through a window across the room, when the splintered end of a 2x4 board came through the glass like a javelin, passing inches from his head and embedding itself in the wall behind him. The twister went straight into the gap between the two houses, but was too wide to just slide through. Each of the houses was caught by the edge of the viciously swirling wind, and was slammed by flying debris. All that was left once the funnel passed was a jumbled pile of shattered wood, shingles, and appliances that had been ripped to pieces. The two strangers were picked up, then beaten and slashed to death by the glass, bricks, siding, and furniture that whirled around them. Their bodies were flung aside, landing almost a hundred yards apart in a field north of town. Their identities would forever remain a mystery. And the tornado was not yet finished with Kanichi Springs.

It crossed Lee Street, and scored a direct hit on the church building that had stood on that spot for several decades. The old building was made of large blocks of solid rock, strong and thick, but the twister was carrying debris from downtown that weakened the structure, broke the windows, and swirled into the foyer and upstairs classrooms with a destructive rage. The roof was torn off, along with the steeple, which was tossed across the parking lot.

The front wall fell in, then the north wall collapsed, burying both sets of the stairs that led to the basement, trapping the townspeople who had taken refuge there. Some of the heavy stones rolled down the steps, then others wedged themselves into the remaining space, creating a barrier that left the residents below helpless to dig their way out.

Next door, the Abbott home sustained damage from flying debris and had a portion of the roof ripped away. The storm then continued across the pasture and demolished Brian Powell's home, leaving his workshop relatively unharmed.

Continuing to grind up trees and residences as it progressed, the violent tornado finally began to rope out and rise back into the clouds, as rain poured from the roiling, angry sky. The storm had lasted only minutes, but it had seemed like an eternity to those who lived through the ordeal. It was still afternoon, and within an hour, the sun was shining brightly on the horrific path of destruction.

***

Talako quietly suggested that someone go to the western and southern cave entrances to check the sky. Brian and Val volunteered, and soon returned with the news that the storm was over. The group returned to the lodge through the pantry, and several of the adults took a look outside. There was minor damage to the vehicles.

The windshield of Erin's Expedition was cracked, and it looked like someone had bounced a hammer all over it, but the dents were mostly superficial. The tanker had similar dents, but after checking it out thoroughly, Mac assured everyone that the fuel was safe. The few tomato plants, the one crop still producing on the deck, were bruised, but Erin had hopes that they would live until the first frost.

Tanner and Ian went as quickly as possible up the mountain, and tried repeatedly to get Ken or Terri on the radio. They heard nothing at first, then thought they heard clicks. Finally, they heard a crackly noise, and what sounded like "help us."

The two men slid and slipped their way back down the slope to the lodge, and gathered the group in the living room.

"We think they're in trouble at the church. We could barely hear it, but it sounded like someone calling for help on the channel we use to talk to Ken." Tanner paused to catch his breath. "I think we better go check on them."

Erin handed Tanner the keys to the SUV, and he, Ian, Vince, and Brian headed to town. The trip was only about four miles, but took well over an hour because they had to continually stop to drag trees limbs out of their way. In several low places, water rushed across the road, but Tanner drove through it.

"Hey, whatever happened to 'turn around, don't drown'?" Ian joked.

"I know these roads like the back of my hand, and this is a big ol' SUV. We'll make it," Tanner assured him.

They finally came out of the woods and could see the damage. The shock of seeing their hometown with a wide path of devastation through it caused several moments of silent staring as they stopped to survey the reality in front of them.

Tanner finally took his foot off the brake and continued down the hill. At the bottom, they had to abandon the Expedition and walk the rest of the way in, due to debris all over the streets. They found the bodies of the two strangers, damaged beyond recognition even if they had known them well. When they got to Lee Street, the damage to the church became visible. The three of them were speechless at the sight of the damage to the building, and hurried over to the pile of stones to check on their friends.

"Ken! Ken! Terri! Are you okay?" Tanner shouted frantically toward the rubble that covered the stairs. The stones were too large for mere men to move, but they tried anyway, scraping skin off their hands as they struggled to remove them.

"Help!" The cry came from beneath the debris, and Tanner shouted back.

"Ken? Is anyone hurt? We're going to get you out, I promise."

"We're fine, but we're afraid to open the door!"

"NO! Don't even *think* about opening that door! It's holding back an avalanche of rock."

Brian took off on foot, running toward his property. All that was left of his house was the foundation. Even the fireplace and chimney were gone, but the metal workshop only had hail dents and several scars from being struck by pieces of the house. He quickly unlocked the door, using the keys that he still carried in his pocket out of habit, and climbed into the cab of the huge backhoe that he had used in his construction business. It started after a few tries, and he drove it as fast as he could back to the pile of rubble that had been the church building, skirting around broken fragments of the town that were strewn all over the pasture.

Waving Tanner and Ian to the side, he used the backhoe to remove the largest of the rocks blocking the staircase. It was slow work; he had to be careful not to move any rock that was keeping other rocks from falling. He also had to keep his heavy equipment off the basement ceiling; the added weight could result in structural failure. The door was holding so far, but a shift in the pile could send the stones tumbling into the basement, and he wasn't sure if the people down there were near the door. Anyone who was nearby if the door gave way could be badly injured. The last thing he wanted to risk was moving so fast that someone got hurt because of his haste. Tanner and Ian started removing lighter pieces of rock from the pile, while still leaving Brian room to work.

The townspeople who had survived the storm in their own homes finally emerged from their shelters, looking stunned by the destruction that cut the town in half diagonally. Several of them ran to the church to see if the people there were okay, and stayed to help clear the smaller pieces of stone away.

It took hours to clear the stairs enough that they felt it was safe to open the door. When they did, they found that all of the people below were okay, considering the trauma they had endured. The children had been very frightened by the storm; the adults were now wondering what they would do for somewhere to live. Ken and Terri asked Brian if he thought they could still live in the fellowship hall, but he just shook his head.

"The structural integrity of the part that's left has been compromised. Four walls help support each other, but there are only *parts* of *two* walls left now. Think about all that weight, the stones that already fell on the floor of the auditorium, which is also the ceiling of the fellowship hall. That floor's been weakened, and if the remaining walls should fall, it could easily cause a cave-in, pretty much guaranteeing injuries or deaths. That ceiling might hold for years, or it might give way tomorrow, or with the first heavy rain we get, but it will almost certainly fail if more stones collapse on it. It's also going to leak, even if it doesn't fall in, because it's cracked badly in places, and the staircases are now open to the sky. Water will pour down those steps and flood the basement. It's not safe down there. I'm sorry. It probably can't be repaired, either, at least under the present circumstances."

"Where will we go? We need to keep this group together, since it's mostly women and children," Terri pleaded. "We can't protect each other if we're scattered out, and there's not much left anywhere in town, from what we can see. Maybe we could live in the school."

Tanner moved away from the cluster of people discussing where to go, and used his radio to contact Erin. She only heard static at first, but she got Vince and grabbed a rifle, then hurried up the mountain to see if she could hear better.

"Tanner? Tanner, are you there?"

"Yes, honey. Yes, I'm here. It's bad. Must have been a twister. The town is pretty torn up, but we got the folks out of the church basement. Two whole sides of the building fell in and blocked the stairs. Everyone's okay, but Brian says it's not safe for them to stay there anymore. When the upper part of the building collapsed, the stones filled the stairwells and we had to dig them out. If Brian hadn't left his backhoe with a full tank of fuel, they'd still be trapped down there. Thank God he was with us instead of at home. His house completely gone. There's nothing's left at all except his workshop. If he had still been in there…."

"Was anyone hurt?"

"We found two bodies out at the north edge of town. No identification, and well, they're so badly mangled we can't tell who they were. As far as we know, almost all of the townspeople are accounted for, so I have no idea who those two were. We're pretty sure everyone else is okay, but we'll have to check to be sure.

But the real reason I needed you is that Ken and Terri want to keep their little flock together, if possible. I can see the school from here. It looks like a lot of windows on the south side are broken, but that's all I can tell about it without a closer inspection. Ernie's house looks okay, too."

"Of course! There's the answer! They can stay in the basement at Ernie's. They'll have the upstairs, too, but will probably stay in the basement a lot, at least at night. That's a wonderful idea. Tell them they have my permission and blessing to use it as long as necessary."

Tanner signed off, and strode back over to tell Ken the good news. "You could stay at the school, but you'd have a lot of broken windows. Even if the ones on the other side aren't broken, anyone could look in and see you with so much glass. You wouldn't be able to hide the women and children from bad guys there. Erin says you can stay at Ernie's house. It looks undamaged from here. There's a secret to getting into the basement, though."

"Ernie's house doesn't have a basement," Ken insisted, looking confused.

"Yes, it does," Tanner assured him, with a grin. "It's just hidden, and therefore, should fit your needs quite nicely. Have everyone grab whatever they can carry, and we'll show you."

The group gathered some of their belongings and walked the two blocks to Ernie's old house, and Tanner took them inside, then showed them the secret latch that allowed the bookcase to roll away from the wall, revealing the steps that would take them down to their new home. He showed the adults how to lock the bookcase/door from the inside so they could prevent intruders from finding them.

"We'll bring you some candles and other supplies, and we'll bring some help to move the furnishings down here so you can all be comfortable. Ernie had a garden space cleared out, but never got around to planting anything because he got sick. It won't take much to get it in shape, and I'm sure that Erin will have seeds to give you so you can grow some food next year. I hope the solar panels on the roof are still intact, so you'll have refrigeration. She said to tell you to make yourselves at home for as long as you need to stay."

"Please tell her that we promise to take good care of the place, and we're grateful to her for letting us use it. I don't think the school would have worked out. It's too big a place to try to keep up with all these kids, and you're right about all those windows. We couldn't stay out of sight."

***

The next day, several of the adult members of the group grabbed their work gloves and loaded into the Expedition and the Explorer for the ride to town. They stopped when they got to the debris that blocked the streets that would take them to Ernie's, and got out to clear away rubble so they could get the vehicles through. They brought food, including part of a deer that Charlie had shot earlier that morning, helped the townspeople move the rest of their things from the church to Ernie's basement, then scavenged mattresses and chairs from empty houses.

"Erin, you'll never know how much we appreciate this. Thank you, sweetie," Yvonne Johnson said as she hugged Erin.

"You're all welcome. Consider this to be your home for as long as you need it. Since the house is on solar, you'll have the small refrigerator in the basement to keep food longer, but please be careful about turning on any lights upstairs. If anyone saw the lights, you'd become a target in a heartbeat. In fact, you should unscrew the lightbulbs in the fixtures upstairs, just to be safe. You can cook on the gas grill, but you should probably do that in the garage so the smoke doesn't give you away. There are some extra tanks of propane for it, too, but conserve as much as you can. Gus is going to make you an oven that uses the sun to cook, and I'll come show you how to use it when he gets it finished. How are you for food now? Do you need anything else?"

"One of the gardens we had was pretty much destroyed, but Ken checked on the other one, and there are still a few winter squash and tomatoes left, and we have some of the food you brought last time. If you can keep bringing meat, we'll be okay for a while. When we're sure that gang is gone, we can walk down to the creek and do some fishing, at least when the weather cooperates. I wish we had more people here with guns."

"We brought a couple of Glocks and some ammo. You're all a part of our community, even if you don't live at the lodge, and we're all friends. Helping each other is what friends do. We have some gang-related business to take care of, but we'll be back soon with more supplies."

Chapter 15 – Two Days Later

Ollie was in a particularly foul mood. They had looted several homes in the area, but their haul had included only some half-empty bottles of liquor, a few food items, and some shoes that some of the gang members needed, but no women. Their supply of food was getting dangerously low, and he knew that without the regular meals he had promised them, and without the females he said they'd get, the liquor wouldn't do anything to help him maintain control of his men. In fact, the liquor might even make the problems worse; men drunk on "liquid courage" were more likely to challenge his authority, and he'd seen a few of the men whispering and giving him sly looks.

It was time to move on. The tiny towns in the area were already stripped bare, and Ollie suddenly realized that staying in such a sparsely populated area for so long had been a mistake. With winter coming on, they needed to find a lot more food, and some place where they could stay warm.

I think I'll go to Arkansas. McAlester is where most of the other guys from the prison probably wound up, so that's no good. Maybe I can find some farmer whose wife put up a lot of food this summer. Just take off on my own, find a likely place, get rid of the owners – well, maybe not the woman, if she's not too old or ugly – and spend the winter relaxing and eating all I want. Food will go a lot further if I don't have to share with these idiots. I'll need to plan how to get away from this bunch, but I'm going, and going soon.

***

The group's plans to launch an offensive against Simmons and his men had been delayed by the weather long enough. Vince's idea had been tuned and refined, and they were more than ready to put it into action. They wound up with two motorcycles for the attack on the gang. Hunter Gibbs had an olive green 2002 Kawasaki KL 250 Super Sherpa that he hadn't ridden in a while, since his dad hadn't wanted him riding it back and forth to Stillwater. It needed some work, but Gus had it up and running in just a couple of hours. Hunter wasn't too happy when he found out that his twin, Heather, would be the one riding it, until he found out that he would be riding the other bike.

Paul Foster had saved his wages from carrying out groceries and made a big down payment on a brand new Shadow Aero cruiser from the Honda dealership in Tulsa, with his dad co-signing the note. It was bright red and a beautiful machine. Paul was eager to give it a try.

A few of the men had a problem with the idea of the women being involved this time. In the first fight, they had been stationed on rooftops and at second story windows, so were not out in the open, but for this one, they would be more vulnerable. Jimmy Gibbs was reluctant to let Heather take part in the plan, until she convinced him that her role was vital to getting the gang out of the house, and actually one of the safer parts of the plan. She was an experienced rider, one who had raced dirt bikes since childhood; none of the other young women knew how to ride a motorcycle. She was familiar with Hunter's Kawasaki, having ridden it many times, and she was determined to help.

Shane made the mistake of trying to give bossy commands to Jen, telling her bluntly, and in front of the others, to stay home at the lodge, but he found out rather quickly that Jen was not one to take orders from anyone. The petite blonde marched up to him and stretched high on her tiptoes in a futile attempt to get right in his face.

"Shane Ramsey, if you think you can tell me what to do, you better think again! We all have a stake in this, and if I recall, *all* of the people who've been raped were *women*. Not that I think those creeps wouldn't rape a man, but so far, the only sexual crimes we've heard about have been against women. So I'm *going*, and that's the end of this discussion."

Shane tried to argue with her, but wound up with her simply refusing to speak to him.

Tanner, at least, had sense enough to approach Erin privately and with a more persuasive demeanor. He found her on the deck, picking the few remaining tomatoes, and came up behind her to wrap his arms around her.

"Erin, please. For me, stay here. I need to know that you're safe."

"Tanner, if I asked you to stay here, would you do it?"

He looked shocked. "Of course not…. Uh, I walked right into that one, didn't I?"

"Yep. So you know my answer. We're all in this together, and if I hadn't gone to the fight in town and *saved your life*, we wouldn't even be having this conversation."

Tanner sighed "Point taken. Please, just promise me you'll be careful. I don't think I could stand it if anything happened to you. You're my life."

"I'll be very careful, but I'm not going to hide from this. We still don't know how many are in the gang now. We could even be outnumbered, but this is something that needs to be done, and the more guns we have out there, the safer we'll all be. And I certainly wouldn't stay safely at home and expect Heather to ride out there as a decoy. I'm not a coward, and I'm not going to be a hypocrite, either. You *know* that I'm a good shot and can help."

Tanner was silent for a moment, then sighed. "You're right. At least we'll have the element of surprise on our side, and hopefully, better cover than they'll have. If we don't have enough camo for everyone, we'd better find clothes that are at least muted green, tan, or brown so they'll blend in."

Erin nodded. "Good thinking. Most of us would just do that without much thought, but we'll need to be extra vigilant this time. We won't be up on roofs for this round."

"Tomorrow morning, I hope we put an end to the Simmons Gang. They've earned what's coming to them.

We've got a good plan, and good people. I'm pretty sure they don't have the quality of guns or the amount of ammo that we have, just what they've been able to scavenge. As far as I am concerned, the time for holding trials is over. This time, we use the *coup de grace* on the wounded, and put those scumbags out of their misery for good."

Ian stuck his head around the corner and motioned for them to follow him. Everyone was in the living room, and Vince had a big sheet of butcher paper with a diagram of the area.

"The farmhouse is here, with the barn over there," he explained as he pointed at the drawing. "The land right around the house is pretty level, as is the driveway, but across the road, there's a ditch, then a pretty high bank. It's uphill all the way on that side. There's not a lot of cover on their side of the road, just a few trees. It looked to me like the owners thinned the woods out quite a bit in front of their house.

"When the punks come out, they'll probably jump in the van to chase the bikes, so we need to set up down the road to the west a little bit. There's a narrow trail that leads uphill on our side, and that's where the bikes will turn off, then Hunter and Heather, you need to get up into the trees as quickly as possible. We figure the van will stop and the gang will jump out to continue the pursuit on foot. There's no way they can drive the van across the ditch and through those trees. That's when we hit them, once they're all out of the van.

"Now, I understand that when you fought them in town, Simmons drove the van and didn't get out. That's what allowed him to escape. We need to make sure that doesn't happen this time. Charlie, we're going to need you in a good spot to shoot Simmons or shoot out the tires so Simmons can't get away. Flat tires on the dirt roads around here won't go anywhere fast, so we'll have him.

"Riders, as soon as you get where you can, ditch the bikes, grab your guns, and find cover. Be sure you stay on the east side of the path, so you aren't hit by friendly fire. There are some big rocks scattered around, and we'll use those for cover, plus we'll have the high ground and they'll be coming up the bank after the riders. Is everyone clear on what to do?"

"What if the whole gang doesn't come out? What if some are still in the house?" Sarah asked.

"We're going to have Will and John covering the house. Anyone steps out, or even looks out a window, they'll take them out. Then, when we've cleared out the vermin from the van, we'll join them, and make sure that anyone left won't survive to cause trouble later. We'll clear the house, the barn, and any outbuildings. We need to make sure that Simmons and Kline are among the dead. They've wreaked havoc on this county long enough.

"Angie will stay with the vehicles, which will be hidden nearby, to take care of any wounded, and the mothers of the little ones will stay here, along with Gus, Talako, Frances, Julia, and BJ. Weather permitting, we'll go tomorrow morning. We need to hit them soon, before they relocate again. So, that's the plan. Anybody see any holes in it?"

* * *

Around midnight, a storm blew in. Thunder cracked and rumbled across the sky, and rain fell in sheets as jagged fingers of lightning arced and crackled. Breakfast that morning was quiet, as all of those who had prepared mentally for an attack on the gang ate silently, realizing that the fight was going to be postponed until the weather cooperated.

The rain continued that day and the next two, causing tensions to build and tempers to be short. Erin and Val nearly came to blows over how much laundry detergent to use. Frances had to step in to calm them down and force a grudging mutual apology. Tanner took Erin on a walk through the caves, trying to calm her cranky, irritable mood. The men checked and rechecked their weapons, nervous energy growing as the dreary hours passed with them all cooped up in the lodge together.

Shane tried to relieve some of the stress by giving a few kenpo lessons. It worked, at least a bit, by letting those who participated work off some steam. Several members of the group packed up sandwiches and took the children to the cabana cavern for a picnic and a dip in the clear pool.

Finally, after three days and nights of rain, the storm moved out and the members of the group woke to sunshine and a light breeze instead of rain and howling winds.

Over breakfast, they discussed whether they should wait for the roads to dry out or just go ahead with their planned attack. Since the motorcycles were a vital part of the plan, and the road in front of the old farmhouse was dirt with only a little gravel, the decision was made to wait one more day, allowing the sun to dry the road out a little.

They filled the day with chores, kenpo lessons, and checking their weapons yet again. Tanner and Ian hiked up the mountain and let the Gibbses and the Fosters know that weather permitting, they would meet at the lodge early the next morning.

***

The stars were still visible when the Fosters arrived the next day with Paul's motorcycle strapped into the back of the truck. Jimmy Gibbs and his twins were a few minutes behind them. Hunter's Kawasaki was already parked on the patio where Gus had worked on it.

Vince went over the plan again, this time in detail, using the map he had drawn on butcher paper. He pointed out where they could park the Expedition and the narrow trail about forty yards past the drive, the one that led uphill into the trees.

"Hunter and Heather are our most experienced riders, at least over rough terrain. They've been up and down these hills on dirt bikes since they were little," Jimmy explained. "I don't like this, but at least their exposure will be over quickly, then they'll be with the rest of us, up the hill and behind cover."

"Okay," Vince continued. "We'll leave the two SUVs here, and walk through the woods. Heather and Hunter will be 'Gemini', the twins. They'll wait near the vehicles until we give the signal on the radio that we're in place. Heather, you bring up the rear. Hunter will rev his engine a lot, like he's showing out, and you'll be behind him, wobbling a little and acting like you're inexperienced, but still having fun. They'll want you alive, and won't shoot at Hunter if you're between them and him. At least, we hope they won't. Go slow, but not so slow that they'll suspect something is up. Once you pass the driveway, watch for the trail on your right, turn up it, and get where you can ditch the bikes and take cover on the east side with the rest of us. You'll each carry a concealed Glock.

"We'll wait until the bad guys are out of the van and coming up the trail before we open fire. We need everyone, except those who are staying here to guard the children, because we don't know exactly how many we'll be up against. Angie, you'll be with the vehicles, and I'll leave it up to you whether you need any of your kids as helpers, or would prefer for them to stay behind. Gus, Claire, Frances, BJ, Gus, Rose, Dana, Julia, and Talako will stay here. That puts nine adults and ten children at the lodge, and leaves seventeen of us for the fight. Keep the kids occupied inside, and together, just in case."

"We've got some kids' videos they can watch, and Val found some popcorn in the cavern. We'll keep them safe," Talako assured Vince.

"Now, let's look at the terrain. The door of the farmhouse lines up pretty well with the driveway, so if they're watching the drive and come out, Gemini may see them. It's fairly flat on that side of the road, but on our side, where we'll be waiting just down the road, there's a ditch, then an incline. The bikes should have no trouble getting across it. There are some big boulders that we can use for cover, but watch for snakes. Stay on the east side of the trail until it's over; we don't want anyone hit by friendly fire. When the bad guys follow Gemini up the trail, Tanner will give the signal to open fire. Wait until you have a good shot, then take it.

"Charlie, you're Toker. You'll be set up here." Vince pointed to a spot just before the trail, but on the other side of the road. "You'll pick off any who decide to retreat.

"Nolan, you and Shane will be in charge of providing immediate care for our wounded, and Angie will be nearby if there are any serious injuries. Any questions?"

"Will we be taking the dogs?" Val wanted to know.

"Not this time. They're all young and barely trained. Tanner hasn't had a chance to accustom them to gunfire, and we don't anticipate needing them for this."

"Also, no prisoners this time. We need to wipe this gang out. Any gang members who survive the fight, including the wounded, will get an assist into the afterlife from me, Tanner, or Charlie. Anybody got a problem with that?"

No one spoke.

***

Erin pulled the Expedition into an old track about a quarter mile from the farmhouse, stopping behind some cedar trees. Sarah parked her Explorer next to it and Heather and Hunter followed on the bikes. Everyone piled out as quietly as possible, grabbing weapons and checking gear.

"I've never been bait before," Heather joked. Her long blonde hair hung down her back like a waterfall and she took off her windbreaker, tying the sleeves around her waist. "I guess we want it to be obvious that I'm female, huh?"

Hunter took off his helmet and ran a hand across his forehead. "Sis, I don't like this one bit. I should be protecting you, not the other way around. Using you as a shield goes against the grain for me."

"I know it does, but that's just the way this plays out. They are much less likely to shoot a hottie like me than to shoot a hairy-legged guy like you." She touched his cheek. "I'm glad you shaved, though. That beard made you look older. This way, they'll think you're just a baby-faced kid." Heather grinned at her brother's narrowing eyes.

"You two cut the comedy routine and listen up." Jimmy interrupted before Hunter could think of a comeback. "Remember, you're supposed to rev the engines, go moderately slow, then get a move on when you get to the turnoff point. Take cover and shoot straight. I love you both and I've been praying for your safety today. Work as a team and don't do anything crazy, okay?"

The twins' expressions turned serious as Jimmy reviewed their instructions. They hugged him tight and promised to be careful.

Heather looked at Hunter, tilting her head and staring into eyes that bore a marked resemblance to her own.

"I love you, brother. I truly do."

"I love you, too. You be careful."

Paul had come to assist his mother with any wounded and to guard her and the vehicles. Angie had been teaching him all she could about emergency medicine, and he'd been studying the books she had collected for their prepping library. He knew that he was ready for more firsthand experience, but hoped sincerely that it would not be today.

***

The others made their way through the woods as quickly and quietly as possible and found the dirt path that the twins would come up. They took positions behind boulders and trees, while Charlie sneaked across the road and got set up where he could see it. He hunkered down behind some big rocks that provided a good sniper's nest for him. Once he was situated, he got on the radio and softly announced, "Toker is smokin'. Repeat: Toker is smokin'."

Vince answered for the group. "We hear ya, Toker. We're ready for some action here, too."

"Gemini is comin' to get some weed. Don't smoke it all before we get there," Heather added.

Moments later, the group could hear the motorcycles cruising at a moderate speed toward them. Hunter revved his motor a few times and popped a wheelie, so that he passed the drive to the gang's hideout just as the front wheel returned to the packed dirt. Heather followed about thirty yards back, gunning her bike a little and laughing at her brother, pretending to be a young woman just learning to ride and enjoying the fresh air.

Behind them, the door to the farmhouse flew open and three men raced down the steps. Two of them ran hard the length of the driveway, stopping at the end. When they saw the two bikes slow for the turn, they took off after them on foot. The other man lagged behind, and as soon as he was out of sight of the house, slowed to a walk, looked around, and slipped into the woods on the south side of the road, headed west, unknowingly moving directly toward Charlie's position.

Gemini dipped down into the ditch, then gunned the bikes to climb the slope, fishtailing slightly in the mud. As fast as two experienced dirt-bikers could, they darted up the incline and ditched the bikes behind some trees, then took up a position behind a large rock, pulling out their Glocks.

The two thugs were winded by the time they ran partway up the hill. Both carried weapons, and were looking for the twins. When Tanner yelled at them to stop, they swung around and shot wildly toward the sound of his voice. It was their last act on earth, as each of them took bullets and fell, one dead and one dying. Vince and Tanner ran over to the wounded man and Tanner kicked the thug's pistol out of reach. The guy was hit in the stomach, chest, and shoulder.

"Where are the others?" Vince demanded. "Where is Simmons? Tell me, you bastard!"

The man looked at him and opened his mouth to speak, but couldn't seem to form any words. Blood suddenly gushed from his mouth as his eyes glazed over. He was gone.

Vince felt an unfamiliar urge to cuss long and loud, but the presence of the ladies helped him hold it in. The others slowly emerged, watching the track for more bad guys, but none came into sight.

Charlie's voice came over the radio just then. "Y'all okay? Is it over?"

Vince answered, "Yes on both counts. Only bagged two birds."

"Well, I could use some assistance over here. I had a live bird fly right into my nest."

"Somebody will be right there. And some are going to check out where those birds were roosting."

Jimmy and Hunter went to give Charlie a hand, while Ian, Tanner, Vince, and Erin slipped off through the woods to join Will and John in observing the house. Tanner signaled the others to wait.

Charlie held a frightened young man at gunpoint; the kid looked about twenty years old and was maybe 5'10", with the lean look that had become so common since the collapse. He was scared to death, on his knees with his hands on top of his head, fingers interlaced. From the wet, spreading stain on his pants, the fear was not an act.

Jimmy patted the guy down and found an old .38 revolver with two bullets in it, and a small pocketknife.

"Who are you and where did you come from?" Jimmy hissed in a menacing voice.

The kid stuttered, "My name is Clint Ellis and I'm from Paris, Texas. I—I was in college at Tahlequah when things went bad and was just trying to get home." He started to cry. "I was hungry and wet when these guys came along and said they would help me. It was stupid to believe them, but I was desperate, so I got in that van." He wiped his nose on his sleeve and took several seconds before he was able to speak again.

"It was my worst mistake. I didn't know, honest. I didn't know…."

"Didn't know what?" Jimmy demanded.

"What they were doing. They kill people and steal their supplies. They brought two girls to the farmhouse and took turns raping them. The younger one died. I let the other one go, but they think she escaped on her own. They've been saying that if they don't find another woman soon, they'd have to use me instead.

They acted like they were joking about it, but from the looks I got from some of them, I think they would have done it. That's why I was running. This was the first time I've had an opportunity to get away from them."

"Where are the others?"

"Most of them left early this morning. They said they were going to town to hunt. I'm sure that means for women and liquor. Everyone went except me and three other guys. We were supposed to guard the place, but I was just waiting for a chance to get away."

***

Ken Abbott put his hand on his lower back and tried to stretch the kinks out. He and a couple of the ladies who were staying with the group in Ernie's basement were in what was left of a garden behind the home of one of the church members. The garden was pretty much done for after the storms and with fall coming on, but there were a few late tomatoes and one or two butternut squash to harvest.

Thank you, Lord, for the mild, rainy summer. This food You provided has helped us feed those who would have died without it, Ken prayed. *Without the rain, we would have starved. Thank you, Jesus.*

The little group picked up their small bags of vegetables and moved through the gate, planning to visit another garden about a block away, in an area that the tornado barely touched. As they started to cross the street, one of the ladies stopped suddenly, cocked her head toward the west, and said in an urgent whisper, "Listen!"

In an instant, all three of them darted toward a hedge that surrounded the yard of the closest house. Ken shoved through a gap in the bushes, holding the thorny branches back with his arm so the other two could squeeze through.

The second woman said, "Follow me," and led them quickly to a narrow space between a small storage shed and the wooden privacy fence that separated that yard from the one next door. Ken grabbed a garbage can and set it in the gap, blocking the view from the street, then signaled the two women to crouch down behind him.

They could hear a vehicle moving slowly toward them, going around the scattered chunks of debris that littered the streets on that side of town. The streets on the other side of town and most of Main Street were impassable, but there was much less damage in this neighborhood. As the sound grew closer, Ken peeked around the side of the garbage container. A beat-up old van came into view, and Ken could see that the eight or nine men in it were looking around like they were searching for something. Ken slowly drew back, and said a quick prayer for the few people who remained in the town, then whispered to his companions, "Stay down and don't move or make a sound. I'm pretty sure that was Ollie Simmons, and it looks like he's got a new gang."

Ken pulled his radio out and clicked three times to signal Claire. They had worked out a simple system of clicks, so that if one of them was in trouble, they could let the other know not to speak.

A few seconds passed, and Ken again clicked three times. Claire answered with two clicks, and Ken whispered into his handheld, "Gang in van. Get everyone downstairs now." Claire clicked twice to let him know she understood, and Ken clipped the radio back onto his belt.

At Ernie's house, Claire hurried to gather the adults and children into the basement. She latched the bookcase/door on the inside so that it wouldn't move, and descended the steps quickly.

"Quiet, everyone. Ken said that the Simmons gang is back in town. Evidently, Ollie has recruited some new punks, and they're driving around the neighborhood, looking for trouble. Let's keep the children still, maybe get out the crayons and let them color. Thank God the littlest ones are asleep." *And thank God Erin brought us the extra guns....*

Ten women, thirteen children, and only two men huddled down to wait. The men and two of the women had guns, but Terri had brought all the sharp knives from the fellowship hall when they had left the church, and she had them ready to give to the women, should the gang enter the house. She believed that Christians had the right to self-defense, and they all knew that the gang members would rape any women they caught. Terri did not intend to simply surrender. She and the other women would fight to protect both the children and their own bodies, if it came to that. The men took up positions at the bottom of the stairs, ready to defend their families and friends.

***

The van continued on Oak Street, headed for the school. Kanichi Springs had a relatively new school building, with classes for pre-K through high school. Ollie was disgusted at the meager haul his gang had been able to find lately, and had decided to see if there was anything left at the school. He ordered some of his men to check the cafeteria first, and any vending machines in the teachers' workroom. He told the others to check every classroom and the offices.

Of course, they were much too late for find anything to eat; the townspeople had cleaned out the pantry in the kitchen months earlier, and broken into the vending machines, too.

The only things the gang found anywhere in the school were a bag of stale potato chips and some M&Ms in the bottom drawer of a teacher's desk, and a small bottle of vodka in the principal's file cabinet.

Frustrated, Ollie told his men to burn the school. They piled books in a heap in the middle of the main hallway and lit some papers, tossing the burning sheets onto the pile, then hurried out to the van.

Faint wisps of smoke wafted out the door as they left, headed for the few shops downtown that were still standing.

Inside the school, the papers flamed and smoked, but failed to set the books on fire. Paper burns well, but not when it is compacted inside a closed book where air can't get to it. The edges of some pages smoldered for a few minutes, but once the loose papers turned to ash, the fire died out.

Ollie drove to the west end of downtown and parked the van in the middle of Main Street, north and west of where the tornado had touched down. That was as far as they could go in the van, due to the debris that covered the street. He sent half of his gang to the north side of the street and the other half to the south, with instructions to search every floor of every building. They found a few things to scavenge here and there, but hardly enough to keep the gang members happy and fed. One man found a case of vodka that had somehow been overlooked when Ollie's first gang had looted the liquor store.

Ken and the two women had waited until they heard the van move away, then sneaked away from their hiding place. Once they got back to Ernie's, Ken tried several times to reach Erin or Tanner on the radio, with no luck. He tapped out the secret knock on the bookcase, and one of the men let them in.

***

Jimmy continued to question Clint about the gang. Clint answered without hesitation, and seemed to be telling the truth.

"You said three others. We only saw two. Who's still at the house?"

"Just the one they call Kline. He always stays behind when they go looking for women. He's a strange dude. Obeys Ollie like a slave, never drinks or smokes, and doesn't like women, but he's sneaky. I don't know exactly why I think that; it's just a hunch, but I believe he's up to something."

"So Kline is the only one in there?" Jimmy demanded.

"Yes, sir. He was taking a nap when we heard the motorcycles. He sleeps like a rock, dead to the world. He was the only one there, I swear."

"Hunter, stay here with Charlie. I'll be right back," Jimmy said, as he turned and headed toward the house.

Hunter watched his dad work his way through the trees until he was out of sight, then turned back to their prisoner.

"So, you say you were a student at NSU. Who's the president of the university?"

Clint looked confused, then blurted, "Nobody, when I left. Dr. Oglesby retired in March and they hadn't found a replacement yet when things fell apart."

"What are the school colors?"

"Green and white."

"And the mascot's the Redman, right?"

"No. We're the Riverhawks now. Redman wasn't considered to be politically correct, so they changed it."

"Were you in a skong[2] at Rookie Bridge Camp at the end of the week?"

"Uh, Rookie Bridge Camp only lasts two days, not a week, and yes. I can't sing, but I did a dance with my color group while some of them sang. Why are you asking all these questions?"

"To see if you really went to NSU. You pass, I guess, since you know about RBC, color groups, and skongs."

"Gee, thanks." Clint shook his head. "You go there, too?"

"Nope. My sis and I go to OSU, but we have lots of friends at NSU, so we know about the traditions there. What was your major?"

"Computer science. A lot of good that'll do me now."

***

"You see anything?" Vince whispered to John and Will.

"Nope. It's real quiet, too," John whispered back.

Erin and Tanner had circled around, carefully stepping over a tripwire that Erin spotted right as Tanner was about to hit it with his foot. They watched the house for a few minutes, then returned to the front to check in with Vince, John and Will.

"You see anything?" Vince asked.

"Nope. Not a thing," Erin replied.

---

[2] A skit with a song

"Listen." Tanner shushed them. "What's that noise?"

Everyone got quiet, then a raspy pig-like sound drifted toward them.

"Snoring, I think." Vince cocked his good ear toward the house. "Yeah, that's somebody snoring. So there's at least one person still in the house."

***

Making his way through the trees, Jimmy finally realized that he should have gone on the road and down the driveway. It would have been faster, and probably safer, since the majority of the gang members were in town. In his rush to tell the others that Kline was in the house, he forgot about the noise-making tripwires around the property.

The one he found with his shin was an actual wire, not fishing line. It was thin and strung between two trees, making it hard to see in the dappled shade of the forest. He tripped and fell, scraping a layer of hide off the front of his leg even through his pants.

That's what I get for not wearing boots, he thought.

The wire caused a cluster of beer cans loaded with pebbles to swing free, hitting an empty metal garbage can at the edge of the yard. It made quite a racket, banging into the can and knocking it over.

Great. That's just great, he scolded himself. *I messed up big time.*

Inside the house, Barry Kline slowly came up from his deep slumber, wondering what in the world had made that noise. Barry wasn't someone who awakened instantly; rather, he went through several levels of grogginess before his brain began to work properly. He sat up, rubbing his eyes and yawning, then stretched and looked around for his shoes, which he put on without tying the laces. He tucked his handgun into his waistband, stood, stretched again, and ambled through the house, curious where everyone was. He noticed that the front door was open, and stepped out onto the porch. Closing his eyes during another huge yawn, Kline opened them to discover four people standing in the drive, pointing guns at him. Jimmy suddenly slipped out of the woods and made the number of guns five.

"Hello, Deputy Sheriff Barry Kline," Tanner drawled. "Have a nice nap?"

"Uh, well…uh, you better get outta here. My men are nearby and they'll kill you all," Kline blustered.

"*Your* men? That's not what we heard. We heard they were Ollie Simmons' men, and they're all in town, except for the three we just killed." Vince smiled, but it never reached his eyes. "Hey, where's your lighter? You know, the one you're always playing with."

"Who the devil are you?" Kline demanded, trying to act like his mental image of himself.

"I'm the guy who's going to kill Ollie Simmons. Now *you* answer a question: where's your lighter?"

"I lost it. I don't know where or when, exactly. What business is it of yours?"

Vince ignored the question and asked another of his own. "Could you have possibly lost it out in the woods when you murdered Chief Johnson and his officers?"

Kline turned white, then a sickly green tinge spread across his broad face, but he still tried to bluff his way around the accusation.

"I don't kn
"I don't know what you're talking about. I didn't shoot those men."

"You don't seem at all surprised that they're dead, and nobody said anything about them being shot. You just gave yourself away, Kline."

The deputy reached for his gun, but he never got there. Convicted by his own words and the fact that he was part of the gang, he went down hard, shot multiple times by four men and one woman.

"Leave him there. It'll give Simmons something to worry about. Let's clear the house, Tanner suggested.

"Yeah, but now what do we do with the one Charlie caught?" Ian asked.

Jimmy replied, "He's just a scared college student who fell in with the gang. He was running away from them when Charlie nabbed him, because they told him that if they didn't find a woman, he was going to be their 'girlfriend'.

They entered the house, and quickly checked every room, but there was nobody else there.

When they regrouped in the living room, Erin looked puzzled. "Vince, why did you tell Kline that we killed *three*?"

"Well, I figured if the Charlie's captive was a gang member, I was just a little ahead of the facts. But a runaway kid? How do we know he's telling the truth?"

"We don't, not for sure, I guess," Jimmy admitted. "He did tell the truth about Kline being the only one left at the house. He said he's from Paris. Isn't Lydia from there? Maybe she could question him, see if that's true."

"Okay, we need to get our people together and decide what to do," Tanner interjected. "The rest of the gang could be back any minute, and we're too scattered to handle it. Let's go."

Tanner pulled his radio off his belt and got hold of Charlie, "Hey, Toker. Bring that bird over to the place where Gemini went. We'll meet you there."

"On my way."

When the group was gathered back on the hillside, Tanner filled them in on Kline, and Jimmy explained what Clint had told them about the gang.

"We have some options, I guess," Sarah mused. "We can wait here, either in the woods or in the house and barn, and ambush the gang when they come back. We can go home and regroup, do something with Clint, and come back another day, but we might miss them again. We could, I guess, set up somewhere along the road and attack them when they come along. Any other ideas?"

"You're getting good at thinking up strategies, girl," Erin teased.

"I taught high school. Enough said," Sarah laughed.

"We should stay and wait for them. We're here now, and they don't know it," Vince insisted. "We can be pretty sure they'll come back before long. If we wait, they may move again, or hurt someone else. I say we hit them today, here. We have the advantages of surprise and concealment. It would be foolish to throw that away."

"We left Kline's body on the porch," Jimmy reminded him. "As soon as they turn in the driveway, they'll know something's wrong."

"That's easily fixed. We can drag him inside or into the woods. But if we're going to hit them when they come back, we better get a plan together quick. We don't know how long we have before they come back," Ian argued.

Clint cleared his throat and sheepishly asked if he could say something. Tanner gave him a suspicious look.

"I think he's legit," Hunter claimed. "I questioned him about NSU and he knew the answers. I even tried to trick him, but he didn't fall for it."

"We were going to have Lydia question him, but I guess you saved us a trip into town," Tanner replied. He stared at Clint for a moment, then gave a curt nod. "Go ahead."

"They're trying a new tactic. I heard Ollie talking to Kline about how they used to go out on raids about mid-morning. Now they go out real early in the morning, because Ollie said that people wouldn't be expecting it.

Usually, they stay out several hours, until they find enough stuff to make the trip worthwhile, so they probably won't be back for a while. There's not much left to loot, and women have learned to stay inside, I guess.

"Ollie always drives, and he parks right in front of the barn. Counting Ollie, there's eight men in the van. All but two are escapees from the prison, but those two just hadn't gotten caught yet. They're always bragging about their drug deals.

"They're all armed, but low on ammunition, maybe three or four bullets apiece. There's one really ugly dude, short, bald, and barrel-chested, covered with tattoos. He has knives. He can throw a knife like nothing you've ever seen before, and he hits what he aims at. He carries three of them: one hangs on a cord. If you see him reaching up like he's going to scratch the back of his neck, he's going for that one. He has one hanging on his belt, and the third one is strapped to his ankle."

"Why are you telling us all this?" Jimmy wanted to know.

"Because he's the main one who says I'm going to be their girlfriend if they don't find a woman soon. He's always trying to get me alone, and he touches me every chance he gets.

"The barn has a loft with a window. The glass is broken out. A couple of shooters up there could really hurt them. Put one or two behind the pump house, and the rest at windows in the house. All of you would have a clear field of fire, but they'd be caught in the middle of it."

"And what do we do with you?" Shane asked with narrowed eyes. "We're not giving you a gun, and I, for one, don't want you behind me when the shooting starts. No offense, but…."

"No offense taken. I understand completely. You can tie me up and gag me during the fight, and leave me in the house. If by some freak accident they win, I'll tell them you killed Kline, captured me and tied me up. I won't be any worse off than I was, and I'll find a way to escape soon."

"You have a good plan, Clint. Are you just talented at planning attacks, or what?" Erin asked.

"When I couldn't sleep at night, which was all the time lately, I'd fantasize about how to take the gang down. I'd imagine people like you coming to rescue me. I'd plan how I'd do it if I was out there myself, with some fighters, how I'd position my people so they'd win the fight."

"Okay. We'll try to make your fantasy come true. Enough talk." Erin looked around the group. "Tanner, get on the radio and let Angie know why it's taking so long. Hunter, Vince, you two go drag Kline's body out of sight. Let's put Charlie and Vince in the loft. Shane and Tanner, you're behind the pump house. The rest, find a spot in the house where you can see the drive and barn.

"Jen and I packed some trail mix, our homemade variety, in our backpacks. Everybody grab a bag and go get comfortable, but in place. We'll hear the van coming, but we all need to be in position when we do. It may be hours, so partner up and take turns resting. Wait until they're all out of the van and in the open, then shoot. Let's go."

Tanner let out a big, long *whoosh* of breath. "I love strong women."

Erin punched his arm, grinning. "You better make that 'woman', buster, as in *singular*. You only get one."

Chapter 16 – Later that Day

Settling down on some loose hay in the loft of the barn, Vince handed Charlie a bag of trail mix, and whispered, "*Bon appetit!*"

Charlie gave him a funny look and asked, "You one of them Frenchies?"

Vince chuckled. "No, it's just a saying. Sullivan's an Irish name. I come from a long line of coal miners and railroad workers."

"Huh. Farley's an old name from England. It means 'fern clearing'. Weird thing to call somebody, huh?"

"Charlie, you got any family left?"

"Well, I don't talk about it much, but I was married once, long time ago. She up and left, took my son with her, and I never did find 'em. I guess she wanted more than I could give her. We wasn't rich, not by a mile, but I provided a decent home and food. I always figgered she ran off with someone, but I guess now I'll never know for sure. My boy was only two, so he won't remember me. He'd be forty now. You got anybody?"

"I have a couple of brothers, but they live in Phoenix and San Antonio, if they're even still alive. Our folks are gone. Cancer got Mom, and Dad had a bad heart. Last time I saw my brothers was at Dad's funeral, almost two years ago. I'm sorry now that I didn't keep in touch better. Got a few cousins, but nobody around here.

I never married. I was real interested in someone, but she loved another guy and he was my friend, so I never let on."

"That's too bad. If we let it, being without family can eat us up. I just try to think of Erin and Tanner as my family, and all the others, too. Ain't no use feeling sorry for myself when I have people like them to love and care about. They been mighty good to me. That Erin has the kindest heart of anybody I ever knew. I knew her uncle, too. Good man. He'd be right proud of that girl."

"Yeah. When Ian found me out on the road and brought me to the lodge, I just knew she'd send me packing. But she said I could stay, just on Ian's word that I was a good guy. I'll never be able to repay her for that. All I could think about was revenge, and I didn't care if I died getting it. I'm still determined to kill Simmons, but now it's more to rid the world of a truly evil man than to get even. Of course, when I see him, I may feel the need for vengeance again. What he did to my sister, my nephew…Charlie, it was brutal. It was vicious. They didn't deserve to die like that."

"I know. That Ollie was bad from the time he could walk. A real troublemaker, and mean as a snake. Say, this ol' man is tired. You mind takin' the watch so's I can rest a bit?"

"Nah. You go ahead, try to sleep a while. I'll wake you when the fun starts."

***

In the big farmhouse, Erin sat with Jen, Val, and Sarah, munching on the last of the trail mix and wondering when the gang would return. They talked softly about their disappointment that the whole gang wasn't there that morning, and speculated about what would take place when the thugs returned. Hours had passed and everyone was getting tired and bored.

"I hope they come back before dark. With no lights at all out here, we'll have a hard time telling friend from foe, and it would be hard to retreat without getting shot at. I think we should all leave the house if they aren't back by dusk, so we won't be trapped in here." Sarah paused. "Maybe we could all wait out there in the woods somewhere, instead of inside."

Clint sat against a wall, hands and feet tied. Erin went over and took the gag out of his mouth.

"Where do you think they are? Any ideas?"

"They've never stayed out this late before, at least since I've been around. That van is really old. Maybe they had trouble with it, or maybe they found some booze or drugs. I don't know."

"We should go out and cut all the tripwires and then, if necessary, we could go out into the woods and regroup," Val offered.

"Cutting the wires is a good idea. We can't set up in the woods to the west, because that's the direction that our guys in the barn will be shooting. We'd have to stay on the east and north sides of the house, maybe out by the drive. I don't like this feeling of being in a bad spot. I'm going to slip out and talk to Tanner, maybe Vince, too. I'll be back in a few." Erin got up and let the others in the house know that she was going outside, then silently sneaked out the back door, crouching down and moving fast to reach the pump house, where she explained their concerns to Tanner.

Tanner nodded. "Shane, hold down the fort while we go talk to Vince." He took Erin's hand, and the two of them ran the short distance into the barn.

"Psst! Vince! Charlie! It's us, so don't shoot. We're coming up."

Erin scrambled up the wooden ladder, followed by Tanner, and found Charlie just waking up and Vince standing to the left of the pane-less window.

"We need to revise our plans, guys. If Ollie and his men come back after dark, we'll have trouble seeing to shoot at them. They'll probably make a run for the house, and all the women we have with us are in there. That sounds to me like a bad situation in the making." Tanner glanced at Erin. "I sure don't want this gal to be taken hostage by the Simmons gang."

Erin cleared her throat. "Val suggested that some of us go cut the tripwires so we can take positions in the woods. Maybe we could go up the drive a bit, then we'd be out of the way of your shots, and you'd be up here, where our shots wouldn't hit you. But the problem still isn't solved, I guess. Once it gets dark, we'll all be shooting blind, and we wouldn't know if we hit any gang members." She looked thoughtful. "I have an idea. We could go ahead and cut the wires, then go back into the woods and try to rest until just before sunup, then if they came back during the night, we can sneak back in and get ready before they're up and around. We might position some people behind the house to cut off that way of escape, and put a few behind the barn, you two up here, and some behind the van, if they park it where Clint said they would. What do you think?"

"The only problem with that is that we'll be right back with the problem we had earlier: we need to get all of them out of and away from the house. If they are inside, they'll have the advantage. But I do think we should at least cut the wires, and right away." Vince answered. "You're right. We need to do something different before the sun sets. What if they don't come back tonight? What if they stay out all day tomorrow? We can't hang around forever.

"Let's keep four or five in the loft, and send everyone else into the woods behind the barn. If they come back, we'll hear them, and if they don't, we'll wait a while in the morning and see what happens. How about if they aren't back by about noon, we think about going back to the lodge. We didn't bring food or supplies, since we thought it would all be over quickly. We should have planned better in case things didn't go like we thought they would."

"I'll go back in the house and get some of the folks in there to go take care of the wires. And I'm going to ask Hunter if he can get to the top of the hill with his bike, so he can radio the lodge and let them know we won't be home tonight. They're probably worried sick about us. He can tell Ken to keep an eye out in town, too.

If the gang stayed in town, Ken needs to know. You guys can stay out here in case they come back." Erin climbed down the ladder and ran for the house. She got Sarah, Jen, and Val to help her, and it took less than fifteen minutes to locate and disable all of the gang's makeshift alarms.

Hunter crept through the woods, crossed the road, and climbed up to where he and Heather had hidden the motorcycles. He started the Kawasaki and wove his way to the top of the hill.

"Gemini here. Home base, you there?"

Talako answered immediately. "We're here, and getting worried. What's going on?"

"We only found a few of the birds we were looking for. The rest haven't returned to their roost yet. So we decided to stay over."

"Is everybody okay?"

"Just dandy. Your favorite cigarette lighter is out of fuel. Permanently."

"That's a relief. We're good here, too. Be careful."

"Will do."

Next, Hunter tried to reach Ken, but got no response. He figured they must be in the basement, and decided to try again in the morning.

An hour later, the sun sank behind the mountains. Erin contacted Angie and Paul by radio, and let them know that they should hunker down in the Expedition for the night. Vince, Tanner, Charlie, and Shane stayed in the loft, and the others, after a brief discussion, sneaked through the trees parallel to the driveway. They found enough cover close by even though the trees were thinner there, and after checking around for snakes, settled in for a long, restless night.

***

Ollie's men seemed determined to drink all of the vodka that they'd found. Several of the bottles were well on their way to empty and he knew that the men would turn on him in a heartbeat if he tried to stop their drinking. They hadn't been with him long, but he wanted to punish every one of those idiots. As more of them became drunk, they began to grumble and complain about the lack of food and women. A couple of them even gave Simmons sly, dirty looks as he sat apart from them, watching, and then a few started talking more softly, glancing his way occasionally. He knew they were about to stage a mutiny; he could see the wheels turning. His hold on them had been the promise of women, booze, and regular meals, but he had failed to provide that, and as a result, their loyalty was shaky. *It's not my fault that there's nothing to be had. Supplies are running out, and this town didn't have much to start with. But I better figure out something fast, because it looks like they're about to rebel.*

The days were getting noticeably shorter and Ollie hated the idea of driving back to the farm with a van full of drunks. They might as well stay in town and sleep it off.

They had a couple of small fires burning in the alleyway behind the liquor store. Simmons stood up and walked over to the little group that seemed the most intent on plotting his downfall. He smiled, and grabbed a bottle. Taking a swig, he handed it back and announced, "We haven't looked around much north of town, boys. There's got to be some houses up that way that still have womenfolk and food. Sleep it off tonight; tomorrow we'll go exploring in a new area where I bet we'll find lots of loot. Not much traffic up that way, so it's probably just sitting there, waitin' on us to come get it."

***

Birds began singing as the sun rose, and the gang still hadn't returned. *I wonder where they are*, Erin thought. *Surely they wouldn't just leave, not with that big tank of gas out there.*

Slipping back across the yard in pairs, they returned to the positions they had taken the day before. All this waiting was wearing on their nerves. The only sounds to be heard other than birds were the various rumblings of hungry stomachs. *We should have brought more water and food. It's going to be a rough day.* Erin wanted to kick herself for not preparing for the possibility that things wouldn't go according to plan.

When they could tell by the sun that it was well after noon, Tanner got on the radio and told everyone to start moving out and heading back to their vehicles They would try again another day, but without provisions, they had to go back to the lodge. He untied Clint and took him outside for a talk.

"You got two choices, the way I see it. You can stay here and wait until the gang comes back, and tell them whatever tale you want, or you can take what provisions are left and head out. Now's your chance to escape. We aren't going to take you with us, because we can't trust you. Maybe you told the truth about everything, and maybe you're the nicest guy around, but we don't know that, so you need to decide what to do."

"I was headed home when they found me, and that's where I want to go. My family may still be alive, and the only way to know for sure is to go check on them. I appreciate that you didn't just shoot me, and that you're willing to let me go. You'll never see me around these parts again. I wish you and your people the best."

"Take care, Clint. I hope you learned some lessons from this."

"Oh, believe me, I did. I sure did."

***

Ollie's men slept until the sun had been up for over an hour, and awoke with serious hangovers. He decided that it wasn't in his best interests to reprimand them for drinking all that vodka before they got back to their hideout. Once they were all up and at least semi-alert, he would take them to the wilderness area in the northern part of the county and see if their luck changed. He had plans to stay in the van, just in case things went sideways. If they discovered any homeowners who wanted to fight back, Ollie planned to leave the gang behind. This time, he would just keep driving.

Around mid-morning, hunger began to override the lethargy that came with drinking too much. Some of the men wanted to head out, so Simmons told them to load up. He didn't know the backroads well, so he just drove north a few miles, then started exploring. The first house they came to was obviously occupied; however, nobody seemed to be home. Ollie and his men circled around to the patio, and discovered that the back door was standing open. They went directly to the kitchen.

Bingo! Simmons gloated. *There's quite a bit of food here. Must be some of those prepper folks who stock up on everything. No booze, though. That's a bummer, but finding some grub will go a long way toward keeping the men off my case. I'll be taking a lot of it with me, but they don't need to know that.*

Leaving his men to stuff their faces with food, Ollie explored the rest of the house. There were candles and figurines on shelves, and paintings and photos on the walls. *This place looks like a family lives here; the biggest bedroom has both men's and women's clothes hanging in it. One bedroom is done up with sports posters, one has "deer hunter" written all over it, and that last bedroom has to belong to a girl. No man would have lacy curtains like that. I wonder where they are. Sure would be good to find a woman or two.*

Above the door in the den, Ollie found an antique shotgun, hanging on a decorative gun rack. He took it, and then searched for some 12-gauge shells. Finding a couple of boxes, he loaded the gun. *Lotta good it did for them to have this gun over the door and not loaded. If they needed it in a hurry, they'd be dead before they got a shell in it.*

When the gang had gathered up all that would fit in the van, Ollie whistled and told them to load up. He drove around a little more, and found a narrow dirt drive that curved up a slope. Figuring that it might go to a cabin or house, he turned and drove up it. At the end of the drive, he and his men were amazed to see a beautiful log hunting lodge, two stories high. *Today must be our lucky day*, he thought, as he parked the van. He was excited about finding this place, and completely forgot about his plan to stay in the van and abandon his men. He slowly got out, leaving the door open, and stared at the lodge. *I just hit the jackpot. This place probably has it all, including women. I can hardly wait. And I'm going to be the one who goes at 'em first. After all, I'm the boss.*

The men crouched down behind the van, watching the house. Whoever lived there must have had some money, so they probably had weapons, too. Nothing moved. Ollie signaled two of the men to go try the door. It was locked, so they tried to break it down, but both men just bruised their shoulders in the attempt. There was still no sign of life. Ollie sent a couple of his guys to see if they could get in the back door, and had some try to break the windows.

Damn. This place is like a fortress. That means there's definitely something in there worth protecting, and maybe even some women. But how to get in there is the question. Simmons stepped back and shot at the front window with the 9mm he had taken from a house in town. The window's outer glass splintered, but the polycarbonate lamination and inner layers held. He shot it again, then again, but was unable to break through.

"C'mon!" he yelled, and ran around to the back. "There's gotta be a way in. Somebody climb up there on that deck and see if you can get in."

There wasn't an outside staircase, so while the others were standing below, staring at the deck, one of the younger men climbed the hill until he was above the pantry, then crossed the roof and dropped down on the deck. He failed to gain entry, but could see evidence that people had recently been in the rooms. He glimpsed bunkbeds and clothing, and could see into the bathroom a little, enough to know that someone had been around and the place had not been looted.

"Hey, Ollie! I can't get in, but I can see stuff. Women's stuff. We gotta find a way in!" the man yelled down to the others.

"You men grab those chairs. We'll use 'em as battering rams and get through those windows in front.

Four men grabbed chairs, and carried them to the front porch. They paired off on each side of two windows, and took turns swinging the metal chairs at the panes. What they didn't understand was that the glass alternated with layers of polycarbonate, and was almost two inches thick. They pounded the windows, over and over, and all they achieved was covering the porch with tiny slivers of glass from the outer pane. Ollie told the men to switch off and let the others take a turn, still to no avail.

Inside the lodge, the dogs had alerted the humans as soon as the van approached. Talako had glanced out the window, seen the van, and immediately yelled a warning. Then he, Gus, and BJ herded the children, women, and dogs into the caves; the three men stayed behind, but hidden by the heavy curtains on the windows. Grabbing a radio and praying a quick prayer, Talako tried to reach the team who still had not returned. He got no response, but Gus suggested that one of them run to the end of the west caves, and see if that would help. BJ, being the youngest of the three men, volunteered, and hurried through the pantry, carrying a flashlight and a radio, and accompanied by Major.

He got close to the entrance, and slowed, listening carefully. He had learned from Tanner to watch the dogs, and if they were tense, to use extreme caution, but the big dog was calm and his tail was wagging, so BJ stepped out. He reached the team in one try.

"Hey, it's BJ. We got company here, and they want to come in uninvited. You guys close?"

Shane answered, "Yeah. We're on our way. Where is the company?"

"All out front now. One tried the deck entrance via the roof earlier. We counted nine, all armed, and they look rough. Trying to bust the windows. We got the kids and women safe, but hurry."

"We'll come in from the side, and we're coming in hot. You keep everyone inside, okay?"

"Will do. Be careful, all of you."

Everyone in both vehicles had heard the exchange. Tanner turned one road before the road to the lodge, and parked the Expedition near the burned ruins of the McCoy home. Sarah pulled her Explorer in, and everyone piled out, including Angie and Paul.

"Here's the plan, such as it is. Spread out, stay quiet, and three of us will go through the woods and up the mountain a bit, staying out of sight from the front of the lodge. That group will cross the roof of the pantry and climb up to the peak of the main roof. The rest will come from the woods on the west, and hit them from that side.

"If this is the Simmons Gang, and Clint told the truth, they don't have a lot of ammo. Let's put Erin, Heather, and Will on the roof. If any try to run, they're yours. Let's go."

It took almost twenty minutes for them to get into position. From the roof, Erin could see some of her friends in the trees, and she gave them an okay sign. Suddenly, the sound of gunfire ripped the quiet, as they opened up on the intruders.

One thug vaulted over the railing of the porch, and hugging the side of the lodge, managed to slip into the woods. He circled around and crossed the driveway, trying to get behind whoever was shooting at the gang. He managed to flank the newcomers, scoring a hit on one who was hunkered down behind a tree, and was congratulating himself on being clever as he raised his old revolver again. Nolan saw movement on his right, but before he could get a shot off, Brian shot the man in the neck.

Ollie saw one of his men start to run, and jumped down from the porch, running with the man, putting the guy between himself and the shooters. The man was hit, but kept running for several feet, then stumbled and fell, leaving Simmons unprotected. Ollie wanted desperately to get to the van and escape, but just then, Charlie realized where he was headed, and shot two of the van's tires. *That was Simmons*, the old sniper thought. *He's going nowhere in that van.*

Ollie dived into the open door of the van anyway, and grabbed the old shotgun, clutching it like a life preserver. He waited for a few moments, then crawled across and got out on the other side, slipping into the woods. He didn't care that he was leaving his men pinned down and dying, but he was determined to escape once again.

Vince saw Simmons enter the van, and guessed his intent. The desire for vengeance he thought had died came back to life suddenly, as he remembered the horrible death his sister and her little boy had suffered. He sprinted south to intercept Simmons, and when he got close, shouted for the murderer to stop. Simmons whirled, raising the shotgun, and fired.

Vince stood there, stunned.

***

Erin glimpsed a tattooed man darting off to the east, and fired twice at him; when he fell, but still moved, she and Heather both shot him again, and he went still.

It was suddenly quiet, the only sounds the moans of someone on the porch. Those on the roof made their way back across to the adjoining mountain, and climbed down to join those coming into the yard from the forest, guns held at the ready. Val limped in, holding onto trees for support until Erin ran over to help her up the steps to the porch. Tanner got BJ on the radio and told him it was over. Only one of the gang members still lived, and he wasn't going to last more than a few minutes. Tanner and Mac checked each body that lay sprawled on the ground, the steps, or the porch.

"Eight. Simmons went around to the other side of the van."

"Yeah. And where's Vince?"

They started toward the trees south of the lodge to look for Vince, and found him, standing over a body without a face.

"What happened?" Tanner asked.

"He would have had me, but that shotgun exploded and got him instead," Vince replied. "There is justice in this world. That's Simmons, and his evil life is over, but I don't have to live wondering if I killed him to get even or to rid the world of him."

The others gathered around, staring at the mutilated corpse. Jimmy went over and picked up the shotgun, staring at the wrecked barrel at in disbelief.

"This is my dad's. We have to go, right now! Dad is home alone while we've been gone!"

Erin and Sarah darted off through the trees to get the SUVs, while Jimmy, his kids, and some of the others went down the drive to meet them when they came back by.

Talako and Gus came out of the lodge, but warned the women inside to keep the children back and not to look out at the carnage. The porch was littered with bodies and covered in blood, which they tried to step around as they went to see what was happening.

Val had a slight wound on her leg, a graze from a bullet, but waved Angie off, insisting that Mr. Gibbs might need her more, so Angie took off down the drive with her bag, The only other injuries were scrapes and scratches from running through the woods.

Erin and Sarah pulled up at the end of the drive, and as soon as everyone was in, they took off toward the Gibbs home. Heather, Hunter, and Jimmy held hands, looking anxious, until they skidded to a stop in front of the house, and Mr. Gibbs stepped out, whole and unhurt.

"Dad! Thank God, you're alright! What happened?" Jimmy blurted, joining his family in a group hug.

"Well, I was out back, in the woods, dumping the chamber pot into that pit you dug, when I heard somebody pull up, then I heard car doors slamming. I figured that since I was alone, I better stay out of sight. I just moved back into the trees a ways, and stayed real quiet until they left. Those hoodlums took most of our food. I don't know what we'll do, with winter almost here. I'm sorry I didn't stop them, but I was outnumbered."

"Oh, Gramps, we're just glad you're okay, and we got the food back. That was the Simmons Gang, and they went to the lodge when they left here," Hunter explained. "We were nearby, and we put a stop to them once and for all."

"Your old shotgun got Ollie Simmons, too," Heather added. "He must have taken it and loaded it, because he tried to shoot Vince, but it blew up in his face."

"Well, I hate to lose my granddaddy's gun, but if it took out a bad guy, I guess I won't mind too much. I always told you that old Damascus barrel couldn't handle modern loads. I bet he got into the shells I use in my new shotgun. That's his last mistake. Were any of our folks hurt?

"Just a flesh wound. Val got grazed, but she's tougher than anybody thought. Let's go to the lodge and get our food back. We can talk more there." Jimmy put his arm around his dad's shoulders, "I'm so glad you decided to dump the chamber pot when you did. That load of poop saved your life. Man, this has been a crazy couple of days. I'm sure happy it's over and all of us are in one piece."

Chapter 17 – A Few Days Later

Brian parked the Bobcat beside the east end of the lodge, and joined Tanner, Vince, and Shane on the front porch. They had finished cleaning up after the firefight; the bodies of the thugs were buried in an unmarked grave that Brian dug about a half mile away, and the shards of glass on the porch had been swept up, as well. The Gibbs family was back in their home with all the food that the gang had taken from them. There was a definite sense of relief felt by them all, now that the gang was no longer a threat.

Tanner and Ian had climbed up the mountain and let the townspeople know that the Simmons Gang would no longer be a problem. Ken asked if Tanner thought it would be safe to go to the creek and fish, and Tanner told him that would be fine, if they took reasonable precautions.

"Don't forget that there were a lot of convicts who escaped, probably all of them that lived through the riot at the prison, and some of them may be in the area. Hopefully, there won't be any gangs as bad as the two that Simmons gathered up, but don't get careless. I'd be cautious about letting the children out without guards. I guess they could play in the backyard, as long as you watch them closely," Tanner warned.

"We'll be careful. Fish would be a nice change of pace. I wish someone in town had some chickens. I sure have a hankering for some fried chicken."

Tanner laughed. "Yeah, we'll keep an eye out for some. Fried chicken does sound good."

***

Gus came out the front door, followed by Mac, and it was obvious that they had something on their minds. Shane got up and gave Gus his chair, then perched on the railing with Mac. Gus looked at Tanner, and grinned.

"How'd you like to be able to talk to folks in town and the neighbors without climbing that mountain every time?"

Tanner's eyebrows shot up. "You got a plan?"

"Of course, I do. Mac and I've been talking, and we're pretty sure that with his radio equipment and expertise, and some of the stuff I got at the hardware store, we can rig a repeater up on the peak, but where it won't be too noticeable to strangers passing through. You'd be able to sit inside and talk to Ken or Jimmy or Nolan anytime you want to. We might need some help with part of it, so if you guys are willing to pitch in, we'll get started right away."

"If we're willing? Heck, yeah, we're willing!" Tanner tilted his head. "Not only is climbing up there a pain, it takes time that we may not have to spare in an emergency. Let's do it!"

"Well, Mac and I have a little more figuring to do, and then getting all the stuff ready. We'll get back to you in a day or so."

***

The children had been forced to stay inside the house for several days due to the weather and the raid on the gang, and then because the adults needed to clean up the mess in the front yard after the fight, before the kids saw the bodies and blood. The youngsters were restless and needed to work off some energy before they drove their parents crazy, so Rose and Dana organized a game of tag in the front yard for the ones old enough to play.

Squeals and laughter echoed through the woods as they darted around, dodging the older boys, who were taking turns being "it", the little girls trying to prove that they were old enough to play with the bigger kids, and all of them making up new rules as they played. Claire sat on the porch nursing baby Ford, and Rose sat beside her, playing a gentler game with Wyatt. Dana was in the kitchen, preparing some snacks for the children when Claire noticed that Ford's diaper needed to be changed.

She got up and took the little guy into the lodge. Just a few minutes later, Wyatt tripped and fell on the wooden porch, scraping his knee. It bled a little, and Rose took him inside to clean it up.

The kids played their game, and one by one, got hot under the mid-morning sun. The boys had shed their hoodies after just minutes of play. Gina and Isabelle eventually took off their colorful jackets and put them on the porch.

Gina, a tomboyish little daredevil, had decided on her own that hiding would be just as good as running from her cousins, so she waited until no one was looking, and slipped off into the woods. She was excited at the sudden freedom, and didn't want the others to find her too quickly, so she ran hard for a few minutes. Like almost all young children, her coordination was imperfect, and as she ran down the slope, she fell. Tumbling and rolling, she finally came to a stop, dazed and disoriented. She just lay there for several minutes, then stood up, and looked around. Nothing looked familiar, so she started walking, exploring the woods and enjoying being outdoors for a change.

Something small moved near a tree in front of her. She crept forward to get a better look, and a small rabbit hopped into view. *Oh, a bunny! He's so cute. I wonder if I can catch him.* The rabbit hopped several yards, and stopped to nibble on some foliage. Gina followed, trying to sneak closer, but the little bunny kept his distance.

He went behind a bigger tree, and Gina decided that she would stay on the other side of the trunk and get really close, maybe even reach around and pet the bunny. She stepped closer, then closer still, trying to be quiet, telling herself to move slowly so she could catch the little ball of fur.

Her foot came down on a twig, causing a snapping sound, and the cottontail took off, bounding across the forest. Gina ran after him, fascinated with the prospect of petting a real bunny, but she finally lost sight of him, and sat down to rest, leaning against a tree.

***

The other children were so wrapped up in their game that several minutes passed before any of them missed Gina, and then they thought she was just hiding. Claire and Rose came back and sat down; after changing his diaper, Claire had put Ford down for a nap, but Wyatt cuddled up in his mother's lap, sucking his thumb. They watched the children for a bit, then Rose suddenly sat up straighter.

"Where's Gina? *Where's Gina?!*" she cried, beginning to panic. The children stopped, and looked around, then shrugged. Claire stood, searching the yard; Dana and Erin came out to see what was wrong.

Rose shouted, running around the yard, yelling her daughter's name into the woods, but there was no answer. Her heart began to pound, a physical reaction to the intense fear she felt. Dana wrapped her arms around her sister, and spoke softly. "Breathe, Rose. We'll find her. She can't have gone far. Let's get the other children inside. Frances and Mother can watch them and we'll get everyone else to search. We'll find her, but you need to calm down. You're upsetting Isabelle and the other kids."

Erin pasted on a smile and told the children that their snacks were ready in the kitchen, then followed them in to ask Julia to keep them indoors. Then she got on the radio and asked all hands who weren't on guard duty to report immediately to the front yard. Mac and Gus replied that they were near the top of the mountain, so she told them what was going on and to just start their search from there, covering the north side of the slope.

When most of the adults were gathered, they organized quickly into pairs, ready to set out looking for Gina. Rose wanted to go, but Will persuaded her to stay at the lodge with Isabelle and Wyatt.

Tanner turned to Ian. "Which dogs are on duty at the cave entrances?"

Ian frowned. "Ranger, Sheba, and Flash, I think. Why?"

"That's good. Blitz and Major have the best noses, and I'm going to try them today, see if they can help us." He put his arm around his sister's shoulders. "Rose, we need something of Gina's, something she wore recently."

"Her jacket's over there. I'm not sure which one she was wearing." Rose walked over and picked up the girls' zip-up hoodies.

Tanner went up the steps and opened the door to the lodge. "Isabelle, which jacket were you wearing today?"

"The red one."

"Are you sure?"

"Yes, Uncle Tanner. Gina wanted the purple one, and I like red best."

"Okay. Thanks." Tanner called Blitz and Major to come, and went back down the steps. "It's the purple one. Hand it here, please."

Rose gave him the bright fleece jacket. He let the two dogs sniff it, then told them, "Find Gina!" Both dogs began running around the yard, then Blitz barked and ran into the trees.

"The rest of you, search your assigned area, just in case, since these dogs have no experience with this. Keep your radios handy. Let's go," Erin urged, then chased after Tanner, who was already following the dogs.

***

Gina was slumped against the tree trunk, sound asleep. The active game and her solo run through the forest had worn her out, and she napped for almost an hour. When she woke up, she looked around, then remembered what had happened. She stood, stretching, and yawned. *I'm having an adventure! I always wanted to have an adventure, just like in the books Mommy reads to us.* A noise nearby startled her, and she peered into a clump of weeds to see if maybe the bunny had made the sound.

Snake! Her mind had barely processed the word before her feet were taking her away from the rattler she had seen. She ran as hard and fast as she could, darting around trees and stumbling a few times, until she could barely breathe from the exertion.

She looked back the way she had come, fearful that the snake was chasing her. In her mind, all snakes were mean and would come after little girls to bite them. As soon as she caught her breath, she started out again, this time walking as fast as she could because she was just too tired to run. She kept going for a long time, then realized finally that she had no idea where she was. *I should go back the way I came. No. No, the snake might get me if I do. Where am I? I don't think I've been in this part of the forest before. I guess I'm lost. I've never been lost before, and I don't know what to do, and I'm really hungry.*

She squeezed between the wires of a fence, and stepping into a clearing, Gina noticed that it looked very strange. Whatever had been growing there had been cut or mowed down, and the dying stubs of the plants smelled funny. She didn't like the smell, so she skirted the patch of decaying plants, watching her feet so she wouldn't get any of the stinky plant on her shoes, and headed back into the trees. When she finally looked up again, she froze. A black bear sat not twenty yards away, eating berries from a bush. The bear wasn't really very big, but to Gina, he seemed huge.

The bear saw her, and placed all four paws on the ground. He lowered his head, swinging it back and forth, then raised up on his back legs, and growled at her. She screamed.

***

Noah smiled as he started home with his catch of fish from the creek. It had been a good day. He had cleaned the shack and emptied the chamber pot into a hole he dug in the woods. He had read a few chapters of an old western that Charlie had left behind, and then he went fishing. Next, he planned to clean the fish, eat a feast, and read the rest of the book.

A piercing scream split the air. It seemed to come from the west, so he dropped the fish and his pole, grabbed his knife out of its scabbard, and ran toward the sound. Someone needed help, and Noah knew that he was the only one in the area. *That sounded like a little kid, but surely not. What would a little kid be doing in the woods?* He ran as fast as he could; the scene he found terrified him. A little girl and a bear stood like statues, just yards apart, staring at each other. Noah was nearer to the girl, so he ran up and grabbed her, shoving her behind him. He frantically unzipped his jacket, and grabbing the bottom corners of the front, held them out to the sides like wings, and released a terrible roar at the bear. Noah stood tall, and tried to make himself look as big as possible as he took a single threatening step forward. He roared again, and the young bear ran off into the woods.

Noah almost collapsed with relief. *I guess the stories were true; black bears, especially young ones, don't really want a fight. Who was it who told me to look big and scary if I ran into a bear? I wish I could thank them.*

"Mister? Hey, mister?" a small voice almost whispered.

"Hey, little girl. That bear is gone now. Who are you, and why are you alone?"

"I got lost chasing a bunny, and a snake almost got me, and then the bear came, and I wanna go home!" Gina began to cry.

Noah knelt and took the sobbing child into his arms. "It's okay now. You're safe now. I'm going to help you find your way home." He picked her up, continuing to murmur comforting words, and carried her to his shack.

"There, now," he said softly as he lowered her to the ground. "My name is Noah, and this is where I live. You can stay here until I figure out how to get you home. Are you hungry?"

Gina nodded, so Noah offered her a choice of canned peaches or canned soup. She chose the peaches, so he opened the can and poured some in a bowl for her. While she ate, he tried to find out who she was.

"What's your name, little one?"

"Gina Diane Lapointe. I'm a twin. My sister looks just like me, and her name is Isabelle Marie Lapointe," she answered proudly.

"Do you know where you live?"

"At the lodge, with Erin. She's going to be our aunt when she marries Uncle Tanner."

Noah hid his surprise. "Is your Uncle Tanner a big guy, really tall?"

"Yes. Do you know him?"

"I might. Does he have some German shepherd dogs?"

"Yes! Blitz, and Flash, Major, Moxie, Sheba, and Ranger. Moxie is my favorite. She's just a puppy."

"I do know your Uncle Tanner. And I have a radio, so I'm going to let him know you're here and safe. I bet he's really worried about you."

"My mommy and daddy might be worried, too."

"Well, I'm sure they are. I have to step outside to use the radio, so you just go ahead and finish your peaches, and I'll do that."

Noah stood in front of the tiny shack, and put the radio up near his mouth. "Tanner or Erin? Anybody from the lodge?"

Gus answered. "This isn't Tanner, but I'm from the lodge. Who is this?"

"Noah, from Charlie's shack. I found a little girl who says her name is Gina, and Tanner is her uncle. She's safe. I have her here at the shack."

"Thank God! We're all out in the woods searching for her. I'm sure some of the others can hear this. Guys, you copy?"

Will's voice came on. "Is she really okay? I'm her dad. And where is this shack?"

Tanner came on before Noah could answer. "Will, meet us at Erin's east fence. We're a little south of you, so follow the fence and we'll find you and show you where the shack is."

As they moved forward, Blitz and Major continued to be excited, sniffing the ground, and running ahead. They were definitely headed in the direction of Charlie's marijuana patch.

Twenty minutes later, Tanner and Erin watched as Will swept his little daughter into his arms and cried with relief.

"Young lady, don't you *ever* go into those woods alone again. Do you hear me?"

Gina rubbed the tears off her cheeks. "Yes, Daddy. I'm s-s-sorry. I was so s-scared! At first, I was having an adventure, but then the s-s-snake and the bear…but Mr. Noah saved me from the b-b-bear."

"You can tell us all about it when we get home, sweetie. Here, stay with Uncle Tanner while I talk to this young man."

Will strode over to Noah and shook his hand, then pulled him into a hug. Tears filled Will's eyes again as he whispered, "Thank you so much. We've been frantic. How can I ever repay you?"

"You don't have to do anything to repay me. I'm just happy that I could help. She's a nice kid."

"She's a good girl, but she made her mom and me age about forty years today. Do you need anything? Food, anything?"

"Well, it does get kinda lonely here. Maybe if someone would come for a visit occasionally, that would be nice. I could use a little more food, too, but not if it will put you in a bind."

Major trotted over and sniffed of Noah's pantleg. Noah stiffened. Tanner noticed, and decided that it was time to help Noah overcome his fear of the dogs.

"Blitz, come," Tanner commanded, and led Blitz over to stand beside Major. "Noah, they won't hurt you, unless I tell them to, and after today, that's highly unlikely. Give me your hand." He leaned forward a little, patting Noah's hand, offering it to the dogs to smell, then spoke to both dogs. "Friend. Noah's our friend."

Chapter 18 – Mid-October

"Now this here's a young hickory tree. The wood is real tough, and it might make a good slingshot. Let's see if'n we can find a coupla Y-shaped pieces." Charlie gestured toward the tree, and let Zeke and Tucker search for several minutes.

Tucker found a branch that resembled a Y, but one side was much smaller than the other. "How about this one, Charlie? It looks like a Y," the boy asked enthusiastically.

"See how this un's not even on the two sides? You gotta find one that's the same, so's it's balanced."

Zeke and Tucker continued to look for just the right shape, as Charlie watched patiently. Finally, both boys found satisfactory branches. Charlie cut them with a small handsaw, and they started back to the lodge, the two brothers chattering about all the things they would shoot with their new weapons.

"Now, don't y'all let me catch ya shootin' songbirds, nor any other innocent critters that we cain't eat. Killin' jest to be killin' is a sin, and boys who think killin' is fun…well, I ain't gonna be happy at all if'n you turn into the kind that would kill for no reason." Charlie gave them a stern look. "I mean it. Don't you be shootin' at nothin' that we cain't eat, 'less ya think your life is in danger."

The boys mumbled their agreement, a little disappointed at the restrictions. They were good boys, though, and giving it a little thought, realized that Charlie was teaching them a useful lesson. When they got back to the lodge, Charlie showed them some strips of rubber he had already cut.

"See this? I done shaped it for ya. I cut up an old inner tube a while back and made a slingshot for m'self, and there's plenty left to make more."

The boys watched carefully as Charlie showed them how to sand the rough edges of the cuts. He handed each of them a piece of sandpaper and told them to get busy, and not to stop until the wood was smooth.

Later, after inspecting their sanding jobs, Charlie showed them how to fasten the rubber to the wood, and then he showed them some small rocks in the yard that would make good ammunition. Zeke got busy collecting stones, putting them in his pockets, but Tucker shot most of the ones he found, saving very few.

As he shot another rock into the woods, Tucker glanced at his older brother. "Hey, watch this! I'm gonna hit that tree right there."

Zeke grinned, and said, "I bet you can't hit it."

Tucker shot, and missed. "I just need to practice more. What're you going to do with all those rocks you put in your pockets?

"Well..." Zeke looked around, and seeing no adults within earshot, whispered, "Someday, when nobody's looking, I'm going to explore the caves. There's that one cave that the grownups say doesn't go anywhere, but it's too narrow for them to go very far into it, so I don't know how they know where it goes. I am pretty sure I can fit through there, and I'm gonna need a weapon, in case there's animals in there, like a panther or something."

"I wanna go, too! I can fit easier than you can, and remember, Erin said not to go anywhere alone."

"Yeah, and Erin also said not to go into the caves. Sometimes grownups have too many rules. Okay. You can go, too, but you gotta be brave, not a big baby about it."

***

A cool, crisp breeze ruffled Erin's long hair. She wore it down for the first time in weeks; it had finally cooled off enough that having her hair on her neck and back wouldn't be too hot. She stood on the porch, looking at the fencing and huge planters that made up her new garden. *I'll be able to grow much more food next year. We'll have room for pumpkins, and maybe some more kinds of squash. I can even grow herbs. Hopefully, we'll be able to eat better and help our friends a lot more, too. I'm so thankful for Gus and Charlie and how hard they work around here. Everyone works, but those two are worth their weight in gold when it comes to projects. I wouldn't trade them for anything.*

Tanner stepped out of the lodge, followed by Blitz and Moxie. "You got enough free time to stand around daydreaming?" Tanner teased.

"As a matter of fact, yes, I do. This time of year is a time of rest for the garden, so I get to rest, too. Winter will be here before we know it, and we'll all have a little more free time, I hope. Do you think we have enough wood cut to last a while?"

Tanner grinned. "Have you seen what's stacked on the patio? Ian and Shane got into a log-splitting contest this morning, and it's stacked almost seven feet high back there. Gus and Charlie are keeping the chainsaw operable, if not in perfect shape. Chains do wear out, and the one we have is just about to that point. Ernie didn't happen to have some extras in the cavern, did he?"

"Not that I know of, but I haven't been through every tub out there. They're all labeled, but some of the labels are on the lids, and other tubs got stacked on top, so I can't see them. Maybe we should look on the inventory list that he left. I'd forgotten about that, with so much going on lately."

"It can wait 'til later. I'd like to talk to you."

"What about?"

"Well," he drawled as he pulled her into his arms, "I believe we have a wedding to plan, unless you've changed your mind."

"Hmmm. Are you hoping I have… or hoping I haven't?"

"If you have, I don't even want to know it. I *want* to marry you, Erin. I want to commit myself to you, for always. I want to spend the rest of our lives loving and having kids, and always, always, knowing that you love me back."

"I do. I always will. So when do you want to do the deed?"

Tanner looked apologetic. "I know that most women want a big wedding in a church, but…."

Erin touched a finger to his lips. "I'm not 'most women'. Yes, when I was a little girl, I dreamed of the lacy white dress, the long veil, flowers everywhere, the beautiful music, and my dad walking me down the aisle. But dreams change. I decided several years ago that if I ever found Mr. Right, I wanted to keep it simple. I did still want to be married in church, but that's not possible anymore, thanks to the tornado."

"So, I'm Mr. Right, huh?" Tanner grinned.

"Oh, yeah. Definitely." She stretched up to kiss him. "I know it will disappoint our friends in town, but I'd like to keep it small. I don't have any blood family, but everyone in the group is my family now. I've thought about it, and I'd like to get married here, in the lodge. There won't be an aisle to walk down, so I won't have to decide who I'll ask to walk with me and give me away. I don't want to hurt any feelings, so let's just skip that part, okay?"

"That's fine with me, although I know that any of the older men in the group would be proud to do it. You're right, I think. It would be impossible to choose one over the others."

"Do you mind if we have four attendants, even though that's a lot for a small wedding? I want Jen to be maid of honor, plus Sarah, Val, and Lydia. Maybe if we have a happy occasion to celebrate, Lydia will decide to come home. I miss her so much."

"Me, too. I'll ask Ian to be best man, of course. We've been best friends almost our whole lives. Shane, Will, and John – that makes my four."

"Do you think Dana and Rose will mind if they aren't in the wedding party?"

Tanner took her hand and kissed her fingers. "No. They won't mind at all, I'm sure of it. Come on, let's take a walk."

Tanner led Erin around the lodge and high up the slope to a boulder where they could sit and talk without interruption. "There really aren't any flower shops anymore, you know. What will we do for decorations?"

"We don't need decorations. I have a nice dress, which just happens to be white, and maybe we can come up with a veil or a hat from somewhere. Frances can make the cake. There's some classical music in my collection of CDs. I'm glad, for many reasons, that Uncle Ernie had solar panels put on the roof, but right now I'm glad because we can use the CD player for our wedding. I'll find something suitable for a wedding march, and I'd like enter down the staircase. If Ken can do the ceremony, we can be ready in a matter of days. It's not like we have to find a venue to rent, and hire musicians and a caterer."

"I'm glad we're waiting until after we're married to be intimate. I won't say we 'decided' to wait, because it really wasn't a conscious decision. It's just the right thing to do, for both of us. I'm looking forward to our wedding night, though. If kissing you is an indication of what's in store, it'll be great."

"I wondered if you were unhappy about waiting. We haven't even had time to talk about that, but I want you to know that I promised my mom when I was just fourteen that I would *deserve* the white dress when I got married. It's old fashioned, but to her, white represented purity, and I've kept my promise. For me, it's what I believe is God's will, and also, it's honoring my parents. I guess I'm not very modern in my outlook, but I'm not sorry I waited for you."

"Neither am I. Besides, under the circumstances, the *where* and the *when* would have been problematic. We're surrounded by a crowd, day in and day out. I wish I could take you on a honeymoon. If I could, where would you like to go?"

Erin considered the question for a moment, then said, "Since we're just dreaming about it, we might as well dream big. I always wanted to go to New Zealand, or tour the Greek islands. In college, I took a class on Renaissance art, and decided that I wanted to go to Florence, Italy someday, and see some of that art. There are just too many possibilities. Where would you like to go?"

"It may not seem romantic to anyone but me, but I'd love to take you to Montana. We'd rent a cabin near Glacier National Park, and spend our days hiking or kayaking down the Flathead, and our nights making love. Or maybe a secluded beach somewhere tropical. We could snorkel and swim, dance the night away at the clubs, or just take long barefoot walks in the sand."

"My, my, that sounds totally romantic," Erin cooed, batting her eyelashes. Then she sobered. "I knew you had a romantic streak, but somehow, it still surprises me. Our lives haven't been conducive to romance lately, have they?"

"No. We work hard around here, to feed our people and our friends in town, and to fight the bad guys and keep us all safe. It seems like we never have time for *us*, but if I had the time and the means, I would show you just how romantic I can be. You bring out that side of me, but I can't always express it with so many people around. I think about what I want for us, and dream that someday, I'll be able to provide for you like you deserve."

"This can't last forever, and even if it does, we'll manage somehow to love each other through it all. I'll be with you, Tanner, no matter what happens."

"Do you remember that right after we met, I was gone for a while?"

"Yes, and I was very disappointed. I looked for you every time I went to town, hoping to see the good-looking giant who rescued me from Ollie Simmons. That was my first impression of you, ya know? Handsome, heroic, and *really* tall."

"When I got back, Grandfather and I camped out one night, and he asked me when I would get married. I told him that I had already met my *chunkash anli*[3], and my heart was hers. He asked me who, and I said, 'the

---

[3] True heart

niece of *Tali isht hollisochi*.[4]' I knew, Erin, from the moment I saw you, that I had found the one my soul loves. I was already interested, after hearing Ernie brag about you, and seeing all the pictures of you that he showed off to everyone. I think he knew, too, or at least he hoped. I have a feeling that he'd be pleased that we're together, and I'm honored at the thought that he would trust me to make you happy. I love you. I've loved you and *will* love you, forever."

---

[4] Silver Pen

Chapter 19 – The Next Two Days

"Oh, Erin! It's beautiful! That's the perfect dress for you." Jen exclaimed. "I wish we all had pretty dresses to wear for your wedding. I don't know what I'm going to wear."

"Do you have matching shoes?" Sarah asked.

Erin turned once more to see her dress in the mirror. "I do. Sparkly white sandals, with a three-inch heel. I have my mother's pearl earrings and necklace, too. They'll be my 'something old', and the dress and shoes are new. Now I need something borrowed and something blue, and a veil or hat. I have a sixpence that Ernie got for me on his last trip to London."

"What about your sapphire ring? You could wear it on your right hand," Val suggested. "Or we could use some of the elastic and fabric from the tubs in the cavern and make a blue garter."

"I like the garter idea. Frances sews, and I'll offer to cook tonight so she can work on it."

"No, *I'll* cook, and Val can help. Let us do things for you, since we can't really do all the traditional bridesmaid things," Sarah begged.

"Okay. Now, what can we come up with for you bridesmaids to wear? Val, you're closest to my size, and I have a dress that might work for you, but it would look strange to have one of you all dressed up and the others in ordinary clothes. Did any of you happen to bring something fancy?"

"No. You had your fancier dresses here because you moved all your stuff before the collapse. We had limited time and space in the Explorer when we left Tulsa. Sarah, you're the same size as Lydia, just taller. I wonder if she has anything. And Jen, you're so petite, I don't know what we'll do for you. Nobody else here is so tiny."

"Maybe one of the ladies from town has a nice dress we could borrow. Isn't one of them really small?" Sarah thought for a second. "I remember what she looks like, but I've gone blank on her name. We'll have to ask Terri who she is."

"*If* whoever you're thinking of has a dress, and *if* her house wasn't destroyed by the tornado, we might be in business. At any rate, I think a trip to town is in order. We need to take some food to our friends, and we can ask when we get there."

"Erin, I'm curious: how is it that you just happen to have a beautiful dress – and white, no less -- on hand when you happened to get engaged to that gorgeous man of yours?" Val asked.

"Uncle Ernie wanted me to go with him to a fancy reception where he was getting an award from the Choctaw Nation for his help with their literacy program. He even went with me to pick it out, and he said he always loved seeing me in white, that it's a good color for me. He even paid for the dress. Then Lillie, his lady-friend, came for a visit, and I bowed out so she could be his date. I just never had another opportunity to wear it before the collapse."

"You sure have all the luck, girl. Well, let's see if we can get some stuff together to take to town." Val stood up, and beckoned the others. "C'mon, ladies. Our 'shopping' trip will be fun."

The four friends went downstairs and got some canned goods and frozen meat to take to Ernie's house. There was a good selection to choose from, due to the success of recent hunting and fishing excursions.

The hunters in the group had almost filled the big freezer in the laundry room with wild hog and venison. Tanner had even killed a turkey with his bow. Ian and Vince had been teaching Micah to fish, and the kid showed a real knack for it; they had several packages to take to the townspeople, without worrying about running low themselves. *Once again, I'm thankful that Ernie had the foresight to put solar on his house and the lodge, so we can have a working freezer,* Erin thought. *Life is good, in spite of everything that's gone wrong.*

Tanner, Ian, and Shane came in and helped carry the supplies to the Expedition, and insisted that they were going, too.

"We're big girls. We don't need you to escort us into town. Besides, the gang is gone. We'll be fine," Erin protested.

"Why should you girls have all the fun? We'd like to spend some time with you ladies. Is that okay with you?" Shane shot back.

Erin looked at her friends, who didn't seem to mind the idea at all. "Well, this is a *shopping* trip, so to speak. We're going to see if we can borrow some dresses for the wedding, so don't start complaining or trying to rush us. It may take some time, and if you get bored, just remember that you *asked* to come."

***

When they pulled up in front of Ernie's house, they could hear the happy voices of children in the back yard. Ken sat on the front porch with a rifle across his knees, and waved a greeting, then stuck his head in the door to tell the others that they had guests.

Terri, Yvonne, Lydia, and the other women came out to exchange hugs and hellos, and with so many to help, they got the food into the house and put away in a very short time.

The townspeople were completely cut off from the outside world, except for what news the lodge group brought, which was only what Mac, Gus, or Charlie heard on the radio. Ken left the front door open so he could hear what was said and still continue his vigil on the porch.

"What's happening these days?" Yvonne asked. "Sometimes it seems like our world has shrunk to just this tiny corner, this torn-up little town. We could be alone on the planet, for all we know."

"There are reports that whoever is running the government is using the military to keep the peace in some areas, mostly the big cities on both coasts, plus Denver, and Houston. We've heard that they used missiles on suspected gang hideouts, but who knows?" Tanner shrugged. "They pulled out of Chicago and

Detroit a long time ago, just gave up and left. Seattle is in ruins, according to Mac's sources, and so is New Orleans. They had another big flood in Louisiana, and added to the unrest in New Orleans, it pretty much wiped them out. Saint Louis is, if the reports are true, mostly burned. They never got the riots under control, and when the rioters started fires, nobody came to put them out, because the first firefighters to arrive got shot.

"You knew that a lot of young adults have been conscripted into a so-called security force, right?" At their nods, Tanner continued. "Well, they call it NERC, the National Emergency Recovery Corps, and Jen's brothers are in it. They got sent to Pueblo. We've heard from them again, and we're pretty sure they plan to escape and try to get here. The last we heard, they said something about Price being terrified of water, so they don't go canoeing on the river, and they mentioned summer camp again, this time complaining about how strict the camp counselors were. We think that meant that they are not being treated as well as they were at first, and that the officers are hard on them. And Price loves water. He was a lifeguard at the NSU pool and swims like a fish. We think that what they were trying to tell us with that one is that they may be coming part of the way by boat. They also said something about assuring their mom that they had plenty to eat. We aren't sure what they meant by that, but figure it either means that they are well fed, or maybe that they have lots of food stockpiled for their trip."

"There've been some bombings, too, if we can believe the radio reports," Erin added. "Supposedly, the Golden Gate Bridge, the Great River Bridge in Iowa, and the bridge across the Mississippi in Memphis were badly damaged, and a couple of skyscrapers in New York, too. They're still standing, but will need major repairs if things ever get back to normal."

"And Tanner forgot to tell you the good news," Erin added.

Tanner grinned, and took Erin's hand. "This beautiful lady has done me the honor of consenting to become my bride."

After the hugs and congratulations subsided, Jen spoke up. "Erin has a lovely dress, but we need to ask a favor. She needs a veil, and do any of you ladies have dresses that we could borrow for the bridesmaids?"

"Jen, Val, and Sarah didn't bring anything except very casual clothes that they grabbed when they bugged out of Tulsa. Val is going to wear one of my dresses," Erin explained. "And Lydia, I want you to be one of my attendants, too. Do you have a dress you could wear? We aren't worrying about colors; matching dresses would be too much to ask, but we would like semi-formal or formal. Short or long doesn't matter, I guess. I just want us all to look pretty."

Lydia raised her head, taking part in the discussion for the first time. She had lost weight, and looked like she hadn't been sleeping well, but the idea that Erin wanted her in the wedding seemed to break through her despondency and get her attention.

"I'd be honored, Erin. I do have several nice dresses. And some of them might fit you, Sarah. You're welcome to wear any of them that you like. I left them at my house, though, because I didn't think I'd need them at the lodge, and I haven't been back to see what damage was done. I hope my house is still there and has a roof on it."

A short, slender young woman looked at Jen, and asked, "What size do you wear?"

Jen shrugged. "I wore a size 4 before the collapse, but like everyone else, I've lost a little. I used to eat like a horse, but now, I eat only one serving per meal, and I am a lot more active than I was. Maybe size 2? I'm not sure."

The other woman smiled. "I think I have something you could wear. In fact, I have two, and you may wear either of them. One's a swirly blue chiffon that I bought when I was taking ballroom dance lessons, and the other is a lilac sheath, with a sequined leaf design across the front. I can see my house from here, and I know it's still standing. Shoe size?"

"I wear a 4 ½ or 5," Jen answered, hopefully.

"Great! I have a pair of silver strappy sandals that will go with either dress."

"Does anyone have some size 7 dressy shoes?" Val asked.

Two women nodded, then looked at each other and laughed. One of them said, "I guess you'll have a selection to choose from!"

Two of the houses were close enough that they could walk to them, so the ladies set off to "shop", each pair accompanied by one of the men. Terri's house being on the other side of town, Tanner and Erin took Terri, Lydia, and Sarah in the Expedition. They skirted around the debris that still littered the streets, and stopped in front of the Abbott house. Terri led them into the damaged home, and they could see that the tornado had spared all but the dining room, which had water damage from the metal roof being peeled back. The rest of the house was musty, but intact.

Terri got on her knees and reached under the bed in the master bedroom, pulling out a long, shallow box. "I keep this where I can get to it, because you would be surprised how many times someone has needed to borrow wedding attire. Young brides without the money to buy a fancy dress, mostly, but they deserve to have a nice wedding, too, and I've loaned the dress out at least five times." As she spoke, she pulled out a lovely veil, attached to a dainty crown of white silk flowers. She shook the wrinkles out of the delicate lace, and offered it to Erin.

"Terri, it's beautiful. This will be perfect. Thank you so much." Erin whispered, tears of gratitude filling her eyes.

"I'm happy to help make your day special, Erin. You've been a good – no, a *wonderful* friend to us all, and anything we can do is just a small way of saying thank you. Now, let's go see what treasures we can find at Lydia's"

Tanner drove back the way they had come, going around the outskirts of town to avoid the worst of the rubble from the twister. The women were stunned by the devastation they saw, since none of them had ventured over to that side of town since the storm. Lydia's house was two blocks from the path of the tornado, and she was thrilled to find it in one piece, but then she remembered the last time she had been there. She had a feeling that the memory of Richie's heroic death would haunt her for the rest of her life, but for Erin, she would go in, and face her grief.

She led her friends to the closet in a spare bedroom where she kept her dressier clothes, which she seldom had occasion to wear since her move to Kanichi Springs. She waved Sarah forward and began pulling padded hangers out, displaying the gowns before tossing them onto the bed. "Here's one that I bought for a charity ball. This one was for an engagement party at the country club in Plano. I bought that mint green one for a dinner we were invited to on a trip to New York, and the coral one I bought just because I liked it. There's a slinky, floor-length emerald green, but it's probably too short for you. These are the newest ones, but feel free to look at any of the others."

Sarah stared at the closetful of elegant clothing. "Lydia, you have so many formal and semi-formal dresses. Were you *rich*?"

"My ex-husband made a lot of money, and we traveled, partied, went out dancing, and spent most of what he made. Then I found out about his little girlfriend, barely out of her teens. She was pregnant, and he married her as soon as our divorce was final. I got a good settlement, and of course, I got to keep my clothes and jewelry. I much preferred the simpler life I had here. I was happy here," Lydia said, looking wistful.

Erin put her arm around Lydia's waist, and leaned her head on Lydia's shoulder. "Please don't make happiness past tense. My sweet friend, you'll be happy again someday. I know it hurts. It hurts us all, but Richie wanted you to be happy more than anything. Grieve, but don't let it rule your life. We miss you so much at the lodge. I hope that when you feel like you can, you'll come back to us."

Lydia took a deep breath, and let it out slowly. "I know. It's still just too new, too raw. I've been doing some counseling sessions with Ken, and that's helping. Just sometimes, it hits me pretty hard, and I can barely hold it together. I feel like I'm shattering into a million pieces. I was afraid to come here today, but you know, I think that facing what happened is going to help me somehow."

Sarah leaned over and kissed Lydia on the cheek. "I appreciate that you are willing to help me pick a dress. I know you really don't feel up to doing this right now, but I do appreciate it. Before I pick one, how about you choose which one you want to wear, then I'll pick from the rest."

"The coral one is my favorite, but I never got to wear it, so I think I'll take that one. I'd suggest the mint green for you, Sarah. With your coloring, I bet you'll look awesome. I have a necklace and earrings that'll be perfect with it, too. I promise, I'm going to do my best to help make this wedding beautiful, and not let my sadness spoil it."

Erin shooed Tanner out of the bedroom, and Sarah slipped out of her jeans and sweatshirt, and into the elegant dress. As she did, she noticed the name of a world-famous designer on the label.

"This isn't something that a teacher in Oklahoma would ever expect to wear. It's amazing," she said softly.

Erin fastened the tiny buttons down the back, then Lydia fastened the necklace around her neck, and led Sarah over to a cheval mirror. "I was right; that shade of green brings out your eyes and makes your skin look all peaches and cream. We'll put your hair up so the keyhole back will show, and you'll look so gorgeous that maybe we'll have another excuse to dress up soon."

Sarah turned her head and gave Lydia a conspiratorial wink. "Yeah. We might, at that."

***

When they got back to Ernie's, the others were already there with a gown and shoes for Jen. Tanner and Erin made plans with Ken to come for him, Terri, and Lydia two days later. Erin explained to Ken that no one would be giving her away, and that they would recite their own vows, but wanted the rest of the ceremony to be very simple. Terri suggested that they go ahead and take the dresses and shoes to the lodge so they would be ready.

When they got back into the Expedition, Tanner said, "Okay, two more stops to make."

"Really? Where?" Erin asked.

"Shane's cabin and my place. He's got a couple of suits to pick up, one for himself and one for Will. When they bugged out from Wilburton, they swung by and picked John up at the college and he was wearing a suit, so he has one. I need to get some things, too, but there's no need for anyone else to get out. We'll be quick."

He maneuvered past the cluttered streets and down the gravel road to Shane's little cabin. Shane ran in and was back in just a few minutes with a dry cleaner's bag containing his clothes, a pair of shoes in his other hand. Then Tanner drove out to his training facility and former home.

The kennel grounds were overgrown with weeds, but there was no sign of any vandalism or looters. Unlocking the door to his quarters, he quickly found a charcoal gray suit and black dress shoes. He chose a white shirt and a red silk tie, as well. Then he took a painting off the wall and opened the safe behind it, removing a small red velvet box and dropping it in the pocket of the suit coat. He locked the safe and replaced the painting. Taking one last look around the apartment, Tanner promised himself that someday, he would rebuild his business, so he could support his wife and the children he hoped they would have.

***

Early the next morning, Erin sat out on the porch drinking her coffee, and thinking about what being married would be like. She had no doubts about whether she and Tanner could have a successful marriage; she was just having a problem figuring out the logistics of being married, in every sense of the word, in the midst of over twenty other people.

People used to go on honeymoons, trips to romantic places, but we can't do that. I don't even know of a way to have privacy for our wedding night. I guess we might ask if we could go to Talako and Julia's house, but I have a feeling that Tanner won't want us to be somewhere that might not be safe. His apartment at the kennel? No, same problem. We've waited for marriage, and I'm glad, but I want that big guy. I've never felt this before, this strong desire, this longing to be one with a man. I want to be with him, but where?

She drank the last sip of coffee, then went inside to find Val, Shane, and Sarah huddled near the spiral stairs, whispering. *They're up to something. I have no idea what, but there's been a lot of sneaky-looking little meetings the last couple of days.*

Tanner came down the stairs, nodded at the little group, and walked over to hug Erin. He gave her a light kiss and held her for a few moments, then said, "What are your plans for the day?"

"Well, I was going to clean the living room some, but the girls have forbidden me to do anything that they can do instead. The garden chores are all finished for the year. Everything that I can think of for the wedding is already done, and Frances wants us all out of the kitchen this evening so she can prepare the cake. I guess I could sew Micah some new pants."

"I have a better idea. Let's go visit Noah and take him some food. It'll get us out for a while." Tanner whispered, *"Alone,"* as he waggled his eyebrows. "We owe him for saving Gina from the bear. We could take something for us to snack on, or even a picnic lunch, and maybe go sit beside the creek and watch the fish jump."

"Actually, that sounds much better than sewing. As distracted as I am about the wedding, I'd probably sew pockets on the knees of his pants. I'm not really nervous, but I do have a lot on my mind."

"I can tell. Okay, I'll make a couple of sandwiches for us, and you sort out what you want to take for Noah. We'll go by the shack first, then go to the creek and have a little picnic, just the two of us."

"It's a date. I want to change these sneakers for my hiking boots, though. I'll be right back."

Erin hurried up the stairs, only to glance out the window and see Vince, Julia, Claire, Shane, Val, Sarah, Jen, and Ian on the deck, looking very much like they were conspiring about something. *I must be getting paranoid, seeing conspiracies everywhere. Sheesh, maybe this is part of my pre-wedding jitters.*

Erin got her hiking boots on, then helped Tanner get things ready for their excursion, and the two left out the front door. As they started down the steps, Erin noticed BJ, Gus, and Charlie huddled around Frances, who seemed to be doing all the talking. When the little group saw her and Tanner, they all straightened up, and acted just a little bit too innocent. *Okay. Maybe I'm not paranoid. They are definitely up to something. Well, my guess is they're planning something for Tanner and me, so I'll just let them have their fun.*

Erin brushed a stray lock of hair out of her eyes and waved. "We're going on a picnic, and to see Noah. We'll be back later!"

Tanner held her hand and they set off, curving northeast around the mountain. The leaves on the trees were turning beautiful shades yellow, gold, orange, and red, and the day was cool, with a slight breeze.

"Let's take Noah's food first, so we don't have to carry it all the way to the creek. I hope he's at the shack and not down at the creek fishing. I like the kid, but today, three's a crowd." Tanner helped Erin cross the fence by holding two strands of the barbed wire apart so she could squeeze through, then he pushed the top wire down and stepped over it.

"Being tall comes in handy sometimes, doesn't it? You can reach things I'd need a ladder to reach. I guess changing lightbulbs is gonna be *your* job, buster."

"Height has some advantages, but it also has disadvantages. It's hard to find clothes that fit, and I have to duck a lot in the caves and walking through the woods. When I was a kid, my mom used to threaten to sew a ruffle on the bottom of my jeans if I kept growing so fast. And I sure got tired of people asking, 'how's the weather up there?' I wanted to just spit, and say, 'it's raining'."

Erin chuckled. "I'm tall for a woman, but I always wanted to be even taller. I knew a woman at church in Tulsa who was just over six feet. I always thought she was so elegant and graceful. I like it that you're tall. It makes me feel dainty and feminine, which isn't something I usually feel."

"You're very feminine, and you're also strong and brave. I think you're just the right height. Tall enough to kiss without having to strain my back, and small enough that I can pick you up and carry you away to my lair, heh-heh." Tanner swept her up and kissed her. "See? You're just right."

Tanner set Erin back on her feet, and put his arm around her, as they continued their hike to the old shack. They found Noah outside, lashing some branches together with rope.

"What are you making?" Erin stared at the ungainly contraption. "A table?"

"No, it's gonna be a bench, I hope. I've never done anything like this before, but I wanted a place to sit when I'm outside. It may not turn out like I want, but if not, I have lots of time on my hands, so I'll just keep trying until I get it right. Charlie left an old handsaw, and I used it to cut the limbs. I've sorta got an idea of how to do it. I just hope it works."

Tanner shrugged out of his backpack, and held it out to Noah. "We brought you some food. There's several cans of veggies and some fruit, and half of a loaf of bread that Sarah made last night. Oh, and there's a couple of books in there you might like."

"Wow, thanks. I was just wishing for something new to read. Let's go inside so I can put this away and return your pack. How's Gina doing?"

"She's well. She had some scrapes and bruises, but I think she learned a lesson. Rose, her mom, wants to meet you. I think they'll be coming to visit you soon, but not until after the wedding. Erin and I are getting married tomorrow."

"Hey, that's great. Congratulations! It's good to hear some happy news for a change. Ian and Micah came to see me a few days ago, on their way back from fishing. They said there's another creek on the other side of this mountain, but they wanted to come try the creek where I fish. They filled me in on all the stuff you guys hear on the radio. It sounds like folks in the cities are going crazy. I can't thank you enough for letting me stay here."

"We're happy you decided to stay, Noah. If you hadn't been here, I can't stand to think about what might have happened to Gina. We owe you, man," Tanner insisted.

They filled him in on the latest news, and asked if there was anything they could do for him, but he said he was doing fine, and congratulated them again on their impending marriage.

"I thought my future was all set. Culinary school, start working in a restaurant, learn all I could, marry my girlfriend, and someday, open a restaurant of my own, but I guess none of that's going to happen now. Under the circumstances, I think I landed on my feet, though; lots of people have it worse than I do."

"We've been blessed. I wish this was over, but until it is, we have to help each other when we can, and try to keep the bad guys from hurting people." Erin looked at Tanner, and smiled. "We have a good team, and Noah, I want you to know that if you get to a point that you want to join us at the lodge, we'll make room for you. You've proven yourself."

Noah stared off into the trees for a moment. "Thank you for that. I think I'll stay here for now, but if I run out of wood or food, and can't get to the creek to fish, I'll take you up on that, if you're sure."

"We're sure. Just don't wait until things get desperate. Use the radio, and we'll send someone to help you get your stuff to the lodge. Then, in the spring, if you want to come back here, you're free to do that."

"Hey, I hate to cut this short, but we need to run. Erin and I are going to the creek and have a little picnic. You take care, Noah. We'll see you again soon."

Erin gave Noah a little wave, then she and Tanner walked down to the stream and found a nice spot to spend an afternoon. Erin was hungry, and according to the growling sounds she heard from Tanner's stomach, knew he was ready to eat, too. He helped her spread a tarp to sit on, and she handed him a sandwich.

"The girls and I were talking not long ago about what we miss from before the collapse. What do you miss, Tanner?"

He thought about the question, then shrugged. "I miss the work I did, helping law enforcement by training dogs. I miss earning a living and supporting myself. I miss hanging out with my friends on a Friday night, and being able to hop in my truck and go somewhere without worrying about the gas and having to watch out for bad guys. But I wouldn't want to get those things back if it meant not having you in my life. What do you miss?"

"Nothing."

Tanner gave her a disbelieving look. "Nothing? You can't think of a single thing that you miss about your life before the collapse?"

"Not really. I edited books from my apartment, went out to eat with friends, shopped, slept, and then did it all again. It wasn't a challenging life; in fact, it was getting kinda boring. Now, I can't remember the last time I was bored. Well, today would have dragged a bit if you hadn't come up with the idea of a picnic, I guess, but really, I needed to get out of the routine I was sinking into before I came here. I'm happier right now than I've ever been, and if I had stayed in Tulsa, I wouldn't have met you."

"Do you really think that's true? I don't. I believe that we were destined to be together, and we would have met somehow and fallen in love no matter what happened in the rest of the world."

"Maybe you're right. I do feel that we were meant to be together, and I know that we'll have a good marriage. Have you written your vows?"

"I have, and I know them by heart. What about you?"

"Yes. I'm so ready to become Mrs. Tanner McNeil. Erin McNeil has a nice sound, don't you think?

Tanner pulled her into his arms and kissed her gently. "I think it has a wonderful sound, and I'm the luckiest man alive."

***

Lydia descended the spiral staircase first, followed by Val, Sarah, and Jen. Each of them looked lovely in their finery, dressed up for the first time in months. When Erin descended the stairs, her beauty took Tanner's breath away. Her hair fell in curls down her back, under the delicate lace of the veil as she took her place beside him. She carried a single red rose that Terri had found on a bush in her yard; Terri had removed the thorns and tied a white ribbon around the stem.

Ken began the ceremony with the customary "Dearly beloved…" and spoke of the meaning of marriage. There was a prayer, then Ken asked them to join hands for their vows.

Tanner's voice was both confident and gentle. "Erin, you are everything that I ever wanted. You make my life complete in every way. I promise that we will be partners in everything and build a life together. I promise to laugh with you and cry with you, to listen to what you have to say, and value your opinions. I promise to give you all my devotion and walk beside you through whatever life brings. I promise to be honest, open, and faithful, to nurture our relationship, and to cherish and protect you always. I promise to grow old with you, and love you forever."

Erin's looked up into Tanner's eyes, and spoke softly. "Tanner, you are more than I ever dreamed a man could be, and you fulfill my deepest needs. I promise to encourage you in every endeavor. I promise to cherish your strong, kind, and determined heart. I will share with you all of life's unexpected adventures and lend my strength to you for all your dreams. I promise to laugh with you, to respect you, and to honor you every day. I will give you my unconditional devotion and faithfulness through the pressures of today and the uncertainties of tomorrow. I promise to grow old with you, and love you forever."

When Ken said, "May I have the ring?" and Ian handed him something, Erin gave Ken a startled look. When they had gone over the order for the wedding service the previous day, they'd discussed the fact that they didn't have rings to exchange. Ken noticed Erin's confusion, but just smiled a bit and continued, talking about the meaning of the circle. He then handed Tanner the ring, and Tanner slipped the lovely, wide gold band set with several small diamonds onto Erin's finger. She looked at him, questioning him with her eyes, but he simply smiled.

The rest of the service was a blur for Erin, until Ken said, "You may kiss your bride," and Tanner took that permission very seriously, causing all their friends to laugh and applaud.

The reception was very simple, just the cutting of the cake, and Koolaid for the kids. The adults got one small glass of wine each, from a few bottles that Ernie had included in his cache.

When Erin finally had a chance for a quiet word with Tanner, she looked at the ring, then at him, and simply asked, "How?"

"I bought that ring about an hour after we met. I told you that I knew immediately, and I really did. That afternoon, I went to McAlester just to shop for a ring. You are my *chunkash anli*, my 'true heart'. When I saw you, all the pieces of my life fell into place, and I *knew*. Look at the inscription."

Erin pulled the ring off and looked inside it. There, engraved in tiny letters, were the words *Chunkash anli* and the initials T.M. and E.M. When her eyes lifted to his, they were filled with love and happy tears.

After visiting with their wedding guests for a little while, Tanner tapped a fork on the side of his wine glass, and announced, "Thank you all for making our wedding special. This has been a wonderful day, a day full of surprises for my bride, and now I'm going to show her one last surprise, for which I again thank you, our dear friends. She may have suspected that something was up, but I'm quite sure she has no idea what, and I am eager to show her, so help yourself to the rest of the cake and enjoy yourselves. Mrs. McNeil and I are going on our honeymoon."

The expression on Erin's face was priceless as Tanner led her across the kitchen and through the pantry.

He stopped to thoroughly kiss her in the cache cavern, and by then, she had regained her voice.

"Where are we going, Tanner? What's going on?"

"Our friends prepared a little getaway for us. That's why I took you on a picnic, to get you out of here so they could work their magic. Come on, I'll show you."

When they arrived at what Erin called the "cabana cavern", she was speechless. There were blankets hanging from wires strung across each end of the cavern, creating a cozy enclosure. A bed, a *real* queen-sized bed, with sheets and a bedspread, stood near the pool. A small table with two chairs sat near a metal fire pit, which had kindling and logs ready to light, and more wood was neatly stacked several feet away. Candles perched on ledges in the rocks, and a lantern hung from the ceiling of the cavern.

Erin took it all in, and could barely speak. "Where did all this come from? The bed, the fire pit?"

"From my grandparents' house. The guys brought it over yesterday while we were on our picnic, and everyone helped set it up. We'll even have our meals delivered by 'room service' three times a day. The guards at the entrance to the cave will stand watch for five hours each, instead of three, so we won't have so many interruptions. They pretty much have to pass through here to get there, but at night, there will be two guards and two dogs, and they'll stay all night. One of Ian's twin mattresses is there, so they can take turns resting. I think they thought of everything, as much as possible under the circumstances."

"'They'? What was your role in this?"

"Well, I might have been involved in the early planning, but our friends took it and ran. Every one of them helped, too. They all wanted to be a part of it, just as a small way of thanking you for all you do, for taking them in. They love you, too, Erin. And they had a lot of fun putting this together for us. We have three days, just the two of us, except for changing guards and people bringing us our meals. And I have some ideas about how we can fill the time."

Chapter 20 – Two and a Half Days Later

"Tanner? Erin?" a voice asked from behind the hanging blankets.

"Shane, this had better be important. You're interrupting the last few hours of our honeymoon," Tanner warned.

"It's important. Urgent, even. Come to the lodge, okay? Mac and Gus have news."

Shrugging, then chuckling, Tanner helped Erin climb out of the warm water of the natural pool. "Welcome to another day at the lodge. I'd have liked to stay here, just the two us, for the entire three days, but I guess it's just too much to ask."

"I've been thinking about something. We could go to the lodge during the day to do our work, and spend our nights here. I'm not ready to go back to sleeping in the women's dorm instead of with you. Maybe we could do our guard duty at this cave entrance, too. This little cavern is pretty comfortable and homey."

"You've been reading my mind. I like the idea. I wonder what Mac has heard that's worth interrupting our honeymoon," Tanner mused as he put on his shoes.

"One way to find out. You ready?"

It only took a few minutes to return to the lodge. Some of the group had gathered, but others were busy with various chores, and Ian had taken Micah, Tucker, and Zeke fishing. Tanner sat beside Erin on the sofa and asked, "Okay, what's up?"

Gus glanced at Mac, and gestured for him to begin.

"As you know, we've been working on a way to improve our reception and transmission so that we can talk to the folks in town, the Gibbses, and the Fosters, without having to climb the mountain. Basically, there are three factors that affect radio performance: the power of the transmitter, antenna length, and the environment.

"Ernie did a good job picking radios. They have removable antennae, which means we could replace the original ones if we had something to replace them with. Or we could rig some copper wire to them. They're powerful, and the antennae we have are pretty good, although there's room for improvement. Our environment is the problem. Radios work best if there is a line of sight between the transmitter and the receiver, but we live in a terrain that blocks transmissions. The lodge isn't quite high enough on the mountain to have line of sight to town. It's not too bad between here and the homes of our friends, but to town? We just can't get through, and if it's an emergency, the time we waste getting a signal could be a problem.

"If we put a bigger antenna on top of the mountain with a repeater, we could talk to Ken and Terri from here. Now before the collapse, there might be some question of whether modifying our radios in certain ways was legal to do, but now, I'd wager there's nobody to say we're doing anything wrong," Mac concluded.

Gus grinned, then chimed in, "If we just increased our ability to send messages with a bigger antenna, it would also increase the number of people who could be eavesdropping. The signal would go out to everyone within range, and that might not be good. The ideal answer to the problem would be a directional antenna that would send out our voices on a beam aimed at our friends, so to speak. It would narrow our transmissions to one area, but that area would get wider the further from us it went. Still, that would be better than having everyone within several miles hear what we say; however, it would also limit our ability to talk to any of us who went to the other side of the mountain for some reason. We decided that an omni antenna would be best, even though there's a slight chance that we might be heard by people outside our group."

"So how much progress have you made?" Erin wanted to know.

"A lot, actually. Between my knowledge of radios and Gus's ability to improvise, we've got an antenna set up on the mountain, with a repeater that Gus rigged up by connecting a digital recorder to a handheld radio. The repeater will relay our voices to our friends. We kinda requisitioned a small solar panel from the flashing light in front of the school, and Gus figured out how to connect everything so the repeater will have power, at least during the day. We put it all in an old electrical box to keep it dry. Without getting too technical, we can now talk to both folks in town and our neighbors from *inside* the lodge. We've tested it thoroughly, and it works. No more running up the mountain every time we need to contact our friends"

"That's wonderful, but how likely is it that someone might overhear our transmissions?"

"To hear us, someone would have to be within range of us, with a charged-up radio, and listening to the correct channel. I think it's unlikely that anyone will be doing that," Mac explained. "Few people have radios, and even fewer have both a radio and a charger, except maybe government folks. But just in case, we all need to be careful about mentioning locations."

"And the next step," Gus said, "is to go to town and rig up a way for Ken and Terri to be able to talk to us from the basement, without having to expose themselves by coming upstairs. We have some ideas on that, too."

"Now the bad part," Mac sighed. "We've been monitoring the news pretty closely, and what we heard this morning is disturbing. It seems that NERC is expanding its operations into rural areas, rounding up people, and putting them to work on "recovery farms." One guy said it seemed that they were especially interested in people who knew how to grow food, like you, Erin, but they're taking pretty much everyone. And the worst part is, they're reportedly in Oklahoma, and headed our way, coming east on I-40. If they send anyone south down the turnpike, we may be in trouble. With all those planters set up in front of the lodge, and a fence around them, it won't take a rocket scientist to figure out that we plan on growing food. They may decide to "recruit" all of us, and take the seeds you have stored, too. We can't let that happen."

Erin rubbed her forehead, where the beginning of a headache was settling in, but her tone was decisive. "Okay. When we know they're in the area, we'll need to move everything that we can to the caves, like extra linens, clothing, the kids' toys. I want this place to look abandoned, and we'll all have to go to the caves if they come here. I want two guards on each of the intersections nearest the property. We need to warn the Gibbs family and the Fosters, and tell Ken to keep eyes and ears out for vehicles. Are there any other people we need to warn?"

Shane lowered his eyebrows and looked at Vince. "What about Jeb, and that old couple we met, and the woman with the little boy? And Noah?"

Vince shook his head. "Jeb will be fine. There's not even a track leading to his place. But the others? I'd hate to see them forced into a camp. I don't think NERC would ever find the shack, but we should tell Noah to stay alert."

"What do you all think about having Noah join us here?" Erin asked.

"I think he proved that he's a decent human being. He done risked his life to save Gina from that bear, and we owe him for that. He seems like a purty good kid," Charlie replied.

"He has our votes," Will vowed. Rose sat beside him, nodding.

"We should stop dusting and sweeping the floors. It'll make it look like nobody's home," Val suggested. "And we need to move the tanker somewhere away from here. I don't know where, but we really need to hide it."

"That's true, Val. We'll have to do some thinking on that one," Mac replied.

"Mac, do you have any radio buddies along I-40 or in Glenpool or Okmulgee who could keep us in the loop on where the NERC troops go?" Erin asked.

"Yeah, I know a couple of people, as long as NERC doesn't catch them. I guess if they go silent, we'd better get ready for trouble."

"I don't want to get into a fight with NERC. Not only are there a lot more of them than there are of us, most of them are just young people who were shanghaied into working for them. We need to find a way to avoid a fight if possible. I want everyone to think about this, and see if you come up with any more ideas of how to keep from losing what we have here. Hopefully, we'll have a little time to prepare." Erin looked around the room, then stood. "And do a lot of praying while you're at it."

***

Using a small garden trowel that he had found at an abandoned homestead, Clint dug a hole about twelve inches in diameter then scooped it out wider at the bottom. Moving over about a foot, he dug a smaller hole that slanted and ran into the bottom of his first hole. The second hole was maybe five or six inches in diameter.

Gathering twigs and sticks, he placed them in the larger hole, and using a small wad of old newspaper that he'd found, lit his tiny fire.

I always heard that a Dakota fire hole is the best way to cook outdoors, and I hope the stories were right. Very little smoke, because the fire burns hotter, and I can make a little rack out of green wood and cook the rabbit I caught in my snare. I think I'm back far enough from the turnpike that all those refugees I saw yesterday won't know I'm around, and I'm downwind from the turnpike, so they won't smell my food.

Clint had made slow progress in his journey home from the gang hideout, going through Kanichi Springs first to look for supplies and finding almost nothing. Somehow, he was losing his enthusiasm about returning to Paris, Texas. He knew that his family might not be there. In fact, it was very doubtful that they had stayed. His dad had a little travel trailer set up on a hunting lease in the northern part of the Texas Hill Country, and knowing him, Clint figured that he probably left with the family at the first sign of trouble. When things started getting tense, his dad, mom, and little sister may have taken a "vacation" and bugged out. They weren't really hard-core preppers, but they did have some supplies put back, and most likely wouldn't have stuck around to see things fall apart.

Clint had only been to the lease a couple of times, and wasn't sure he could find it again, especially since it was well over a hundred miles away. The more he thought about it, the more he wished he had asked those folks back at the farmhouse if he could stick around, not necessarily with them, but in the area. At least he would have shelter in one of the abandoned houses or barns in or near Kanichi Springs. Nighttime temperatures were already low, and his food supply wasn't going to last much longer. If he made it to Paris, he might find that his family was gone and had taken all their supplies with them. He was afraid to think about the other possibilities, that his family had gotten sick like so many people had, or that they had fallen victim to a gang. He just couldn't figure out what he should do.

While the rabbit cooked, Clint got out a tarp and four bungee cords, and made a small shelter out of the tarp by folding half of it under, and fastening the top side to two trees, about three feet from the ground, and leaving the rest on the ground to sleep on. Using the grommets closest to the fold, he hooked the tarp to two other trees, right at ground level. He hoped it would protect him from the wind during the night.

After he ate the meat, Clint disposed of the rabbit bones by burying them some distance away from his camp. He gathered more sticks and piled them a couple of feet from his Dakota hole, then stretched out in the back of his makeshift tent.

The sun was just starting to lighten the morning sky when Clint awoke to the distant sound of voices. Lots of voices. He rose and quickly broke down his camp, put on his pack, and slipped through the woods to see what was going on. Nearly to the turnpike, he crouched down behind a cluster of cedar trees, and peeked through the branches. There were hundreds of people, all carrying bundles or pulling wheeled suitcases, headed south. *Refugees? I guess things must be bad in Tulsa, but why do they think that it will be better wherever they're going?*

An older man who looked like an aging Mr. Clean, and a tall, bearded guy about forty broke away from the swarm of people, and started toward another cedar tree, very close to Clint's hiding place. Clint thought the man looked familiar, but he couldn't place him. The two men unzipped and peed, talking the whole time.

"You think we can keep ahead of those government types if we stay on the highway? I think we should take off, get away from any major roads. They'll catch up to us and put us all in a camp," Beard Man insisted.

"I agree. What bothers me is that all these folks are headed south, and what's down there? More towns where the government is rounding people up. If NERC is headed east from Oklahoma City like we heard, and south from Tulsa, like we *saw*… and then there's that group we passed yesterday who said that NERC is coming north from Paris, too. We could be walking right into a trap.

"Let's just find a spot to sit down, act like we're tired, and let the biggest part of this bunch move on. If some of them see us take off into the woods, they might follow us, and I don't want company. Too many people leave too big a footprint for the feds to follow, and there's a few people in that horde that I don't trust. They have sly eyes, and they're always checking out what other people have. I think we'd be better off on our own."

Mr. Clean rubbed his lower back, and made a show of acting like he was in pain, then sat down against the trunk of an elm tree. "If anybody asks why we're sitting here, we'll tell 'em we need to rest a while because my back is bothering me."

"Do we go east or west?" Beard Man asked.

"East, I think. But I'm open to suggestions."

Clint was in a quandary. Should he try to sneak away, or stay put? If they discovered him, would they be angry or feel threatened? How long would they sit there, and would they see him when they headed into the trees? He could still hear the two men talking, if he listened closely, so he decided to eavesdrop for a few more minutes and see what else he could learn.

"Finn, how far into the wilderness do you think we should go to be able to evade NERC?" Mr. Clean stretched his legs out and crossed his ankles. "We need to find somewhere safe and where we can keep warm this winter, and we need to do it quickly."

"We'll go until we find a place that feels right, I guess. It seems like all the bad came out in people when the economy collapsed. It's like they were all waiting for a chance to rob their neighbors and loot stores. I hated having to close the restaurant, but after deliveries stopped, I couldn't keep it open. All those years of work, and now, I'm not a chef anymore. I'm just another homeless guy on the run. My 'dream' is dead."

Clint's brain took less than a second to process the man's words. Finn and a dream. He did know the man. Not well, but enough that he was sure he was one of the good guys. *Finn's Dream! I ate there several times. Great food, and lots of it, and outstanding service, too.* The restaurant was noted for helping homeless people by paying its staff well enough that they didn't have to rely on tips. Instead of leaving money on the table, patrons were encouraged to put any tip money in a jar next to the register, and the money went toward feeding the street people in Tahlequah. Clint had seen in the newspaper that Finn even received an award from the city for his charitable work.

Deciding to make his presence known, Clint came around the cedar tree and approached the two men.

"Excuse me, but aren't you Finn, from Finn's Dream? I used to eat there as often as possible, before NSU shut down. I guess I didn't recognize you with the beard."

"Yes, I'm Finn, but there's no more Finn's Dream. I had to shut it down. I remember you. You came in with three or four others on Tuesday nights, didn't you?"

"Yeah, that was my study group. We treated ourselves to a fine meal after our sessions in the library. I'm sorry that your restaurant closed."

"Thanks. I am, too." He gestured toward Mr. Clean. "This is my friend, Larry."

Clint shook Larry's hand, and said, "I'm Clint."

"Are you headed south with this bunch?" Larry asked.

"No, sir. I was headed south, but paralleling the turnpike. Seems to me that traveling on a major road is a good way to get picked up and put in a camp, or maybe killed by a gang. We aren't far from the prison. A lot of convicts escaped; I fell in with some of them, and barely got out alive. I figure they'll be looking to take whatever other folks have, and since most folks are traveling on roads, that means roads aren't safe. I've also just about decided that going south isn't any better than going north. My family has probably left town and gone to dad's hunting lease, and since I'm not sure where that is, I think I'm going to go back to a little community I passed through last week and settle in until spring. The place is mostly empty, so I'd have shelter, and it's quite a ways from the turnpike, so there's not many people passing through."

"Well, young man, we wish you luck. We've been thinking about making a turn to the east, into the wilderness area. We're hoping to find a place to call home for the winter, which will be here in just a few weeks. It looks like most of the refugee bunch has passed, so maybe it's time we parted ways. It was good to talk with you, Clint. Be safe."

"You, too, sir. If you don't find what you're looking for, come northeast to Kanichi Springs. The town got hit by a tornado, but there's still several of houses standing, and hardly any people at all. Best of luck to you both."

Chapter 21 – Third Week of October

"Mac, have you heard anything new on the radio?" Erin finished drying her hands on a towel, then snatched a slice of the bread that Frances had just baked.

"My buddy who lives just this side of Henryetta said that the NERC trucks stayed on I-40 and kept going east. I kinda expected them to turn either north or south on the turnpike, but they didn't. They just kept going straight, and didn't even stop in Henryetta. Maybe they had a full load and needed to take their captives to a camp. I don't know. But I heard from a fellow in Okmulgee that NERC is headed south on Highway 75 and picking folks up all along that route. That may be why the trucks from the City didn't turn.

"There's been a few more incidents of violence against Muslims, and a homemade bomb went off in a mosque in Texas. There are reports are that a lot of people from Mexico have crossed the border, but going south this time. Maybe things are better down there, or at least they think they are. The only other news from around here that I've heard is that several buildings in downtown Tulsa have burned."

"Well, I guess it could be worse. Tanner just heard from Lee Gibbs on a handheld that they're moving in with the Fosters. Neither family has enough people to get everything done without help, and the Fosters have that huge house. Jimmy and Lee will sleep in the guest rooms, Heather will share a room with Amaya, and

Hunter will be in with Paul and Quinn. I'm glad, since it'll put them a little closer to us, too."

"Has anyone talked to Noah lately?"

Erin sighed. "Yes. Tanner and I walked over and checked on him yesterday. We invited him to stay with us, but he says he likes it out there, except for being a bit lonely. He's enjoying fishing and we loaned him some books. I insisted that if we hear of trouble, he'll need to come here, and he said he would, but he still doesn't know where 'here' is. So we told him to follow the curve of the mountain around, and he'd find us. I worry about him being alone," Erin admitted. "He has some camping skills, but surviving a winter without electricity and a grocery store nearby? I don't think he really understands."

"Well, if it starts to snow or sleet, we'll just go get him, whether he wants to come or not. He's a good kid, and in my mind, a true hero. I can't imagine what Rose and Will were going through when Gina went missing. I would've gone insane if it had been Kyra lost in the forest."

***

After meeting Finn and Larry, Clint made a firm decision to return to Kanichi Springs and see if he could find somewhere to stay through the winter. If he survived until spring, he could always decide then whether to stay longer or try to locate his family, but right now, the first priority was to get settled in a place where he could stay warm.

He was traveling parallel to the Indian Nation Turnpike, staying far back in the trees, but where he could occasionally see the road. He knew that soon it would be time to veer off to the northeast, but for now, being close to a major road kept him on course. Progress was a little better than it had been before his about-face, mostly because he was sure that he wanted to go back. He hadn't been certain that going to Paris was best, ever since he saw all the refugees. He estimated that he had seen well over a thousand people trudging along, carrying everything they had in a backpack or a duffle bag. Their apparent hopelessness was really what made him decide to reverse course.

Each evening, when the sun got even with the tops of the trees across the road, he would move a few hundred yards further into the forest and set up his camp. He had very little food left, even though he had hoarded it as much as he could stand, and supplemented it with fishing and catching small game in his snares. *I sure wish I knew what plants and berries around here are safe to eat. Guess I should have paid attention when they had those nature classes at summer camp. I never thought that knowledge would do me any good, but look at me now.*

The last day before he planned to turn more to the east, Clint heard a rumbling sound that had become unfamiliar in the past few months, but he still recognized it. Trucks were coming. He crouched low and scurried west until he could see the road, staying hidden in a cluster of trees. About twenty trucks like the ones he had seen transporting troops in the movies, passed single file. Clint could just make out the NERC logo on the doors, and he suddenly understood that those were some of the trucks that took people to camps. The trucks slowed and got off at an exit Clint could barely see. He ran as fast as he could, trying to find out which way they went. *East! I've got to warn the folks who came to stop the gang. Oh, I hope those trucks have more stops to make before they get to Kanichi Springs!*

Hunger forgotten, he raced back into the woods, rushing to make it back to those folks who had been kind to him and fair enough to let him go. They had given him a chance, and he was determined to repay them. In his mind, he believed that most people would have assumed that since he was *with* the gang, he was *like* the gang, and deserved to die.

***

It took most of three days for Clint to cover the distance to Kanichi Springs, and when he finally stumbled into town, he was filthy, scratched, and bruised, as well as weak from hunger and exhausted. Wandering down Main Street, he searched for signs that someone was around, but the silence was profound. He turned and started back west a block north of Main, on Oak Street, and as he staggered forward, he thought he heard voices.

Ken and Terri came out of a house, Terri carrying a few blankets and some towels, and Ken loaded down with a case of mason jars, some filled with pickles and others containing pears. There was more food stored in the home's pantry, which somehow looters had overlooked. The owners of the house had been among the first to leave town, and the people staying in Ernie's basement needed whatever they could find before winter came. Ken had been reluctant to "scavenge" from the neighbors, because to him, it seemed to put him on the same level as the gang members who had looted the town, but after discussing it with his little flock, he decided that it was a necessity to gather up all they could.

At least we aren't killing anyone in the process, he thought. *Or raping innocent girls. And the people whose homes we're searching have been gone for months. The gang didn't care if people were here or gone. They just took everything. Maybe I'm rationalizing, but we're desperate, and just doing what we must do to survive. If the owners ever come back, I'll try to make it up to them.*

Clint raised an arm, and tried to shout, but only a croak emerged. Terri spotted him just as he fell forward on the sidewalk, too exhausted to even try to get up. She dropped the blankets and ran to him; Ken carefully set the precious food down, and hurried to help.

"Hunter. Tanner. Jimmy," he croaked, over and over. "Gotta tell 'em. Gotta warn 'em."

"Son, what's your name? Are you sick?"

"C-c-clint. No, not sick. Gotta tell 'em."

"Do you know Tanner and the Gibbses?"

Clint couldn't answer. His mouth was too dry, and the weakness that had plagued him for the last mile or so prevented him from speaking. His head lolled back as he almost lost consciousness.

"Terri, go get help. We'll put him in one of these houses for now. Bring water and something for him to eat. Maybe then we'll be able to find out what he's trying to say."

Running to Ernie's house, Terri burst through the door, and told Yvonne what she needed. Terri got a jar of filtered water, while Yvonne dipped up a container of soup, then the two women walked back down the street to where Clint was leaning against Ken, struggling to think clearly.

A few sips of water, and a couple of spoonfuls of soup later, Clint was able to clear his throat and ask, "Do you know how I can find some guys named Tanner, Jimmy, and Hunter?"

"Yes, we do. How do you know them?"

Clint took a little more soup, and seemed to be gaining strength by the minute. "They helped me escape from a gang near here. They gave me some supplies and let me go, but I had to come back."

"Here, eat some more, and drink more water," Yvonne ordered, her grandmotherly instincts coming out.

When Clint finished the soup, and had taken several deep breaths, he was able to continue. "I had to come back, to warn them. I saw some trucks coming this way, and they are rounding up people. It said 'NERC' on the sides of the trucks. I've heard of them. They make people go to camps and work like slaves on farms. Gotta warn Tanner."

"Where did you see these trucks? Up toward Henryetta?" Ken asked.

"No, south. I went south, and they got off the turnpike just a couple of exits from here. You folks better stay out of sight, too. When they see the town, they may go on, since the tornado damage is obvious. Maybe they'll think everyone is gone. Where can I find Hunter and Tanner? There were other people too, but I don't know their names. Are they here? Please help me find them."

Clint's strength was waning, as the exhaustion caught up to him again, but Ken promised that he knew where to find Tanner and would let them know. Then he and Terri helped Clint into one of the houses, and Yvonne agreed to stay and sit with him for a while.

Ken stepped outside and got on the radio. "Tanner, Erin, anybody there?"

"Yeah, Ken. Charlie here. How ya doin'?

"We're all fine here, Charlie, but we have a visitor. A young man pretty much collapsed, but managed to tell us that, uh, the group that Jen's brothers are in is headed this way, *from the south*. He says he met you guys and you helped him get away from some bad dudes recently. I think he's the kid Tanner told us about, the one who was going to be a 'girlfriend' to the gang. Says his name is Clint."

"Holy moly, Ken! He left, headed south to search fer his folks. Why'd he come back?"

"To warn you. He seemed very determined to let you know there's danger. He's pretty much passed out right now, and it looks like he's had a rough time of it. We've got him in an empty ·house near us, and we'll keep him here until you decide what you want to do."

As soon as he got off the radio with Ken, Charlie hurried outside to find Tanner and Erin. Tanner was splitting wood and Erin and Ian were stacking it on the patio, adding to the large amount they already had.

"Hey, you guys, take a break. I got news."

Moving over to the table, they all sat down, and Charlie told them about Ken's message. "He said he thinks it's that there Clint fella from the gang. He's plumb wore out, and could barely speak the words, but he said NERC trucks was on the turnpike, headed north, and turned off just south of our exit. We need to be getting' ready quick, 'cause they could be here anytime."

"Okay, let's think this out. What needs to be done first, and how do we help our friends?" Erin asked.

"We need to notify the Fosters. I don't know if the Gibbs family is with them yet or not, but they need to decide what they can do to stay out of sight. We need to move everything we can into the caves immediately." Tanner stopped a moment to concentrate. "I think we need to try to erase as many signs that someone has been living here as we can."

"And we'd better get Mac's tanker moved right away. We talked before about doing that, but never got it done. We have to figure out a place to put it and get it hidden quick," Ian reminded them.

"Yes, You're right. I can't believe we've procrastinated about that. Ever since the Simmons Gang got wiped out, we've gotten lax in taking care of business, and we can't afford to let our guard down." Erin looked thoughtful. "We can move all the stuff the kids have, the mattresses on the floor that the little guys have been sleeping on, and all the sheets and blankets to the caves. If they're all stripped down, the bunks'll look like they haven't been slept in lately. We'll move all the supplies that we've brought into the lodge back to the cavern, turn the water off and drain the water out of the toilets to make the place look winterized, too. Somebody needs to disconnect the solar power or remove all the light bulbs, or they'll figure out that the place has electricity.

"Let's try to eat up everything in the fridge that we can, and unplug it, too. And maybe Gus can rig a way to get electricity to the cave. We need to move the freezer out of the laundry room. There's too much food in there to waste, and too much to eat in a day or two. They won't see the solar panels unless they climb up the mountain behind the lodge and look at the roof." Erin glanced around the patio. "We can take the cushions off the chairs here, and maybe bring some leaves from the forest and scatter them out. We've been sweeping it almost every day, and it would have more leaves on it if nobody was home."

"Ian, see why I'm crazy about my wife? She's beautiful *and* smart," Tanner teased. "We also could leave the door unlocked, or they may try to break in. We don't want them to figure out that the windows are bulletproof and the doors solid steel. Maybe even leave the front door partially open, like someone left in a hurry."

"I'm thinkin' we should take that latch off the pantry shelf. We'll lock it from the cave side, but if'n they see the latch, they'll know there's somethin' funny 'bout that shelf. No use callin' attention to it." Charlie added.

"Charlie, that's a good idea. How about you take care of that? Where can we hide the SUVs? I think they need to be gone, too. Or could we just siphon the gas out, remove the batteries and some other parts, and make them look like they're abandoned? No, wait. They're too new to look like junk cars. I'm just thinking out loud, but I'd hate to have anything happen to our best transportation." Erin shook her head. "We can cram most of us into those two vehicles, but we can't get many people into the others if we ever need leave here, so we've got to protect those two SUVs."

"Okay, let's tell the others, and get this show on the road. We don't know how much time we have before they start looking for people around here," Tanner said. "I'll let our friends know, and Ian, how about you get with Mac and a few of the other guys and figure out what to do with the vehicles. Charlie, you and Gus and BJ get on the solar, plumbing, and remove that latch.

The ladies and the rest of the men can start moving stuff into the caves. Put the boys to work, too. I wish we didn't have all this freshly cut wood out here. Maybe we can put it in Ian's truck and hide it somewhere."

The lodge became a hive of activity, as everyone rushed to get their assigned jobs finished. Tanner got the Fosters on the radio, and it was decided that they would do the same sort of preparations to make their place look uninhabited, and would move into the forest and camp out until the NERC trucks left the area. Noah insisted that he would be fine so far from any roads or paths, and promised to do without a fire for a few days, in case the smoke might give away his location.

Tanner then let Ken know that they were getting prepared, and that they would come into town that afternoon and bring enough food to last several days. Ken agreed that it would probably be a few days before the government trucks arrived, but he would go ahead and get word to the families who weren't staying in Ernie's basement so they could find a good place to hide.

"Ken, if there isn't a safe place for them, ask Lydia if it would be okay to use the basement of her shop. The store survived the storm with only broken windows, and she'll know what I'm talking about. It's her story to tell, though, so ask her privately."

"Okay," Ken responded, in a puzzled voice. "There's a definite need for prayer right now, too. If we want to stay free to make our own choices, don't forget that there's power in prayer."

***

Only two families in town needed to find a place to hide, but Ernie's basement was already crowded, so Ken took Lydia aside and asked her about her basement. For the first time since Richie's death, her face lit up with a grin, and she actually chuckled.

"Ken, it's a perfect solution, if there's not water in there. In the far corner of my shop's basement, there's a small door, with boxes piled up where it's not visible unless you're standing right in front of it. It leads to a tunnel that goes under the street to the empty building next door to Gus's auto shop. There was damage to those two businesses, but the tunnel should be fine, and I'm sure the NERC people will never find it. I didn't even know it was there, and neither did Tanner or Ian, and they grew up here. Anyone who stays down there will need candles or flashlights, though, It's dark, and a little musty, but it'll be safe. I don't mind letting that secret out if it helps our friends."

"You're kidding. Why would there be a tunnel under the street?"

"Gus said the guy who owned those buildings was a bootlegger back when Oklahoma became a state, and he had the tunnel put in to hide the liquor. Folks in town kept quiet about it, and it was eventually forgotten."

"Well, the Lord works in mysterious ways. Thanks for this, Lydia. I'll go check it out, and if it's dry, tell the families about it."

"Let's get Terri, and I'll go, too. It'll be good to get out for a little while. And it's time I started to shake off the depression and self-pity, and begin doing my share around here. I'll always miss Richie and be sad about what happened, but in this world, we don't have time to wallow in it. I want to feel alive again, and helping with this is a first step."

Chapter 22 – The Next Several Days

"Good grief! We forgot to take down the doorbells and lights!" Erin stood, hands on her hips, staring at the offending alarm system. "Those signs that mention caves would give us away for sure. Gus, could you get some guys and get all that out of sight, please?"

The group had accomplished most of the tasks that they had set for themselves. Shane and Ian took food and candles to town, then returned to help load the wood into Ian's truck. Gus and his crew, which consisted of BJ and Charlie, moved the freezer to the cave, strung a hidden cord for it, and took care of the electrical and plumbing systems, while everyone else toted linens, mattresses, food, and clothing to the caverns. Mac and Vince moved the tanker to an old track on a nearby property, taking it as far into the woods as possible and covering it with the camo nets. Then they took a couple of old leaf rakes and did their best to remove the tire tracks in the high grass where they had turned off the road.

Will and John loaded car batteries into the Expedition and the Explorer, and drove over to put them back into the vehicles that were parked at the McNeil's. Sarah, Talako, Rose, Dana, and Val moved the cars and pickups to an isolated old hunting lease that Talako knew about, and they all hiked back through the forest and made their way to the lodge via the north cave entrance.

All of the children had been told that if any adult called out a warning, they were to immediately go to the cave and be as quiet as they could be.

Dinner that night was whatever had been in the refrigerator, which was cleaned and unplugged afterward. Light discipline was a way of life for them already, but the adults were extra vigilant right before dusk in making sure that they extinguished all the candles they were burning.

The mood was somber, but alert. Erin doubled the number of guards at the cave entrances and the front corners of the property. Tanner put a dog with each pair of guards, and kept little Moxie inside.

At night, everyone who wasn't on guard duty slept in the caverns. Since the radios were line-of-sight, Gus and Mac made sure that an adult was positioned at each big turn in the caves. That way they could relay messages rapidly if an emergency arose.

After twenty-four hours of sleeping in the caverns and spending the day in the lodge, they decided that it would be best to just stay in the caves all the time, rather than risk locking the pantry entrance with someone on the wrong side. They left the entrance open, however, for the outside guards to use if the NERC trucks were spotted.

On the fourth day, early in the afternoon, Val's voice came over the radio. She was standing watch with Vince on the southeast corner of the property.

"Hearing a rumble in front of our position. Can't see anything yet. Wait…yes, it's who we expected. Go, go, go!"

Sarah and Ian, the guards on the southwest corner, signaled for Blitz to follow them, and ran to the nearby cave entrance. Vince and Val got Sheba, and darted up the drive, across the yard, and into the lodge. They were almost to the pantry when they heard Dana yell something out the patio door.

"Tucker, NO!" she screamed, and ran after her younger son as he made a dash around the corner to grab some small rocks from the driveway.

Dana reached him just as the first NERC truck pulled into the yard, and knew that they were caught. Uniformed NERC agents jumped out carrying rifles, and ordered her over to the trucks.

"Who else is here? Where are the others?" an older man demanded.

"We're alone. Just the two of us," she said, pinching Tucker and giving him a warning look. "There's no one else."

The man, whose nametag said "Sgt. Higgins", looked at her with obvious suspicion, then signaled four of his troopers to search the lodge.

Inside the caves, Vince locked the shelf into place, and turned to find John running toward them. He looked frantic, and very frightened.

"Have you seen Dana or Tucker? I can't find them anywhere."

"John, I'm sorry, but Tucker ran out and Dana went after him. The trucks were pulling in just as they rounded the corner."

John lunged for the locks, and Vince grabbed him, forcing him back. John tried to break free, but Vince had both arms wrapped around him, and held on tight.

"No, John!" Vince hissed. "You'll give us all away, and that won't help Dana. We'll find a way to get them back, but you *can't* go out there! You *can't!*"

Tanner, Erin, and Talako arrived just then, and John nearly collapsed from the shock of knowing that his wife and son were captives of the "government agency".

Talako nodded for Vince to release John, and waved all of them back further into the caves.

John seemed wilt and began to cry, tears rolling down his ravaged face. "Why in the world would he run out there at a time like this?"

"Dad, I think I know." Zeke approached, looking ashamed. "We were planning to go explore the narrow cave, and I told him that since we were going to be stuck back here for a while, we might finally be able to slip away, but he couldn't go unless he had ammo for his slingshot. He didn't save many of the rocks he found. He used them all for practicing, and I guess he thought this would be his last chance to grab some." Zeke's eyes fill with tears. "I'm sorry. I'm so sorry, Dad. It's my fault."

John took the sobbing boy in his arms, and held him tight. "It's only partly your fault, son. Tucker made some bad decisions, too."

Talako took John's hand, and waited until John looked at him. "Son, my daughter is a strong woman, an *ohoyo* like her mother. She's smart, and at her best in a crisis. She'll keep Tucker safe until we can rescue them, but we can't go rushing out there and get into a firefight against who knows how many armed agents, and endanger any innocent civilians they've already rounded up. Dana will keep her head, and we'll begin immediately figuring out what to do, but we've got to be smart about this if we want to get them back. And *you* have to be strong for Zeke, because that's his mother and brother out there. Don't let him see you give up hope."

Erin put a hand on John's shoulder. "I'll do whatever I can to help, and so will the others, I'm sure. We've faced down hardened criminals, and that bunch of young kids in uniforms won't stop us. First, we need to know where they're taking all the civilians, and then, we're going to get your family back. And that's a promise."

***

The NERC agents cleared every room of the lodge, and reported to the sergeant that there was no sign of anyone else.

"What supplies did you find?" Higgins demanded.

"None, Sergeant. There was nothing except furniture. No indication that anyone has been living there recently," a baby-faced young man replied.

"Put the woman and boy in the last truck, and we'll continue our search." He gave the lodge a hard stare, as though he could see through the walls, then turned and climbed into the lead truck.

Dana sat under the canvas top in the back of the transport truck, and looked at the other people who had been rounded up by NERC. There were only a few familiar faces, since she hadn't lived in the immediate area for several years. She merely nodded at the three she remembered from her childhood.

The convoy of trucks continued west, then turned north on the road that went past Mac and Claire's burned out home. They slowed and stopped on the road near the entrance to her grandparents' driveway. Only the lead truck pulled in and stopped in front of the house. The same four young NERC agents searched the house, and finding nothing, they returned to the head of the line and went a little further up the road, stopping at the Foster home.

Dana held her breath as she peeked out a small tear in the canvas, hoping that her friends were well hidden in the forest. The searchers got in by breaking a window, and were inside for several minutes. The came out carrying two big boxes, and reported to the sergeant. The boxes went into the back of the lead truck, and they continued north to the next road before turning back east.

Leaning over and whispering in Tucker's ear, Dana instructed him to go along with whatever she said, and keep quiet otherwise.

"Don't tell them anything at all. Do you hear me? *Nothing*, except that you and I were just passing through and found that empty lodge to stay in overnight. Don't mention that there was anyone else there. Don't even think the word 'cave'. Stay close to me, and don't talk to *anyone* if you can help it. We need to stay together, because if we get a chance, we're going to escape. Tucker, I mean it. You stay close to me, no matter what."

***

Mac, Gus, and Charlie sat around the radio base unit and listened. They had moved it temporarily back into the lodge, but left everything else in the caves in case NERC came back. Mac was trying to find someone who might know where NERC was taking the people they captured, but so far, nobody seemed to know. Finally, a new voice came on, and asked for the guy wanting information about NERC camps. Mac responded immediately, asking the man what he knew.

"There's a camp, 'bout twenty tents, with a fence 'round it, near the Stigler airport. I can see it from my cabin, but I make sure those guards don't never see me. Seems like a lot of folks there, and ever' few days, they load a bunch of 'em up in trucks and take 'em north. The trucks always come back empty two days later. I don't know where they're taking 'em, but folks ain't kept here for very long before they ship 'em out."

"When was the last time they did that?"

"They left yesterday mornin', so they'll be back tomorrow evenin', I reckon."

"Where's the entrance to the camp? Can you tell us anything else about it?" Mac begged.

"There's a gate on the south side, and one on the west side, but they use the south one, mostly. The fence ain't electrified, far as I can tell. I seen folks touch it and nobody got shocked. It's chain link, with barb wire on top, 'bout seven or eight foot high. You planning a raid or somethin'?"

"Or something. Are there trees close up, or is it open? How many guards? Any dogs?"

"Never seen no dogs, but they's guards walkin' the fence, going in opposite directions. Trees growin' pretty close to the fence on the east side, down on the south end of it. No guard towers, or anythin' like that. That's all I know. Best of luck to ya. Give a holler when you can and let me know how it went."

Mac thanked the man, then shut the radio down. The three friends carried the radio equipment back into the cave and went to tell Erin and Tanner what they had learned.

***

"We have to move fast on this. The man said they don't keep people there long before they take them somewhere else, and the round trip takes two days, so we might never find them if we wait too long," Mac insisted.

"We can't take a large group, either," Erin reminded them. "We need to use stealth, not overpowering force. We're probably vastly outnumbered, even if all of us went, and a firefight is out of the question. Too many innocent people around, and we don't know who the real bad guys are. I can't help thinking about Jen's brothers, and I don't want to shoot at kids who are there because they got drafted into doing something they don't want to do. They're victims, too. So how many of us and who, that's the question. Then how to get there and how to get home."

"Motorcycles are too noisy and we only have two, but going on foot is too slow. We have to take a car or a truck, I think," Tanner suggested. "As to who, I think we need the best on this. There's no room for error and there's a lot at stake."

They sat on a mattress in one of the western caverns, wanting to have a plan before telling the whole group about the camp. The silence grew, then Tanner spoke up.

"Shane, for sure. He's deadly, with or without weapons, and can move like a ghost. John will insist on going, and I don't blame him. He's good with his fists, and thinks fast. I'm going, and I think our fourth should be Vince. He's proven that he has a good head for dealing with a crisis."

"Those are good choices, Tanner. You won't get an argument out of me; I was about to suggest the same four." Erin grinned. "As hard as it may be to believe, I'm not going to demand to go, too. I'm not the best person for this, and I know it."

"Okay. So how do you get there?" Mac asked.

"We ask Sarah to let us use the Explorer. It runs pretty quiet, and it's smaller, so we could hide it easier than we could the Expedition. It's big enough to hold all of us, and being that bronzy color, if we have to hide it, it'll blend in with the forest." Tanner looked thoughtful. "We take it to a short distance from the camp, and hide it, then slip in and get Dana and Tucker, and get back to the Explorer as quickly as possible, then drive it as fast as we can back here. We'll need to cut the fence. I think Gus has wire cutters we can borrow. We'll be smarter this time, and take supplies in case we have to stay over for any reason, too. We can't plan it in detail until we see the place, but it seems to me that finding them in the camp will be the hard part."

"What I'm worried about is that when they escape, the NERC officers will figure they'd come back here. I hate the idea of having to live in fear from now on." Erin sighed. "Oh, well, we'll have to deal with that later. Right now, I just want them back here, safe with us. This is so hard on John. Julia and Talako seem surprisingly calm about it all, though."

Tanner gave her a slight smile. "Their faith is strong; besides, don't you know that Indians never show emotion?"

"Yeah, right, Mr. Romantic. You never show a soft side, huh? Really, tell another one."

Mac grinned, but sobered quickly. "It's as good a plan as we can have at this point. I think it's time to tell the others and get ready to go. Tanner, we'll be praying for you all."

They left the small cavern and made their way to the northernmost cavern, the one with the pool and spring. Most of the group were there, and were eager to help in the rescue.

"This may disappoint some of you, but we think that a small group will be more effective for this mission. Only four will be going, and the four are John, Shane, Vince, and me. Are you willing?" Tanner glanced around at the other three men. All of them nodded, just as he knew they would. "Sarah, may we use your Explorer?"

Sarah stood up. "Let me make this clear to everyone. I don't consider it 'my' Explorer anymore. It belongs to the group, because without this place and all of you, I'd almost certainly have died in Tulsa. You don't even have to ask. It's yours to use as needed. It's four-wheel drive, too, and don't worry about scratches and dents if you have to go off road, either."

"Thank you, Sarah. Now, we'll need supplies for a few days, so we don't make the same mistake we made with the Simmons Gang. We go prepared from now on. Food, first aid supplies, extra gas. Frances, if you would get some food put together, and Mac, if you'd find us some gas cans, we'll go by where the tanker is and fill up with fuel. The four of us will be busy getting our weapons together, and we'll go as soon as we have things ready, hopefully within the hour."

***

Dressed in camo, the four men traveled the back roads, skirting around the town of Stigler. As they approached the airport, they searched for a place to hide the SUV, finally settling on an old garage at an abandoned house just off Airport Road. The overhead door was down, but the side door to the garage was unlocked; they parked, closed the big door, grabbed their weapons, and set out on foot. The man on the radio had described the camp accurately. It was near the airport, and a band of forest angled northeast from the road to well past the corner of the camp. They stayed in the woods until dusk, watching the guards and learning their routine. Two pairs of guards walked the perimeter in opposite directions, just inside the fence, and passed each other on the east and west sides about every ten minutes. They stopped on the north and south sides, and surveyed the area for a few minutes on each round.

Civilians stood in clusters and pairs around the yard, and after just a few minutes, John spotted Dana and Tucker, talking to a woman who looked familiar to him for some reason. They strolled as they visited, but it was obvious that they were headed toward the part of the fence closest to the woods, which also happened to be where their rescuers waited.

Dana stopped, and after a few more minutes of conversation, the woman smiled, patted Tucker on the shoulder, and turned to go toward the tents. Dana watched her go, then said something to Tucker, and the two continued to stroll casually toward the corner. The sun dropped behind the horizon, and Dana took Tucker's hand, slipping into the shadows of the evening.

A loud bell rang in the center of the camp, and the internees began to slowly drift toward their tents, but Dana and Tucker dropped to the ground, lying in the ankle-high grass.

Shane sneaked forward, motioning to the others to stay put, and began to cut a hole in the fence. He was almost silent about it, but Dana heard the *snip, snip* sound, and turned her head to look.

"See? I told you they'd come after us," she whispered to Tucker, who grinned and nodded.

The guards approached from the north, along the east fence, but Shane could see that Dana knew he was there, so he motioned for her to come. John appeared beside Shane, and as Dana and Tucker wormed their way closer to the slit in the fence, John helped Shane hold it open for his wife and son to come through.

Tucker clung to his father, but John put a finger over his lips, then murmured, "There'll be time for a reunion later. We need to go. Tanner and Vince are over there in the trees. Not a sound, son. Hurry, but stay down. Now, go!"

The guards were getting closer, talking quietly, and not being very alert, in Shane's opinion, but he knew that they might notice the hole in the fence, even in the darkness, and sound an alarm. He got down and slithered through the gap, waiting. When they passed within a yard of him with no indication that they were aware of his presence, he sprang to his feet and put a hand on each of their heads, ramming the heads together hard enough to knock them both out. He darted through the slit and swiftly caught up with his friends.

The Explorer was right where they left it; John slid into the back seat, followed by Dana and Vince. Tanner drove, with Tucker curled up in the back cargo area, and Shane in the front passenger seat. They maintained silence until they were well away from the camp, then Dana took John's hand and reached over to kiss him.

"What's that for?" John asked.

"Did you see the woman we were talking to?" At John's nod, she said, "That was the nurse who worked in the hospital nursery when Tucker was born. She said she was content to go with NERC, because she has no family and thinks that NERC will at least feed her."

"So? I don't get it."

"She also said, and I quote, 'That handsome hunk of yours will rescue you, missy. Don't you ever doubt it. You married a *real man*.' And I told her I knew that, and I had a feeling you were coming tonight. She said 'you love him real good when you get home, and show him you appreciate him'. I told her I would, but after I gave you the news."

"What news is that?"

"We're going to have a baby."

***

John was still grinning when they arrived back at the lodge. The news that Dana was pregnant was welcome; they'd wanted more children, and hoped this one would be a girl.

Tanner pulled up in front of the lodge and let everyone except Shane out, then drove the Explorer to their hidden parking area, and the two friends walked home. When they got near the north cave entrance, Tanner whistled, then called softly, "It's Tanner and Shane." BJ and Frances were on duty with Flash providing backup. Frances stepped out and hugged the two men.

"How'd it go? Did you succeed?"

"Yes, ma'am, we sure did. Shane did most of the work, but we got them back safe and sound."

"I'm so glad to hear that. We've been praying that all of you would come back to us. You must be exhausted. Go now, and eat your dinner. Val cooked a deer roast, and it's wonderful."

Tanner nodded. As he and Shane continued through the cave, he was quiet for several minutes, then finally gave voice to his concerns.

"You realize, I'm sure, that we just opened a can of worms."

Shane gave him a wry look. "I do, but we had no choice. We had to do it. We couldn't leave Dana and Tucker in the hands of NERC. I think that organization started out like most government programs, with good intentions and maybe even some beneficial actions at first. But like other programs, they got carried away and started trying to run people's lives. For their own good, of course."

"Of course. And probably within ten minutes of our leaving the camp, they discovered that two of their detainees had escaped. The other two guards would have come around and found their compadres with knots on their heads. I'm not saying you shouldn't have done it; knocking their heads together bought us that ten minutes. But now, they'll be looking for the escapees and whoever helped them, and unless I miss my guess, they'll come straight here, the place where they picked Dana and Tucker up."

"Yep. And that means we'll have to stay in the caves indefinitely. We may not ever be safe in the lodge again, because we'll never know when they might swing by to check on the place. How will Erin grow our food, if we can't leave any sign that the place is occupied?"

"And our guards have to be extra vigilant. We'll be looking over our shoulders from now on, I'm afraid. But we did what needed doing," Tanner assured him. "There's no price I wouldn't pay to keep my family secure, and this group *is* my family. At least we have the caves as a hideout. We'd be in trouble without them.

"We'll figure this problem out, just like we've figured out the rest of our problems. The one thing we can never do is give up. We won't give up our freedom, and we won't ever give up hope."

Author's Note

Yakoke[5] for reading *Kiamichi Storm*. I hope you enjoyed it. If you did, I would greatly appreciate it if you would write a review on Amazon.com. If you have comments or questions for me, feel free to contact me at chenryauthor@yahoo.com or find me on Facebook under C.A. Henry. I love hearing from readers. I'll be right here, working hard on the third book in the series, *Kiamichi Journey.*

The map of the caves in *Kiamichi Storm* has been revised to include the caves that had not yet been explored in *Kiamichi Refuge.* The cave that goes northwest from the cache cavern is not easily accessible due to narrow passages and low ceilings in several places, and it dead ends without any opening to the outside.

"The City", as Oklahomans know, is Oklahoma City. It is the capital city of Oklahoma, the only state in the union with oil wells on the lawn of the governor's mansion and other government buildings.

Many of the older stores in small-town Oklahoma have basements, and it is not inconceivable that there could be a tunnel or two under the streets. The state also has some of the strictest liquor laws in the nation. It was illegal to sell liquor in Indian Territory, and when Oklahoma became a state in 1907, the state

---

[5] Thank you

constitution contained prohibitions against the sale of hard liquor, so bootlegging was rampant even before national Prohibition. Oklahoma never ratified the 21st Amendment, which repealed Prohibition, and did not allow the sale of hard liquor *at all* until 1959, and since then, only in liquor stores, which cannot sell anything *other* than liquor, wine and room-temperature beer. Twenty-five of Oklahoma's seventy-seven counties still do not allow the sale of liquor by the drink in restaurants. Grocery and convenience stores may sell cold beer, but nothing stronger than 3.2% alcohol. There is a state question on the November 2016 ballot to allow grocery stores to sell wine and stronger beer, and to allow liquor stores to sell cold beer and items other than liquor.

Oklahoma's Kiamichi Mountains are quite lovely at any time of the year, but if you get the chance, the best time to visit is in the fall. The colors are gorgeous, and you just might fall in love with the region and its many lakes, recreational areas, and quaint towns. There's even a Bigfoot Festival in Honobia for those who enjoy live music, arts and crafts, delicious food, family activities, nature walks, and riding four-wheelers. It's held in late September every year.

If you would like to know more about the Choctaw Nation, visit choctawnation.com. The Choctaw are a noble people who have contributed much to our country, including providing code-talkers during World War II. I am proud to claim my Choctaw ancestry.

In Book One of this series, *Kiamichi Refuge*, I didn't include an inventory of what Uncle Ernie had stashed in his supply caches. I felt that most readers would find it to be a tedious interruption to the flow of the story. One reviewer applauded the lack of such a list, but another one wished that there was more information on prepping, including an inventory.

Reading a long list is not most people's idea of fun, but that being said, I've always been one to mentally ask myself, "what if..." and in this case, I realized that maybe I *can* make both of those readers happy, with an inventory list that doesn't interrupt the story. On the following pages, you will find a comprehensive list of what survival expert Uncle Ernie hid in his cavern, and in his basement in town. If you are interested in or need such a list, it starts at the end of this note. If you don't want to see it, just don't look.

I didn't include amounts for any of the items, simply because every group's needs will be different, depending on the number and ages of people in the group, the climate, and the physical surroundings. Ernie's list is fairly comprehensive, but may not include every single thing that every person in the country might need when the excrement impacts the rotary air impeller.

[All notes and recommendations come from Uncle Ernie. He hoped that you know that no list can possibly be totally complete for every family's situation. This list is meant to get you started, and you certainly don't have to buy it all at once. If you don't have a lot of money, start by adding a few canned foods to your grocery basket each week or month. Anything you can accumulate is better than nothing. Decide your personal or family priorities, and start prepping.]

<u>**Drinking**</u>
Water containers of various sizes
Water filters   Sawyer, Berkey, LifeStraws, etc.
Coffee beans
Tea
Powdered milk
Tang
Koolaid or other flavoring mixes
Liquor, wine
Hot cocoa mix
Wine, beer, and liquor if you inbibe

The Kiamichi region has streams, springs, and lakes, so I didn't store a lot of water, just containers and the means to make it fit for human consumption. If you live where water is less abundant, you'll need to store water. A *lot* of water.

Food- Meats and Proteins
Canned beef
Canned chicken
Canned ham, Spam
Canned wild salmon
Canned turkey
Canned clams
Freeze-dried meats
Dehydrated eggs
Egg powder
Jerky
Canned beans of various kinds
Dried beans

Food- Grains
Hard white or red wheat   white will store
longer
Rice
Barley
Pasta
Oatmeal
Popcorn

Nuts
Almonds
Sunflower seeds

Pecans   Keep frozen if possible, or use within a few months

Peanut butter

Veggies-Canned
Peas
Green beans
Beets
Carrots
Mushrooms
Corn
Hominy
Pumpkin
Spinach
Tomatoes   peeled, diced, sauce, paste
Green chilies

Veggies- Freeze-dried
Onions
Celery
Mushrooms
Peas
Broccoli
Cauliflower
Green beans

Fruits-Canned
Peaches
Pears
Apricots

Cherries
Rhubarb
Oranges
Pineapple
Apples

Fruits-Freeze-Dried
Raisins
Prunes
Apricots
Apples
Strawberries
Banana chips
Blueberries
Raspberries

Foods-Pickled
Olives
Pickles   sweet, sour, dill, hot
Peppers
Pickled veggies of your choice

Foods-Dairy
Dehydrated butter
Canned butter
Sour cream powder
Dehydrated cheeses

Foods-Soups
Dry soup mixes

Bouillon cubes or powders beef and chicken
Canned soups, especially those used in recipes

Foods-Baking
Cocoa
Baking soda
Cornstarch
Fruit preservative
Yeast
Honey
Sugar
Stevia
Brown sugar
Molasses
Maple syrup
Chocolate syrup
Corn syrup
Vanilla extract
Almond extract

Seasonings
Parsley
Sage
Rosemary
Thyme
Basil
Cayenne ground and crushed
Celery seed
Dill seed
Dill weed

Chili powder
Cardamom
Cilantro
Chives
Cream of tartar
Cumin
Worcestershire sauce
Coriander
Curry powder
Cloves
Paprika
Black pepper
Nutmeg
Cinnamon
Marjoram
Mustard seed
Garlic powder
Salt
Oregano
Turmeric
Taco seasoning
Bay leaves
Allspice
Ginger
Italian seasoning
Steak seasoning
Onion salt

These will be worth their weight in gold in a long-term disaster, for your use and for barter.

Food-Extras
Jellies and jams
Hard candies
Jello and pudding mixes
Vinegar
Miracle Whip   has a long shelf life
Prepared mustard in various flavors

Kitchen Needs
Manual can openers
Manual coffee grinder
Steel wool pads
Matches
Lighters
Magnesium fire starters
Dish detergent
Towels and dish cloths
Manual grain mill
Canning jars
Canning lids   Tattler lids can be reused. Other
types are one-use only.
Canning rings
Jar lifter for canning
Water-bath canner
Pressure canner

Goods from the Paper Aisle

Toilet paper
Facial tissues
Paper towels
Paper napkins
Coffee filters
Paper plates
Paper bowls
Plastic cups
Plastic ware
Plastic wrap
Zipper bags in various sizes
Waxed paper
Aluminum foil
Trash bags
Toothpicks

Sanitation
Five-gallon bucket with lids

Laundry soap, such as Zote's, Ivory, or Fel's Naptha

Borax powder

Washing soda   Mix with soap and borax, and use a tiny amount to do a load of laundry. You may also mix with a lot of <u>hot</u> water (melts the soap) to make a liquid detergent.

Bleach (unscented) or crystalized chlorine

Crystalized lasts much longer. Keep dry until you are ready to use it.

Lots of cheap washcloths for when you run out of toilet paper. That's what some of the buckets and bleach are for, too. Look up "family cloths".

Defense
Rifles with scopes
Knives, including machetes
Handguns
Ammo
Pepper spray
Shockers   like flashlights that also will knock a big man on his backside, stun-guns
(and learn how to use all of the above)

General household
Light bulbs
Flashlights
Candles
Rechargeable batteries
Battery chargers   solar, crank, plug-in
Glowsticks
Rags, sponges
Fire extinguishers
Hand tools
Scissors
Rope
Staple gun
Zip-ties in lots of sizes
Insect repellent

Mousetraps
Fly swatters
Fly tapes
Oil lamps
Oil wicks
Garden hoses
Wire
Nails
Screws
Siphon hose with bulb
Bungee straps
Rubber bands
Paper clips
Magnifying glass   has many uses, including starting a fire
Hand mirror   can be used as a signal
Buckets with lids

Personal Hygiene
Bar soap
Shampoo
Q-tips
Tampons
Mini and maxi pads
Hand lotion
Combs and brushes
Unscented body oil   Scents may give your presence away to a bad guy.
Scent-killer body wash   for when you hunt deer or hogs

Lip balm
Vaseline
Razors
Tweezers
Bath towels
Wash cloths
Nail clippers and files
Toothbrushes and dental floss

Need I mention that during a long-term disaster, taking care of your teeth is essential to your overall health? Imagine not being able to get help for a toothache. Ignore your teeth and they'll go away.

Medicine/First Aid
Pain relievers
Anti-diarrheal medicines
Laxatives and stool softeners
Bandages – all sizes
Gauze – pads and rolls
Tape – paper and cloth
Hydrogen peroxide
Rubbing alcohol
Antibacterial creams and ointments
Antifungal sprays and creams   for athlete's foot, jock itch, toenail fungus
Birth control   condoms, the Pill, spermicides
Cold medicines
Flu medicines
Sinus/allergy medicines

Antacids
Children's versions of most medicines listed
Epsom salt
Throat and cough lozenges
Cough syrup
Moleskin
Surgical instrument kit
Burn ointment
Vitamin and mineral supplements
Sunburn relief   aloe vera gel
Poison ivy cream
Dramamine
Fish antibiotics   100% identical to human antibiotics, no prescription needed
Airways
Alcohol wipes
Cotton balls
Thieve's Oil blend   antibacterial, antifungal
Tea tree oil (melaleuca alternifolia)   used for wounds, fungal infections, scrapes
Peppermint oil   put a few drops in a glass of water and drink for stomach/heartburn relief
Butterfly bandages/steri-strips
Dental mirror and pick
Temporary dental filling kits
Activated charcoal
Stethoscope
Snake-bite kit   I recommend The Extractor
Vicks Vapo-rub
Preparation H

Surgical masks
Safety pins
Sutures
Clotting powder
Bentonite clay
Diatomaceous earth
Pregnancy tests
Ipecac

Sleeping

Blankets
Pillows
Sheets
Sleeping bags
Inflatable mattresses
Space blankets
Tarps
Hammocks

Clothing

Underwear
Socks   cotton and wool blend - nothing beats wool in the winter
Long underwear
Jackets/coats
Gloves
Hats
Rain suits
Boots   hunting, hiking, or combat style, sturdy and comfortable

Shoes   boots and shoes will be hard to replace if there's trouble, so have extras

Bandanas
Work gloves
Pajamas
Shorts and long pants
Short and long sleeved shirts

You should have at least three complete sets of clothing for each person, and if possible, a full set of camo leafy-wear for each person, including gloves and mask. Remember that kids grow, so have larger sizes available if there are children in your group. Cargo pants have lots of pockets and come in camo.

Baby Gear
Cloth diapers   even if you can afford them, where do you have room to store disposables?

Plastic pants
Baby wash
Teething rings
Toys
Diaper rash ointment
Towelettes
Formula
Bottles
Bottle brush

Repair or Replace

Iron-on and sew-on patches
Tent repair kit
Wood glue
Super glue
Duct tape - a lot of it
Caulk
Patterns for simple clothing in all sizes
Fabric - denim, cotton, fleece, twill, in camo colors, preferably
Buttons in various sizes
Needles   various sizes, and curved needles, too, for tent or furniture repairs
Thread
Elastic in various widths
Snaps
Grommets and grommet tool
Treadle sewing machine

Gardening
Rooting hormones
Seed starter soil
Pots of all sizes
Hand trowel
Hoe
Shovel
Spade
Composter
Garden gloves for each person
A large and varied seed bank, frozen or refrigerated - don't just stock seeds for foods *you* like.

Others may like things you don't, and variety is good. If you can afford it, a greenhouse is a wonderful thing.

<u>For Pets</u>
Dog food
Cat food
Bird seed
Kitty litter
Litter scoop
Bowls
Grooming brush
Your preferred method to deter/kill fleas and ticks

<u>Staying Sane</u>
Bible
Books   fiction, nonfiction, children's
Jigsaw puzzles
Games   Scrabble, Monopoly, Clue, Yahtzee, Connect Four, dominoes, etc.
Decks of cards   poker, Uno, Crazy Eights, Go Fish, etc.
Crossword puzzles
Word-find puzzles
Coloring books
Crayons, colored pencils
Jump ropes, balls, simple toys for kids
Notebooks
Pens/pencils/markers

Paper   plain white, lined, and construction
Glue sticks
Craft kits
Yarn, embroidery floss, and needles for knitting and crochet

Continuing Education
How-to books on:
Survival
Medical and first aid
Canning
Gardening
Preserving food
Sewing
Basic homesteading skills
Butchering deer, and other game
Cooking outside

AND:
Textbooks for high school subjects
Most Americans could teach lower grade subjects without a book if they had to, but high schoolers can do independent study. If things have really gone primitive, they won't need calculus and chemistry, but they will need basic science and math knowledge, and the rest of their learning will be practical things they need to know to survive. They need to know history and economics so they understand that what is happening is something that has happened before, and they'll have ideas how to prevent it happening again when they rebuild society.

I suggest purchasing an e-reader and use it strictly for downloading all types of books for survival, educating kids, and all the classic literature, which is mostly FREE from Amazon. Download the Constitution, the Declaration of Independence, and other documents.

Wouldn't it be a tragedy if we lost Shakespeare, Poe, Jules Verne, Robert Frost and all the other great literature and poetry from the past? I have hundreds of books on my dedicated Kindle. And I have another Kindle full of popular fiction of all types, whether I like a genre or not. Someone in my group might enjoy reading a book that doesn't appeal to me. You may also have solid, non-electronic books, but remember, you can carry thousands of books on an e-reader if you have to bug out. How many solid books can you carry?

Communicating and Getting Where You're Going

Small notepads and something to write with, to leave messages and take notes

Several handheld radios (at least one for each group member)

Backpacks

Fanny packs

Maps   you *need* a topographical atlas of your state, at the very least

Compass

Ham radio   because if it's the end of the world as we know it, it won't matter if you're licensed.

Spray paint in two vivid colors   Use one to mark turns for friendlies who are joining you, and the other to confuse the bad guys who might be trying to find your bug-out location.

Made in the USA
San Bernardino, CA
14 July 2020

75462659R00193